Phoebe and Her Unicorn

Phoebe and Her Unicorn

Dana Simpson

Andrews McMeel
Publishing®

a division of Andrews McMeel Universal

INTRODUCTION

i would dearly love to claim at least some connection to the origins of Marigold Heavenly Nostrils, the innocently arrogant unicorn who preens so charmingly through Dana Simpson's delightful comic strip bearing her name. And perhaps I can. Scholarly articles have been written, after all, about the fact that prior to my 1968 novel *The Last Unicorn* there were no female unicorns to be found in any of the world's varied mythologies. And in the early pages of that book I did write "Unicorns are immortal. It is their nature to live alone in one place: usually a forest where there is a pool clear enough for them to see themselves—for they are a little vain, knowing themselves to be the most beautiful creatures in all the world, and magic besides . . ."

A little vain . . . Marigold would be an appalling monster of ego, utterly self-concerned and completely unlikable, if it weren't for her sense of humor and her occasional surprising capacity for compassion—both crucial attributes when bound by a wish granted to a nine-year-old girl in need of a Best Friend to play invented superhero games with, to introduce to slumber parties and girl-talk gossip and to ride through the wind after being called nerd and Princess Stupidbutt one time too many. For Phoebe is a remarkably real little girl, as bright and imaginative as Bill Watterson's Calvin, as touchingly vulnerable as Charles Schulz's Charlie Brown. And if these strike you as big names to conjure with, I'll go further and state for the record that in my opinion *Phoebe and Her Unicorn* is nothing less than the best comic strip to come along since *Calvin and Hobbes*. Simpson is that good, and that original.

Part of the charm of *Phoebe and Her Unicorn* is the way in which Simpson plays her two characters' opposed world views—immortal and contemporary— against each other, along with their egos: for Phoebe's determination to be recognized as Awesome quite matches Marigold's impregnable superiority to the entire human species. Consequently, both delight in sticking the needle in where they can, and on this ground they are equals. There is real affection between them, but it grows by degrees. Simpson takes her time with this, always remaining in full control of her material, including artful cultural references and the gradual development of additional characters and themes.

The temptation is to quote at least every gag and panel, but that would be wrong. Enchantment doesn't retail well at secondhand; like Robert Frost's definition of poetry, it gets lost in translation. I'll simply suggest that you go read *Phoebe and Her Unicorn* in a serious hurry.

Like now!

— Peter S. Beagle
Oakland, California
September 2013

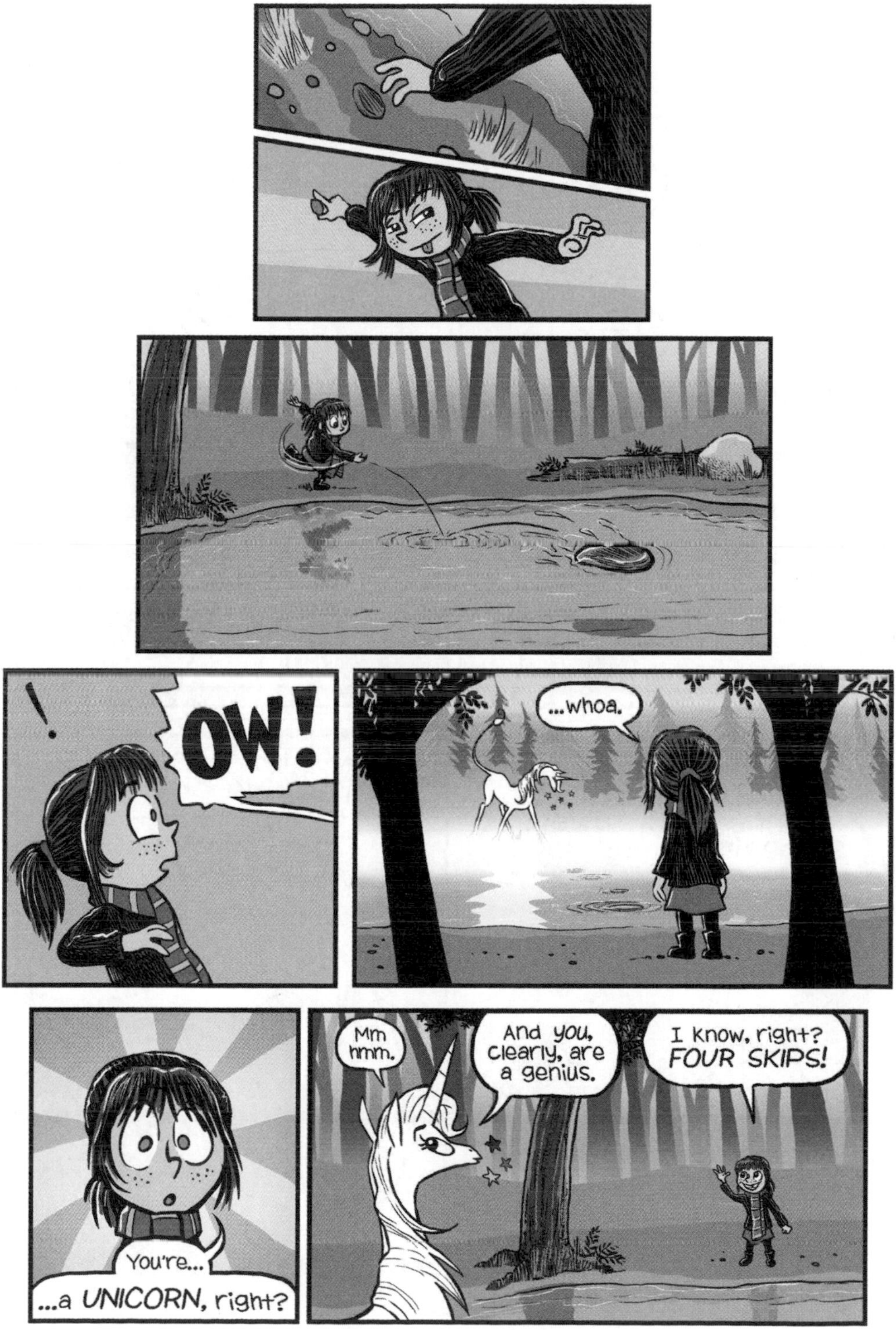
!
OW!
...whoa.
You're...
...a UNICORN, right?
Mm hmm.
And you, clearly, are a genius.
I know, right? FOUR SKIPS!

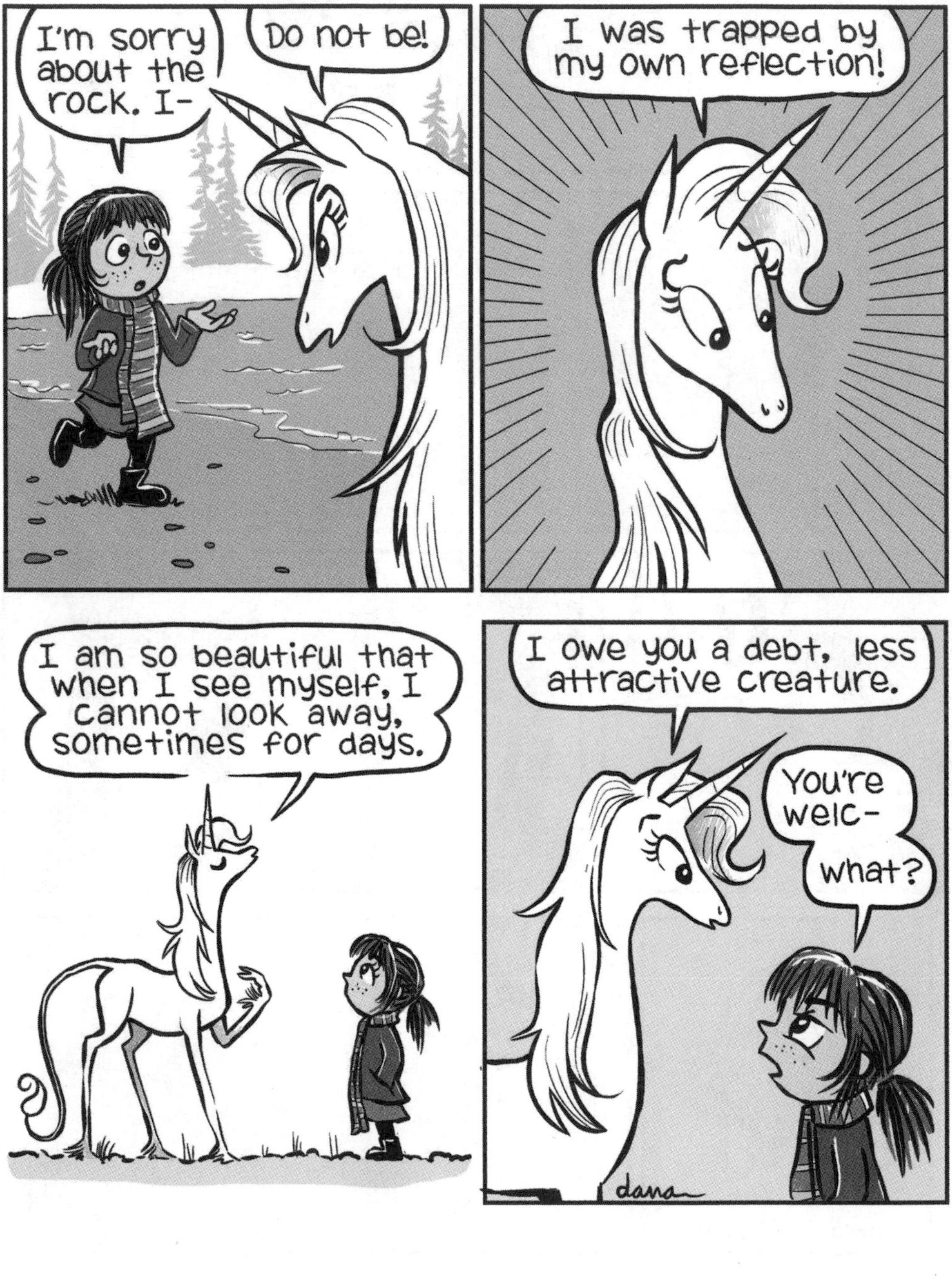
I'm sorry about the rock. I-
Do not be!
I was trapped by my own reflection!
I am so beautiful that when I see myself, I cannot look away, sometimes for days.
I owe you a debt, less attractive creature.
You're welc-
what?
dana

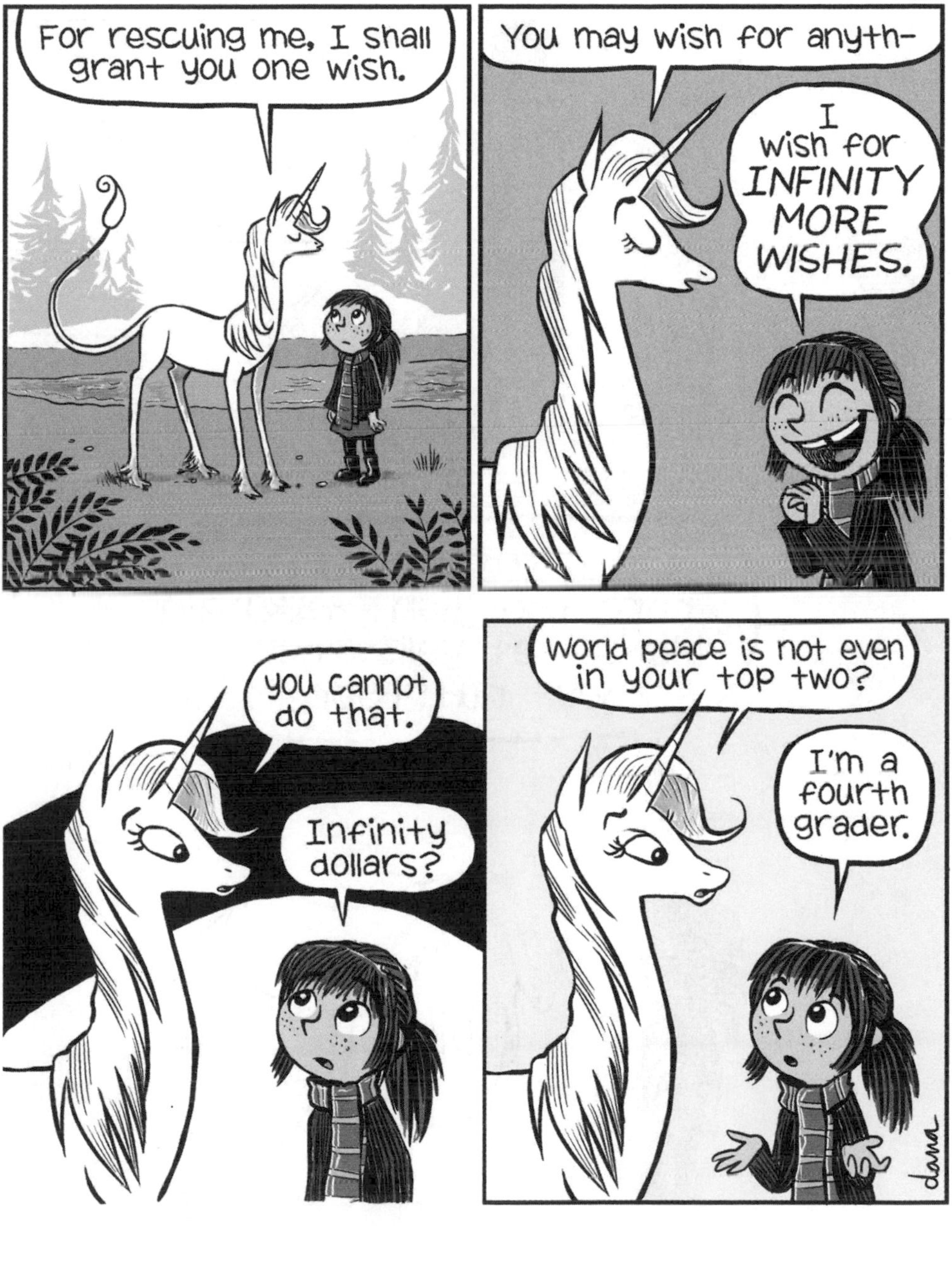
For rescuing me, I shall grant you one wish.
You may wish for anyth-
I wish for INFINITY MORE WISHES.
you cannot do that.
Infinity dollars?
World peace is not even in your top two?
I'm a fourth grader.
dana

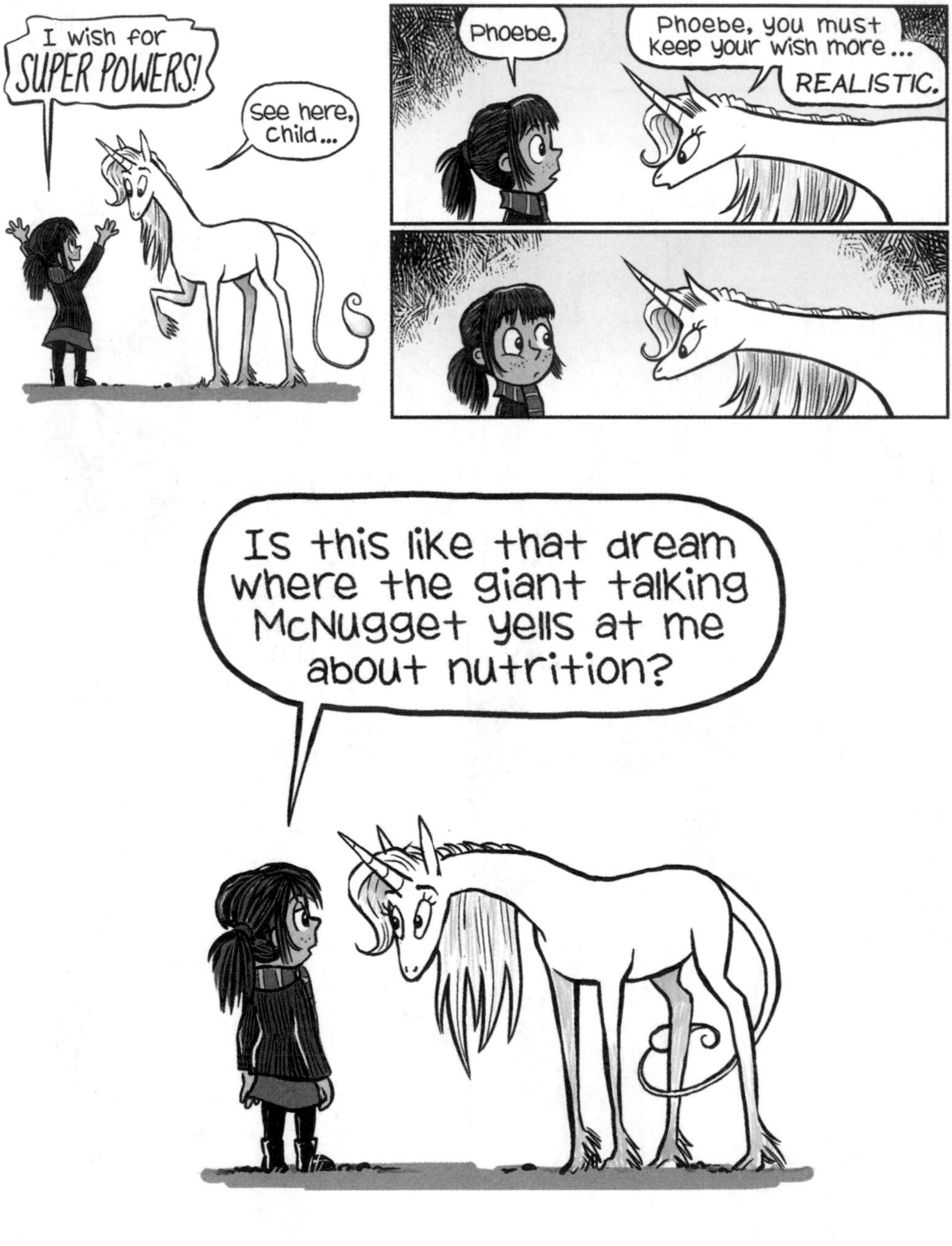
I wish for SUPER POWERS!
See here, child...
Phoebe.
Phoebe, you must keep your wish more... REALISTIC.
Is this like that dream where the giant talking McNugget yells at me about nutrition?

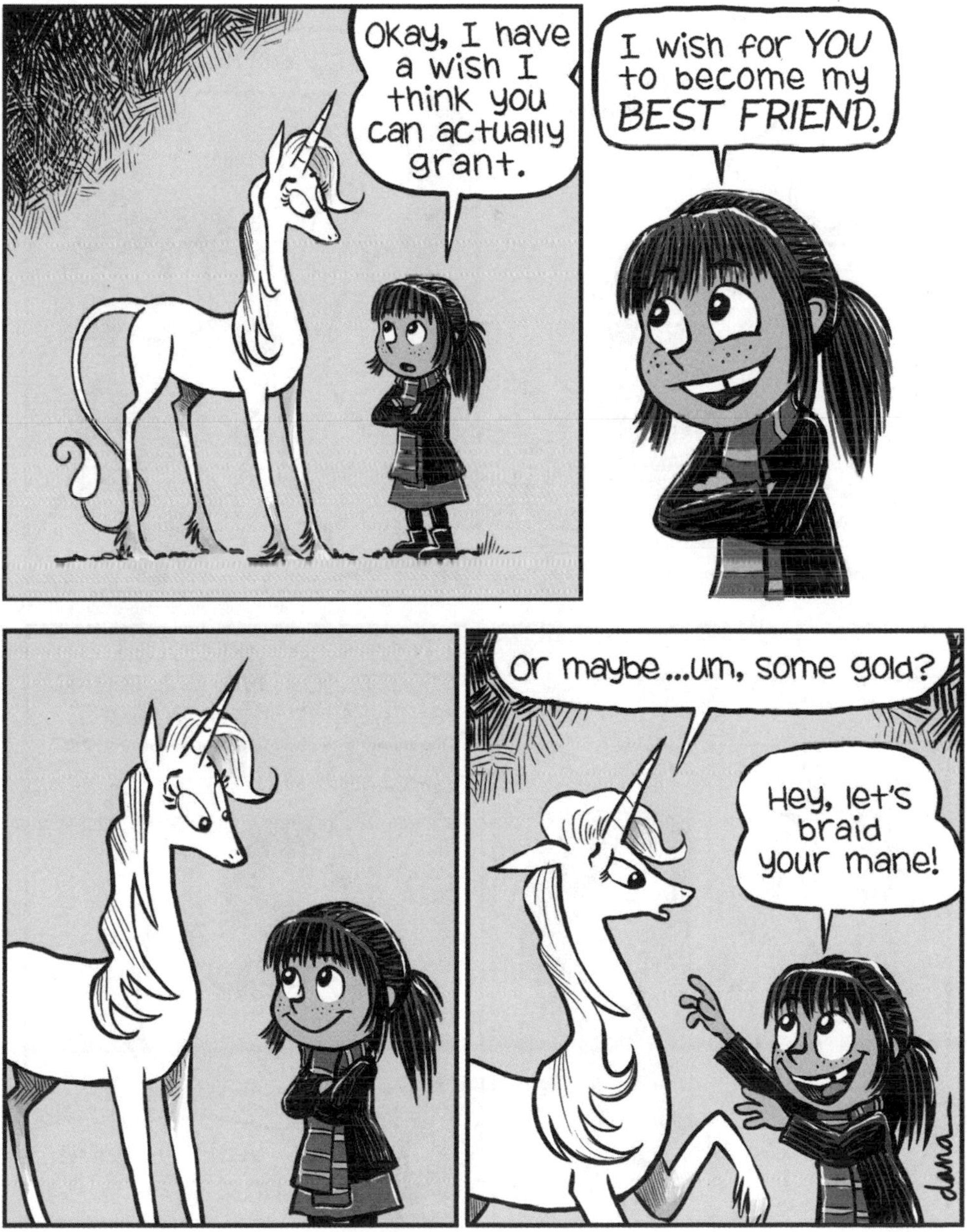
Okay, I have a wish I think you can actually grant.
I wish for YOU to become my BEST FRIEND.
Or maybe...um, some gold?
Hey, let's braid your mane!
dana

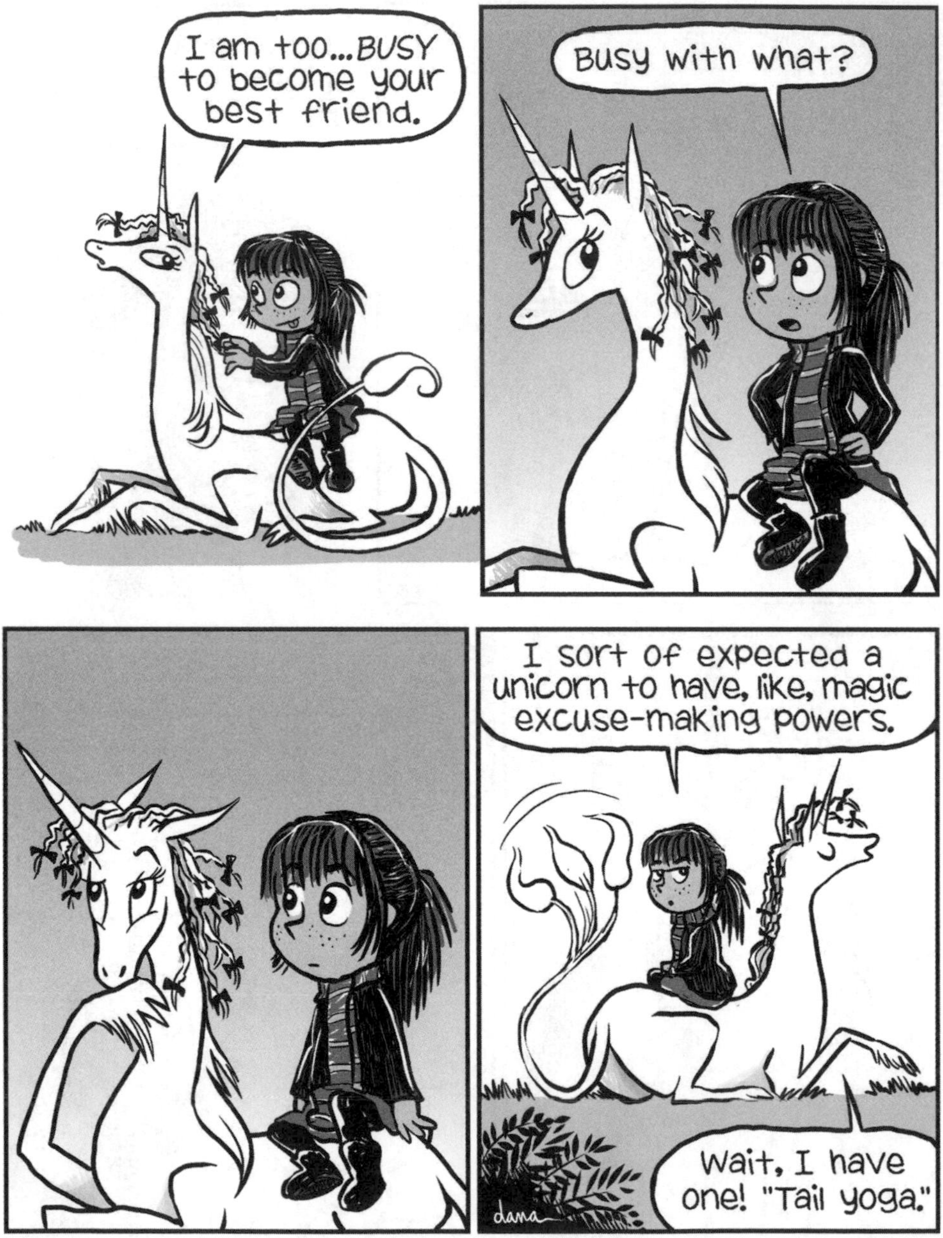
I am too...BUSY to become your best friend.
Busy with what?
I sort of expected a unicorn to have, like, magic excuse-making powers.
Wait, I have one! "Tail yoga."
dana

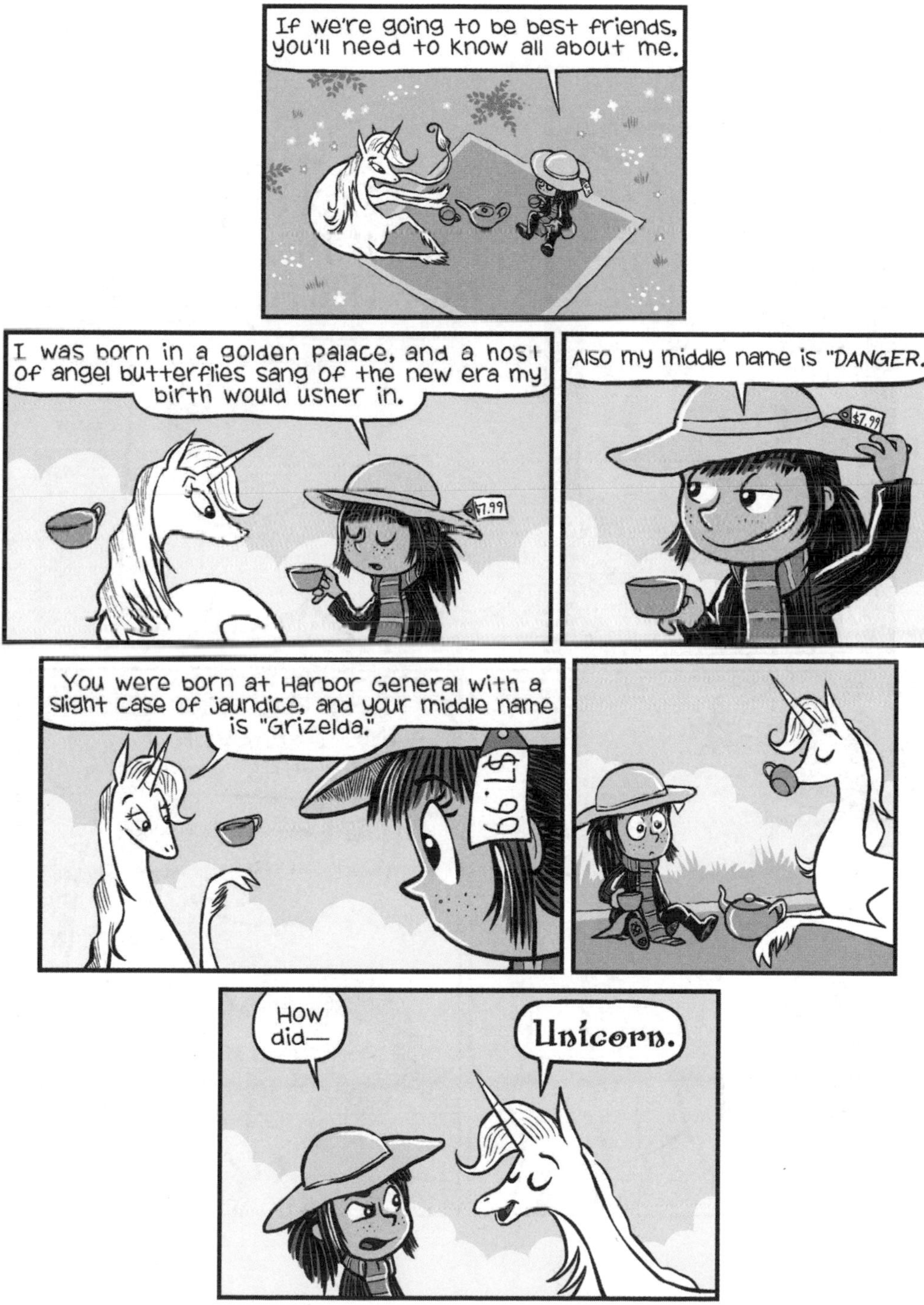

If we're going to be best friends, you'll need to know all about me.
I was born in a golden palace, and a host of angel butterflies sang of the new era my birth would usher in.
Also my middle name is "DANGER."
$7.99
You were born at Harbor General with a slight case of jaundice, and your middle name is "Grizelda."
$7.99
How did—
Unicorn.

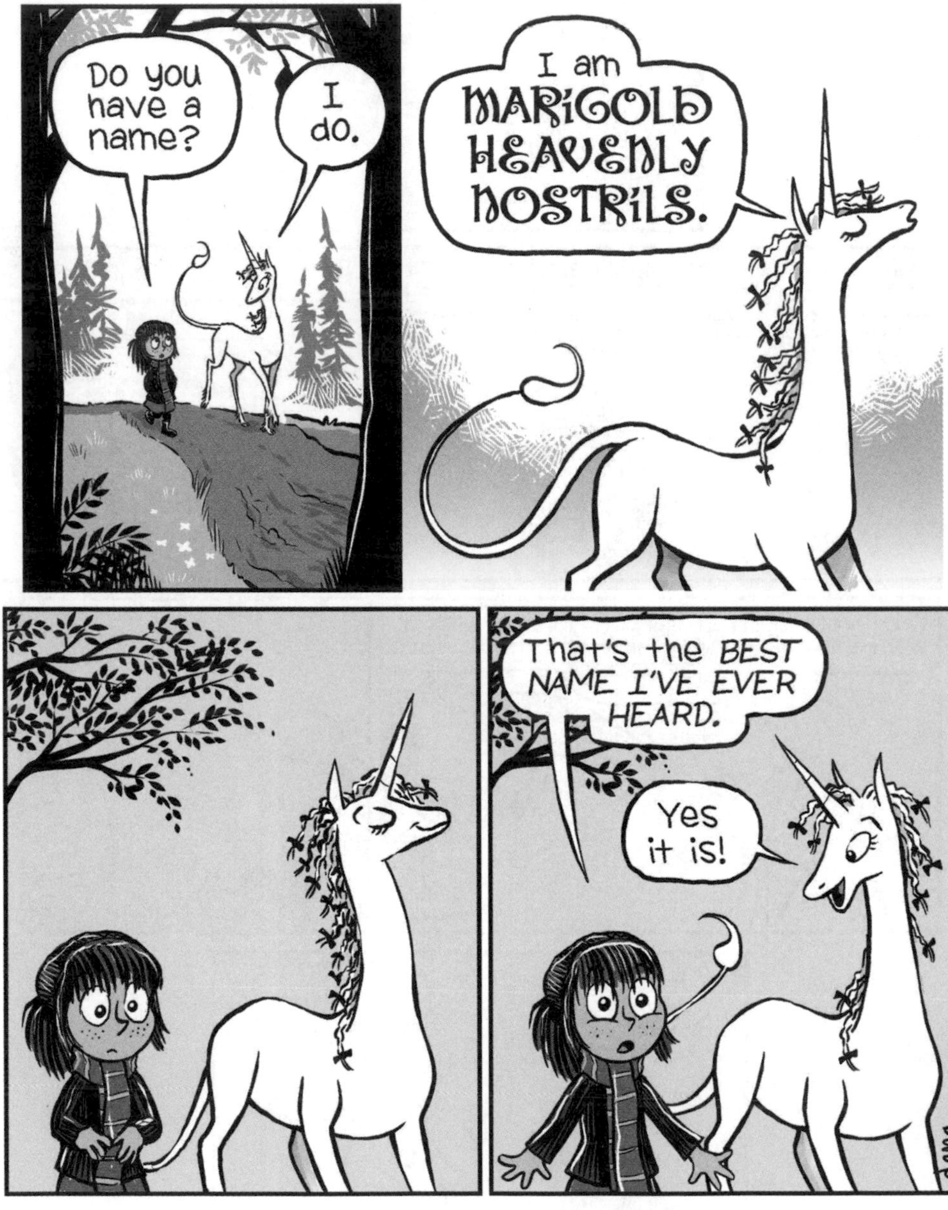
Do you have a name?
I do.
I am MARIGOLD HEAVENLY NOSTRILS.
That's the BEST NAME I'VE EVER HEARD.
Yes it is!
dana

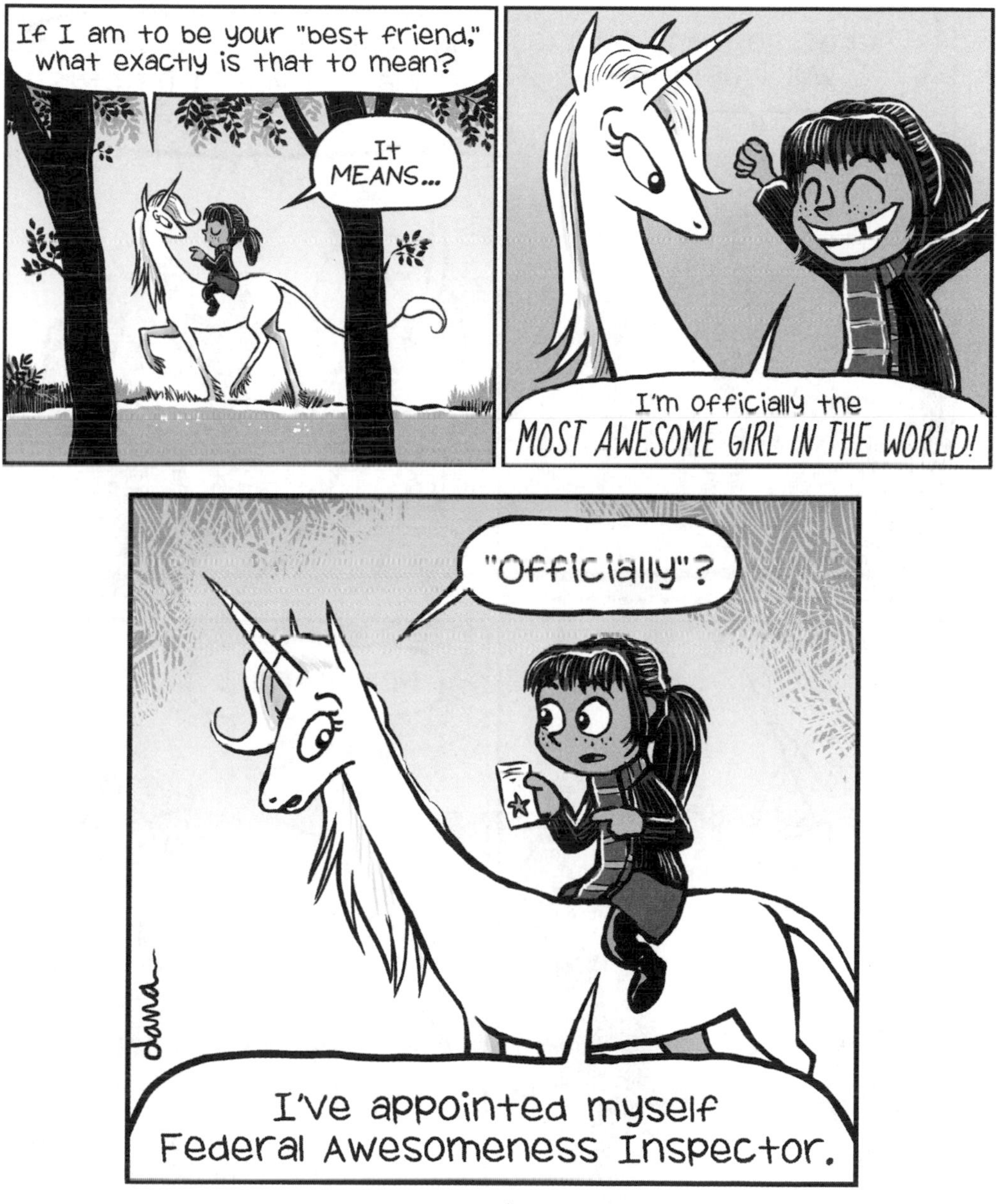
If I am to be your "best friend," what exactly is that to mean?
It MEANS...
I'm officially the MOST AWESOME GIRL IN THE WORLD!
"Officially"?
I've appointed myself Federal Awesomeness Inspector.
dana

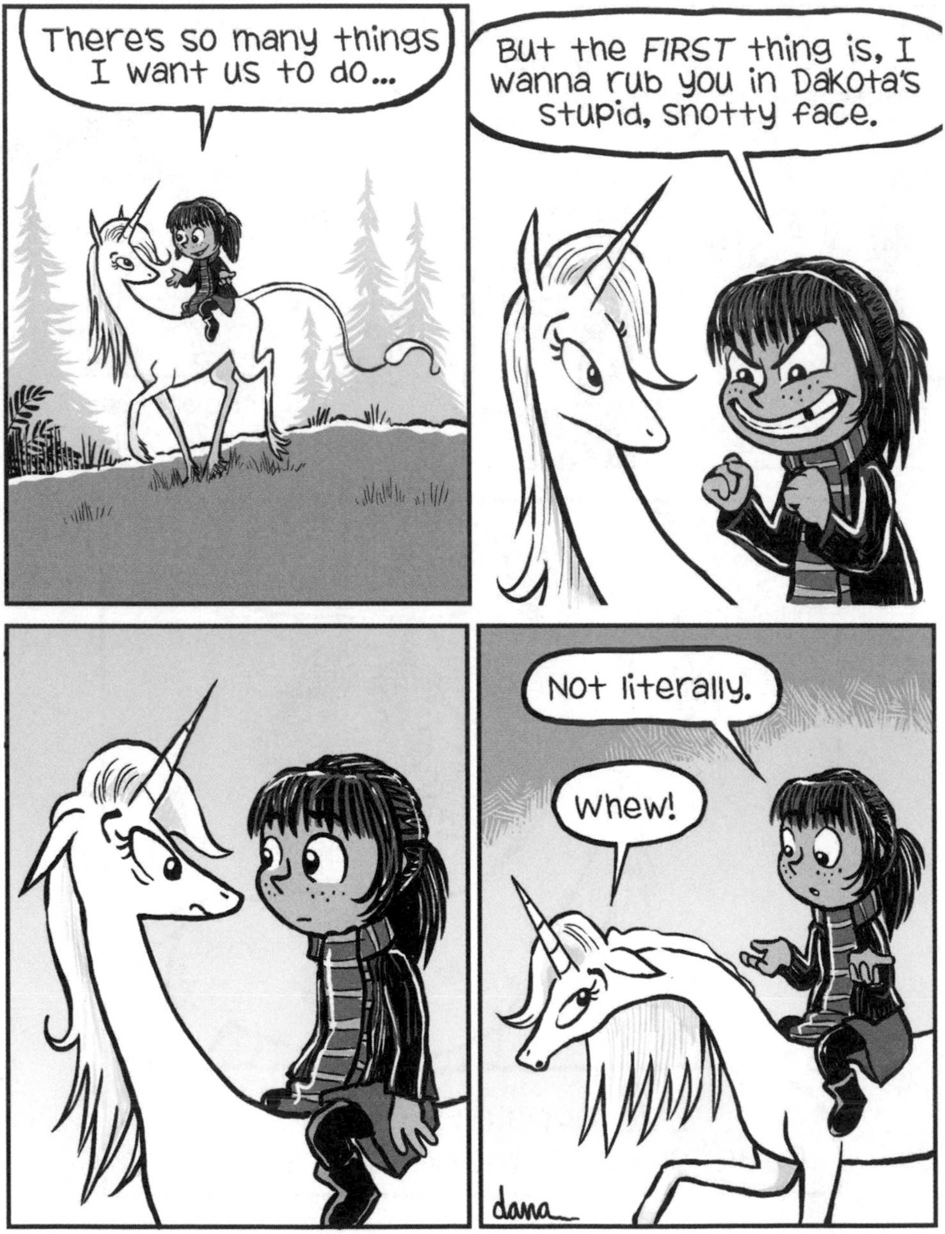
There's so many things I want us to do...
But the FIRST thing is, I wanna rub you in Dakota's stupid, snotty face.
Not literally.
Whew!
dana

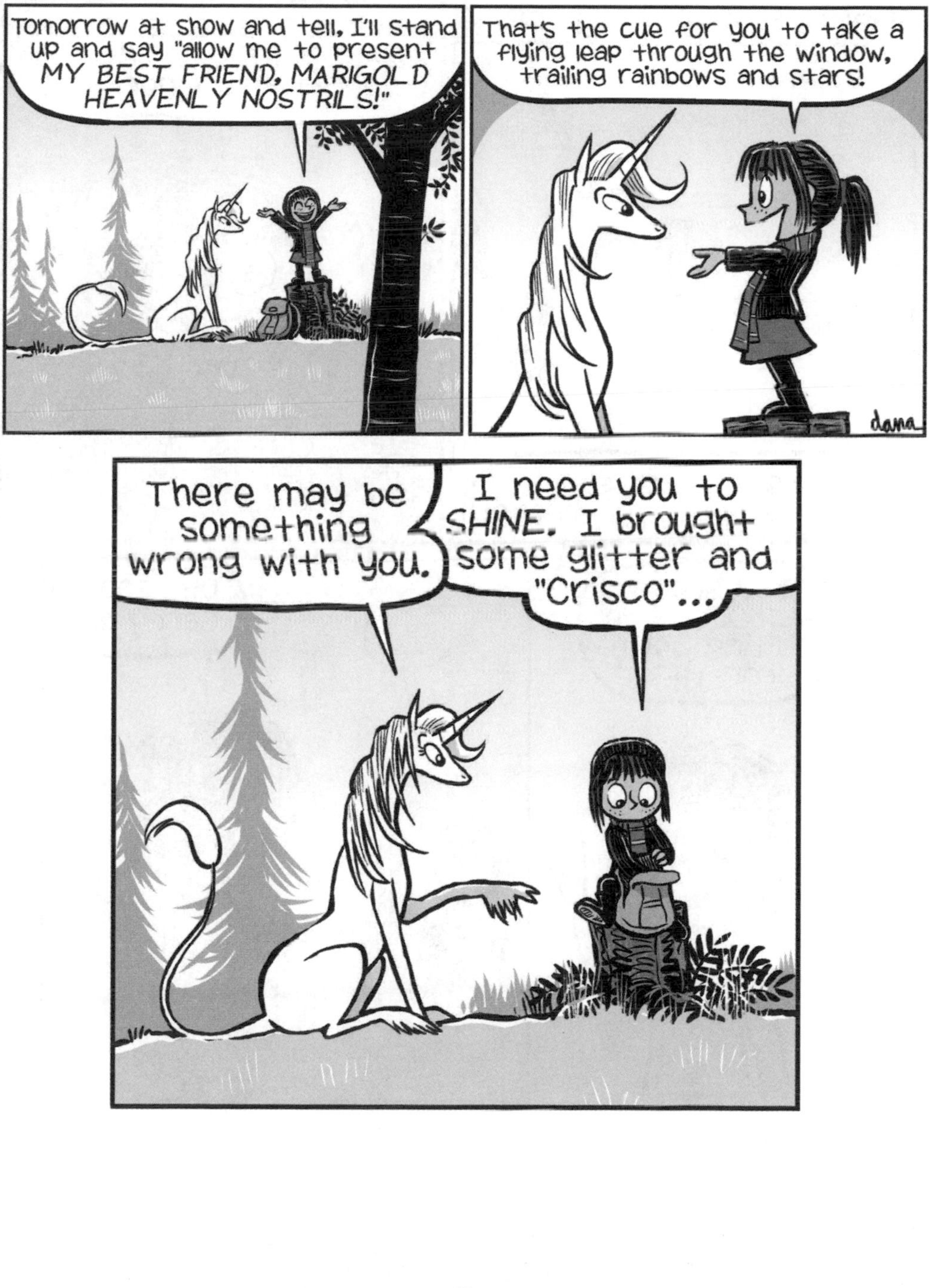
Tomorrow at show and tell, I'll stand up and say "allow me to present MY BEST FRIEND, MARIGOLD HEAVENLY NOSTRILS!"
That's the cue for you to take a flying leap through the window, trailing rainbows and stars!
dana
I need you to SHINE. I brought some glitter and "Crisco"...
There may be something wrong with you.

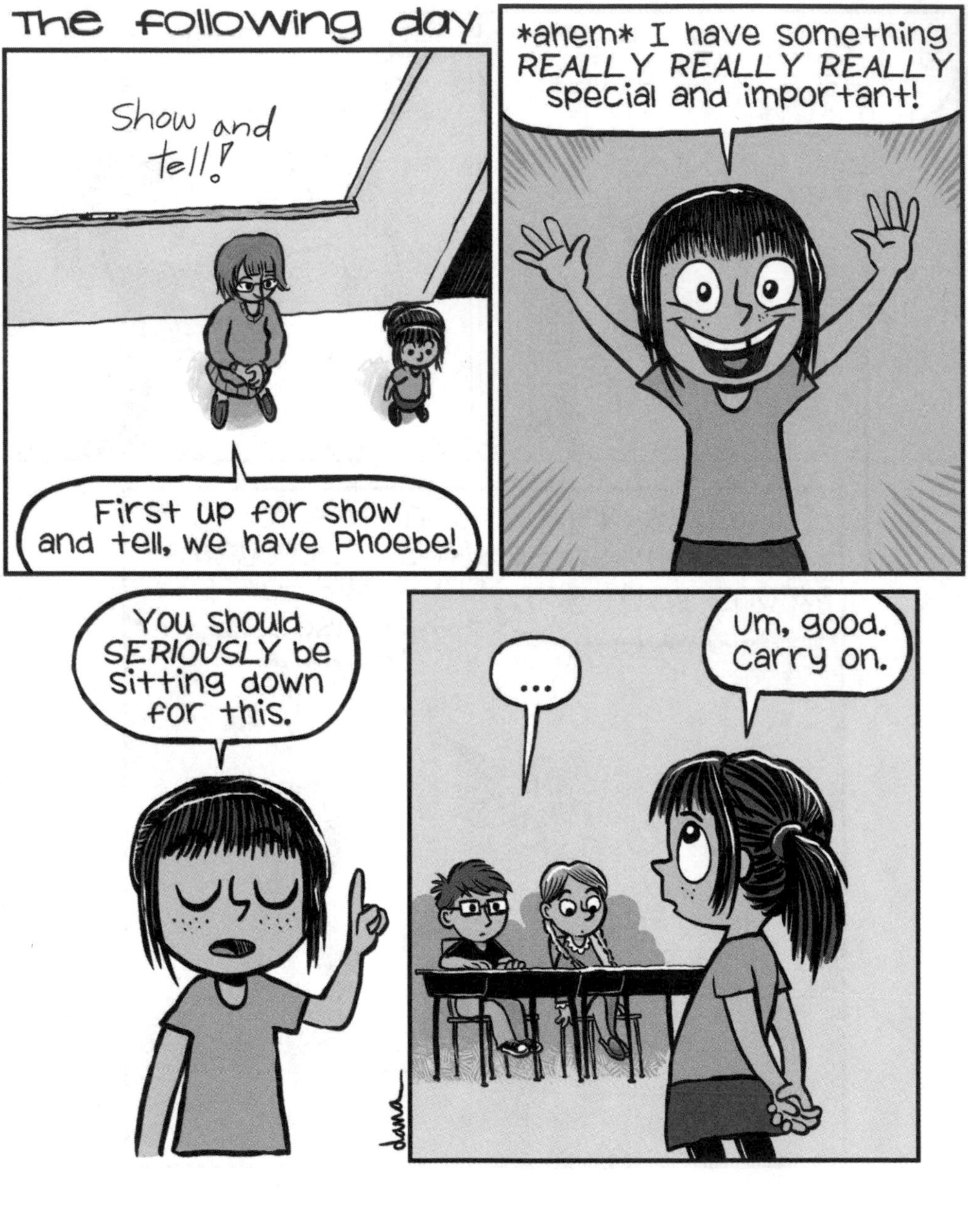
The following day
Show and tell!
First up for show and tell, we have Phoebe!
ahem I have something REALLY REALLY REALLY special and important!
You should SERIOUSLY be sitting down for this.
...
Um, good. Carry on.
dana

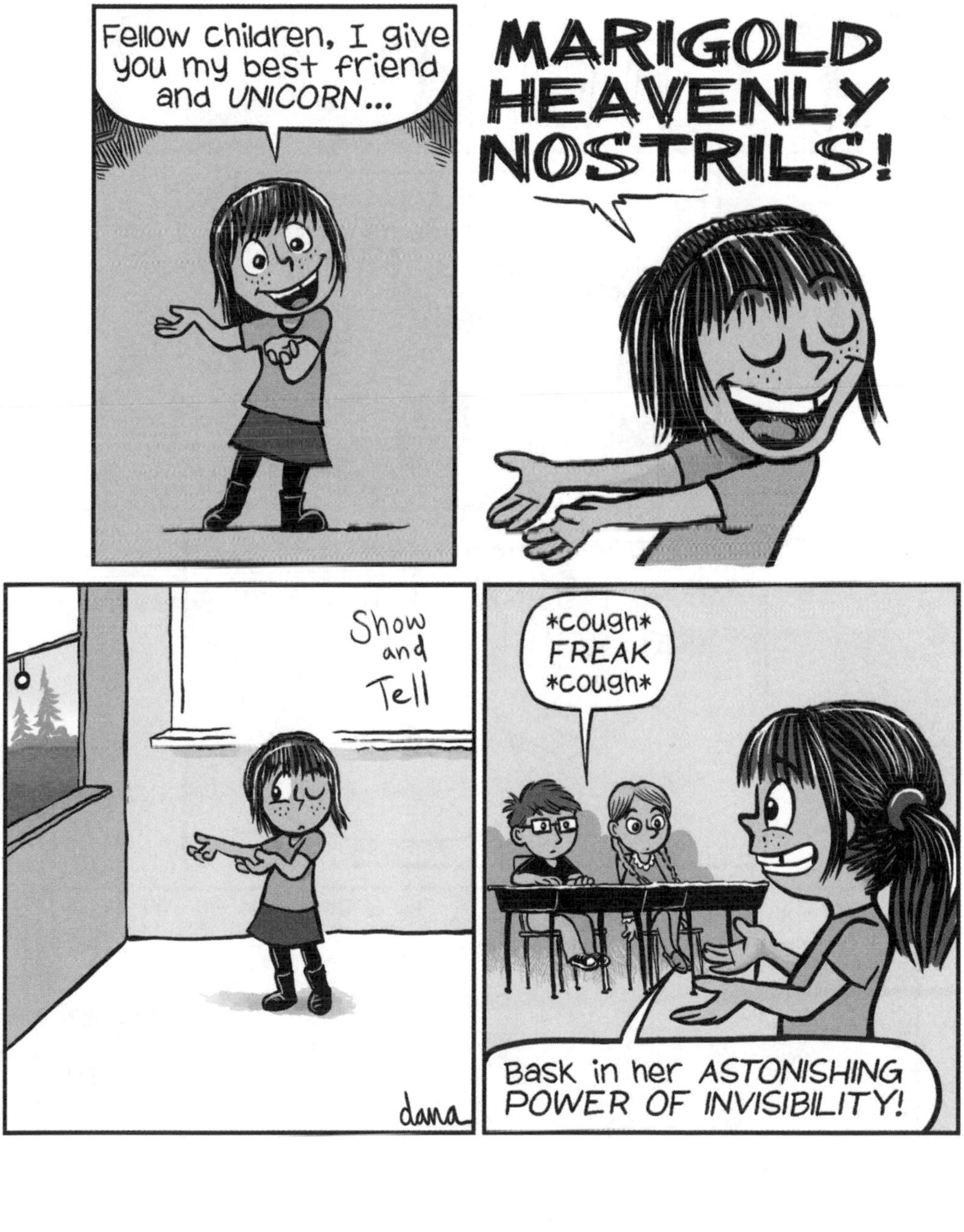
Fellow children, I give you my best friend and UNICORN...
MARIGOLD HEAVENLY NOSTRILS!
Show and Tell
cough FREAK *cough*
Bask in her ASTONISHING POWER OF INVISIBILITY!
dana

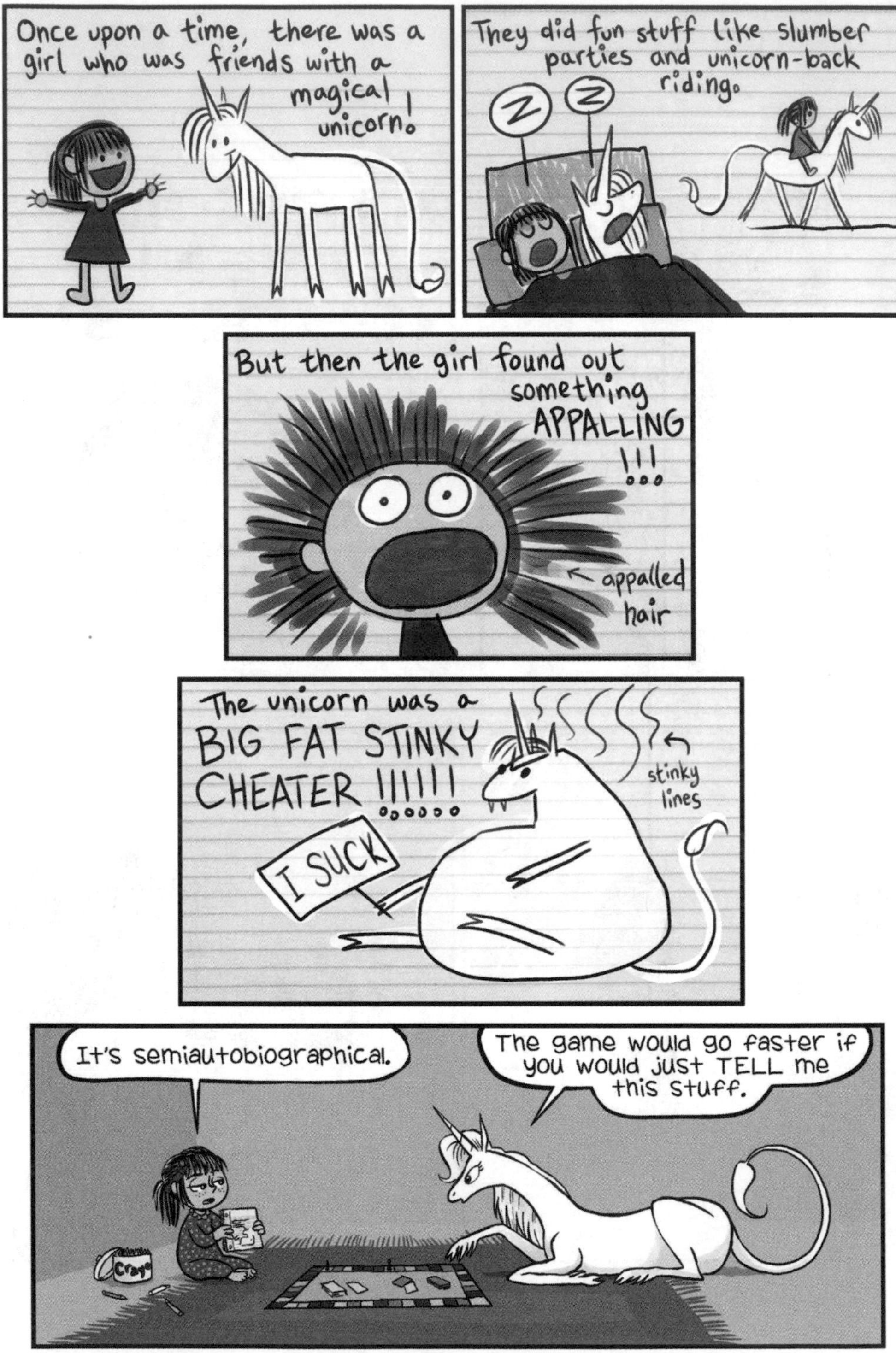
Once upon a time, there was a girl who was friends with a magical unicorn!
They did fun stuff like slumber parties and unicorn-back riding.
Z
Z
But then the girl found out something APPALLING!!!
appalled hair
The unicorn was a BIG FAT STINKY CHEATER!!!!!!
stinky lines
I SUCK
It's semiautobiographical.
The game would go faster if you would just TELL me this stuff.

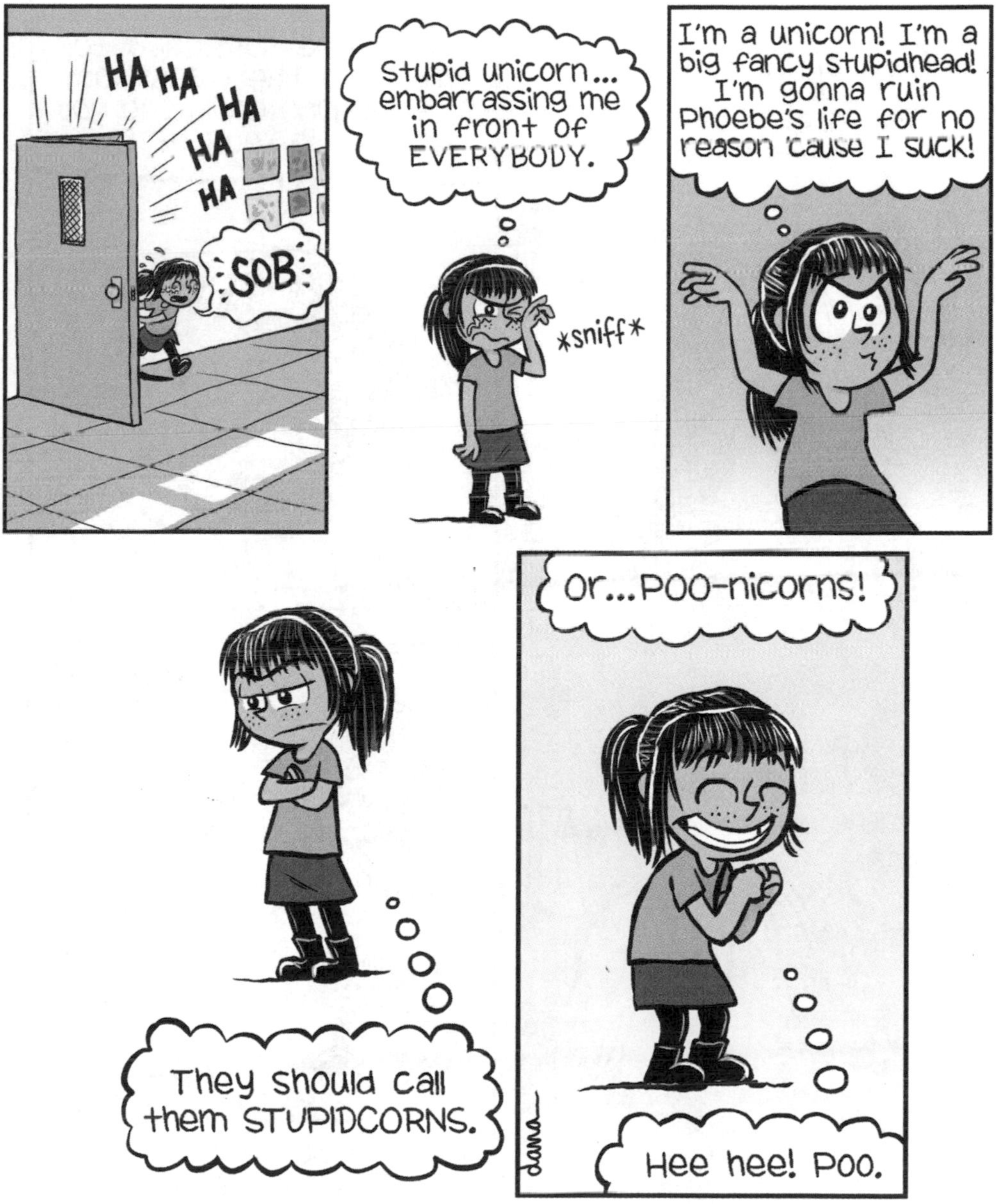
HA HA HA HA HA
SOB
Stupid unicorn... embarrassing me in front of EVERYBODY.
sniff
I'm a unicorn! I'm a big fancy stupidhead! I'm gonna ruin Phoebe's life for no reason 'cause I suck!
They should call them STUPIDCORNS.
Or...POO-nicorns!
Hee hee! Poo.
dana

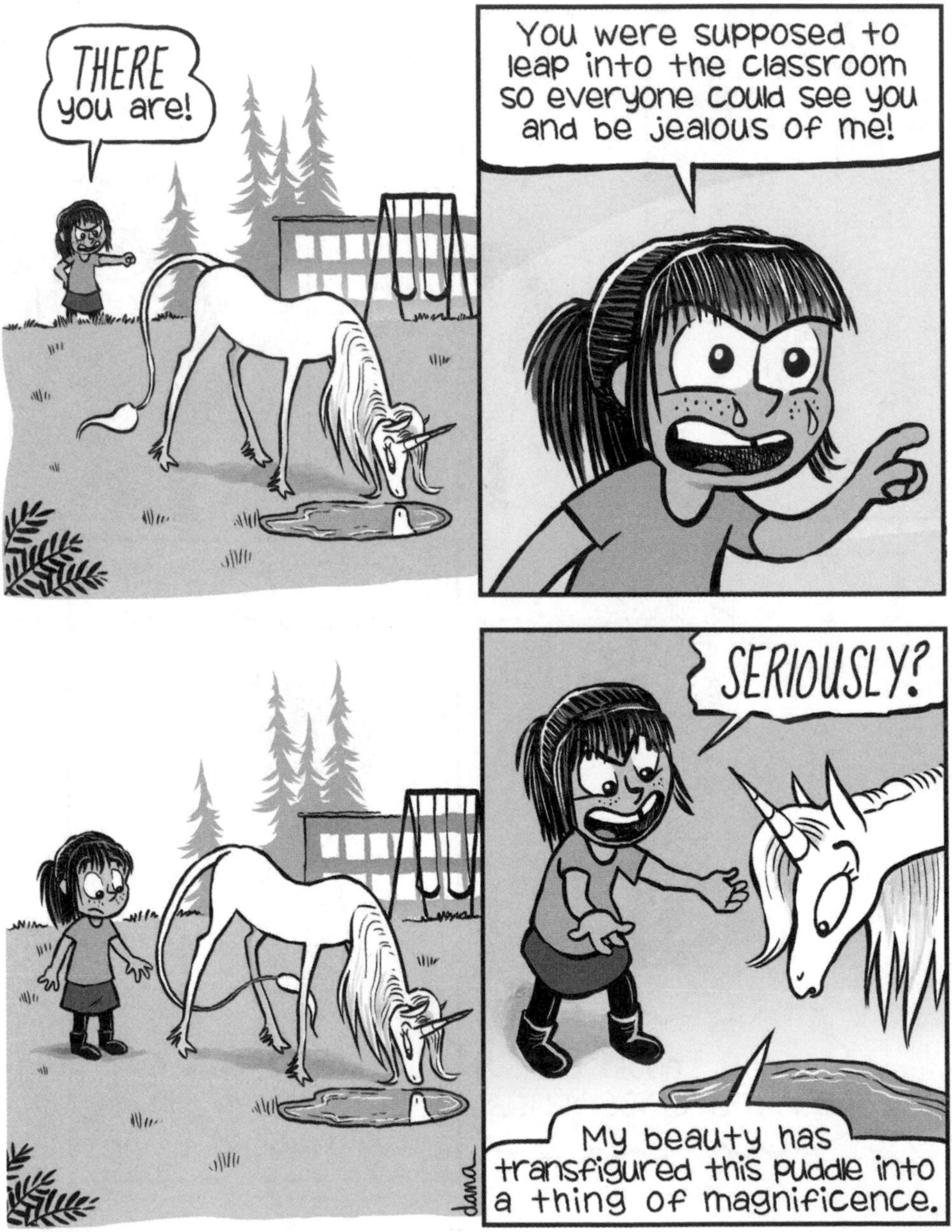
THERE you are!
You were supposed to leap into the classroom so everyone could see you and be jealous of me!
SERIOUSLY?
My beauty has transfigured this puddle into a thing of magnificence.
dana

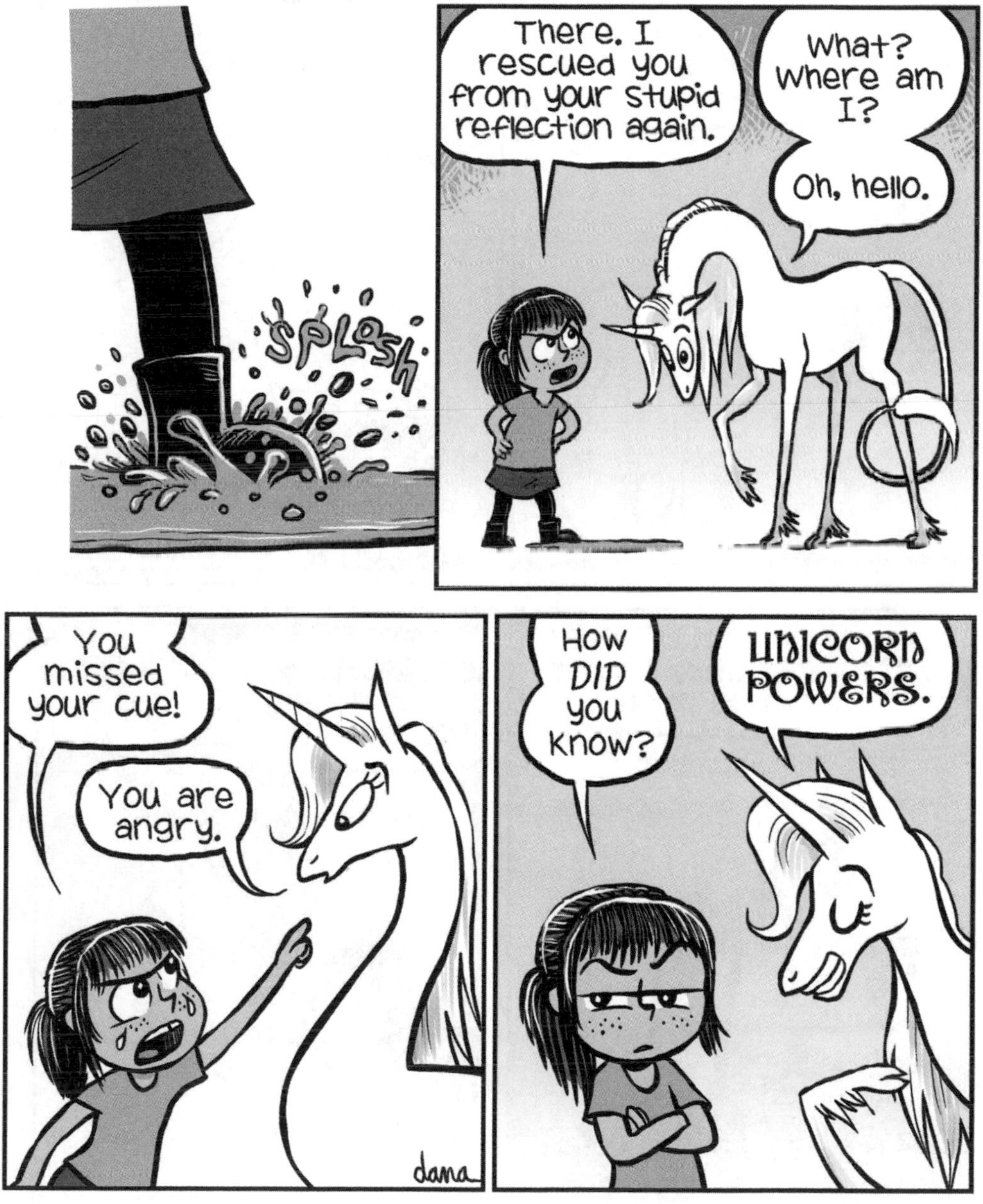
SPLOSH
There. I rescued you from your stupid reflection again.
What? Where am I?
Oh, hello.
You missed your cue!
You are angry.
How DID you know?
UNICORN POWERS.
dana

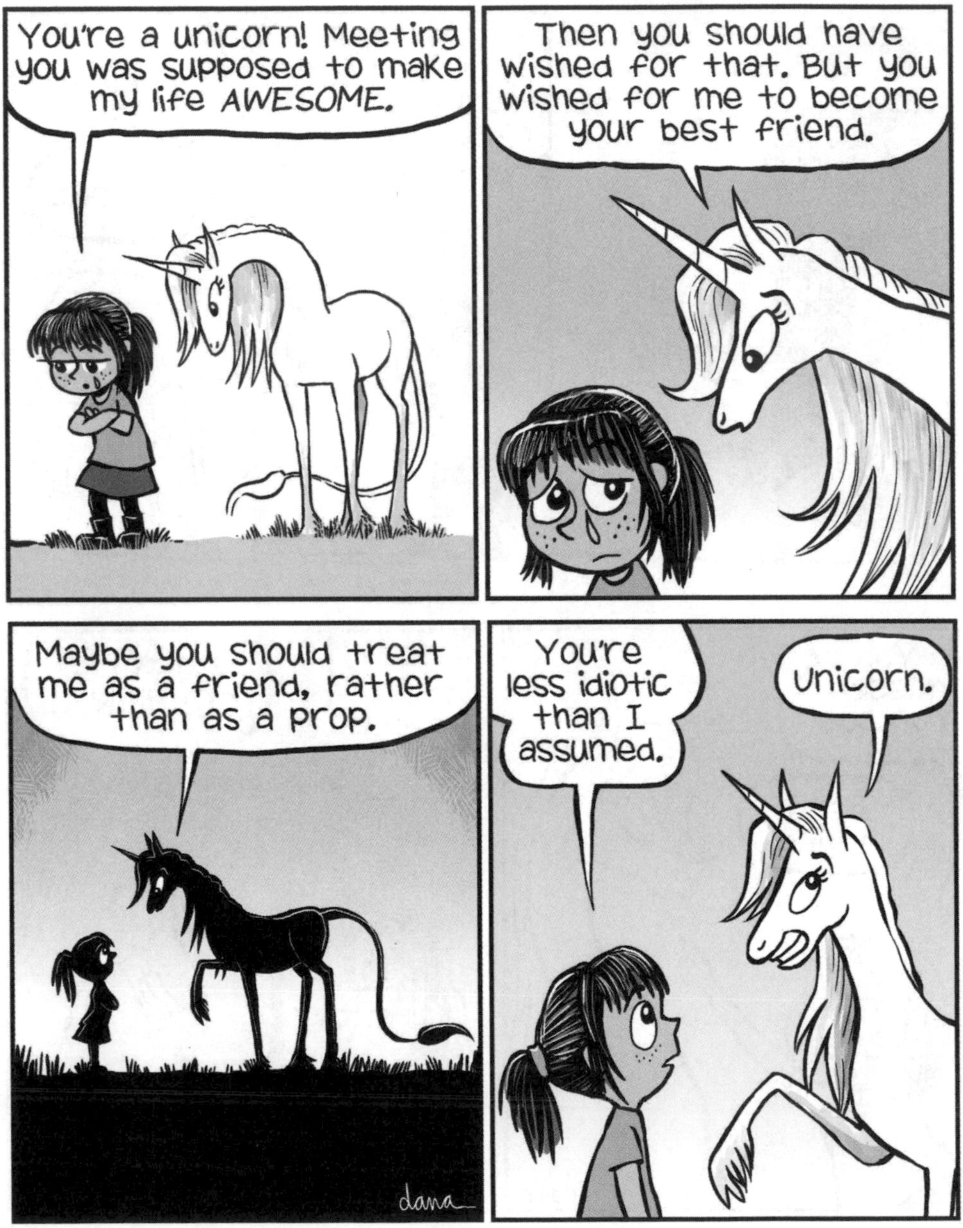
You're a unicorn! Meeting you was supposed to make my life AWESOME.
Then you should have wished for that. But you wished for me to become your best friend.
Maybe you should treat me as a friend, rather than as a prop.
dana
You're less idiotic than I assumed.
Unicorn.

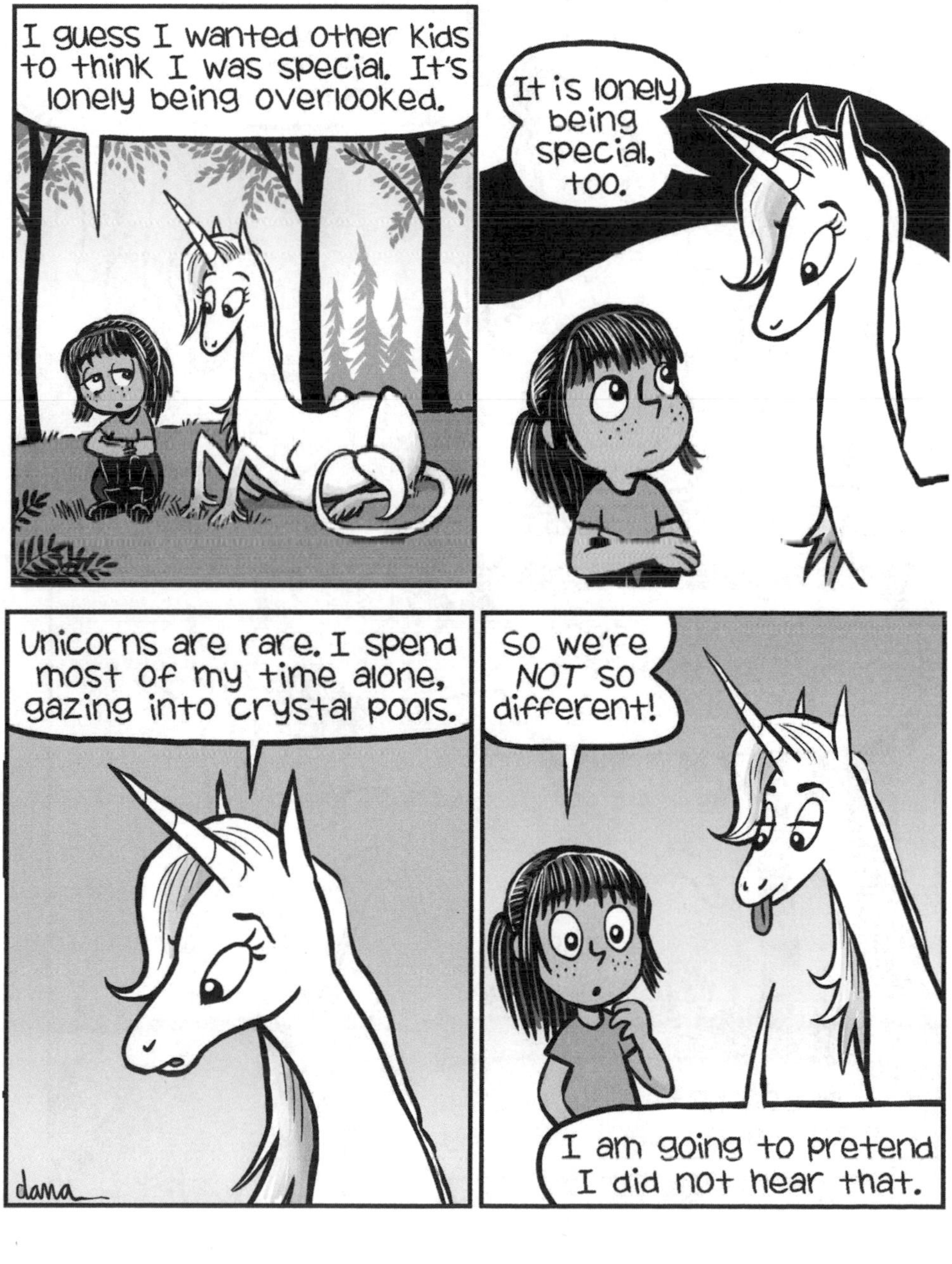
I guess I wanted other kids to think I was special. It's lonely being overlooked.
It is lonely being special, too.
Unicorns are rare. I spend most of my time alone, gazing into crystal pools.
So we're *NOT* so different!
I am going to pretend I did not hear that.
dana

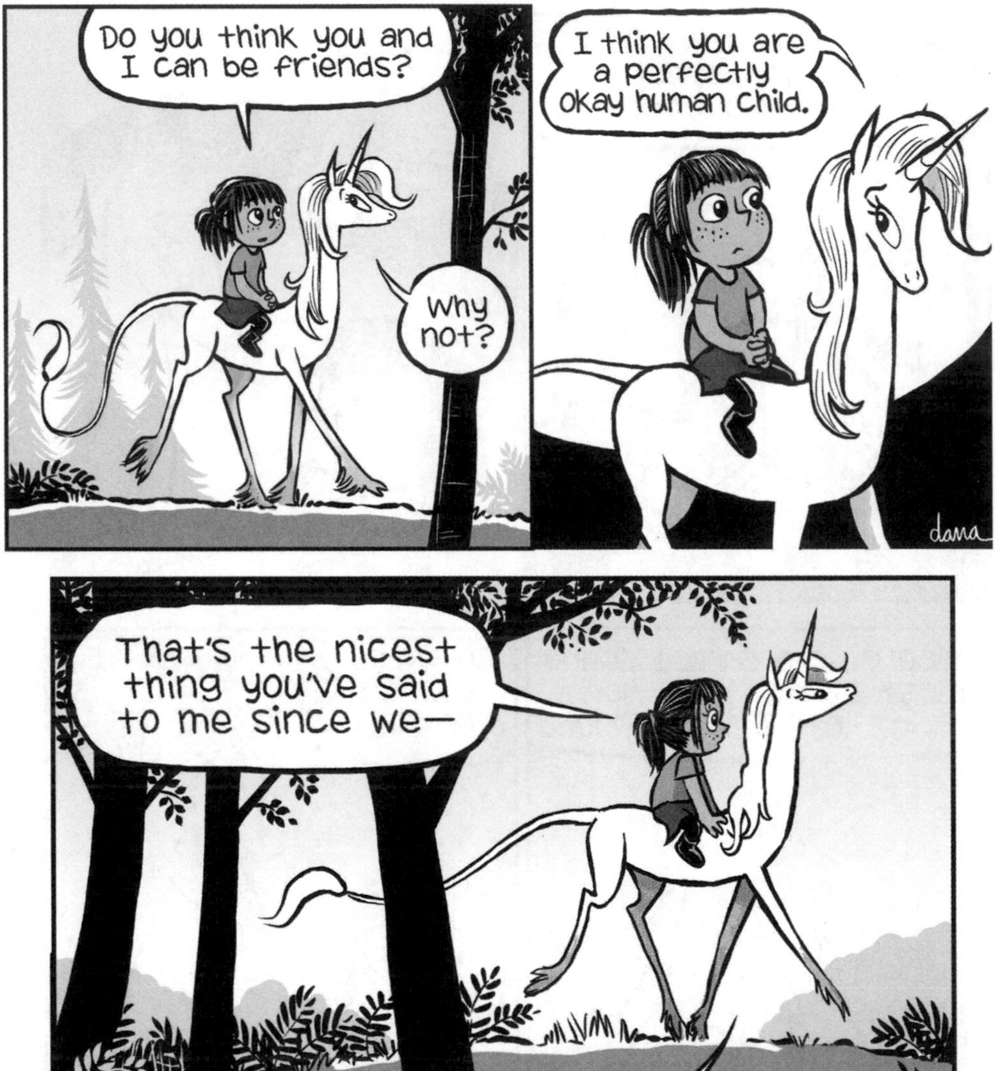
Do you think you and I can be friends?
Why not?
I think you are a perfectly okay human child.
dana
That's the nicest thing you've said to me since we—
A presumptuous, bossy, snot-faced sort of okay.

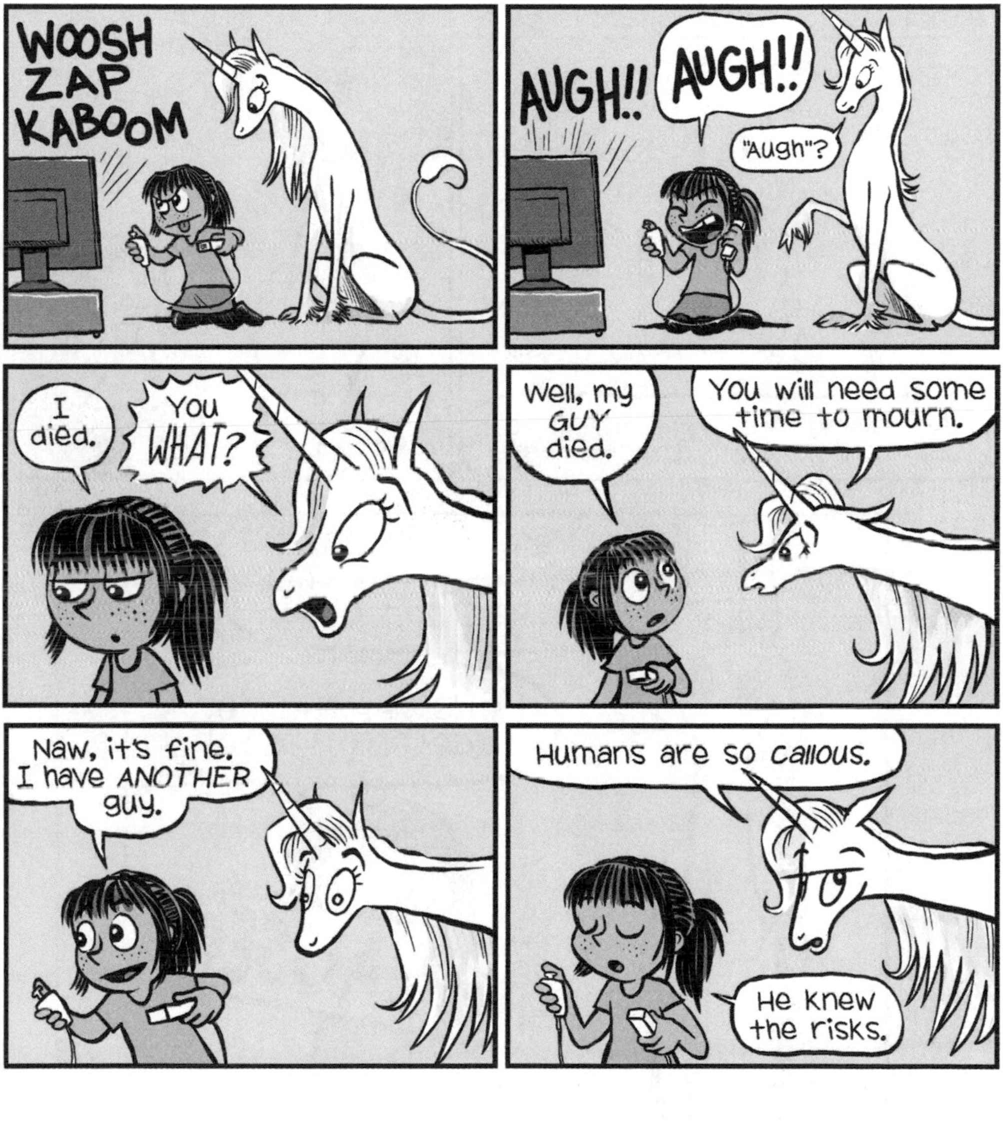
WOOSH
ZAP
KABOOM
AUGH!!
AUGH!!
"Augh"?
I died.
You WHAT?
Well, my GUY died.
You will need some time to mourn.
Naw, it's fine. I have ANOTHER guy.
Humans are so callous.
He knew the risks.

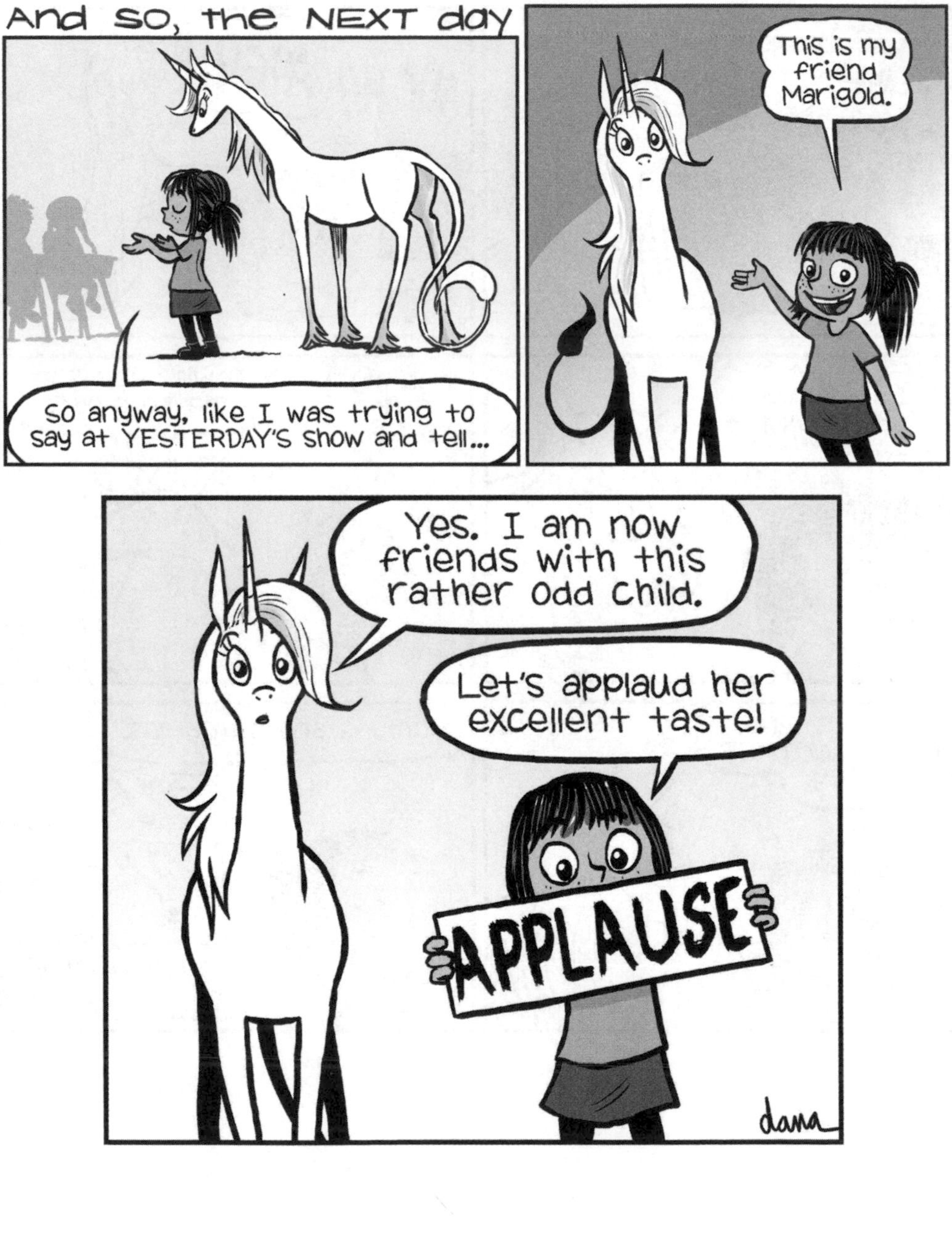
And so, the NEXT day
So anyway, like I was trying to say at YESTERDAY'S show and tell...
This is my friend Marigold.
Yes. I am now friends with this rather odd child.
Let's applaud her excellent taste!
APPLAUSE
dana

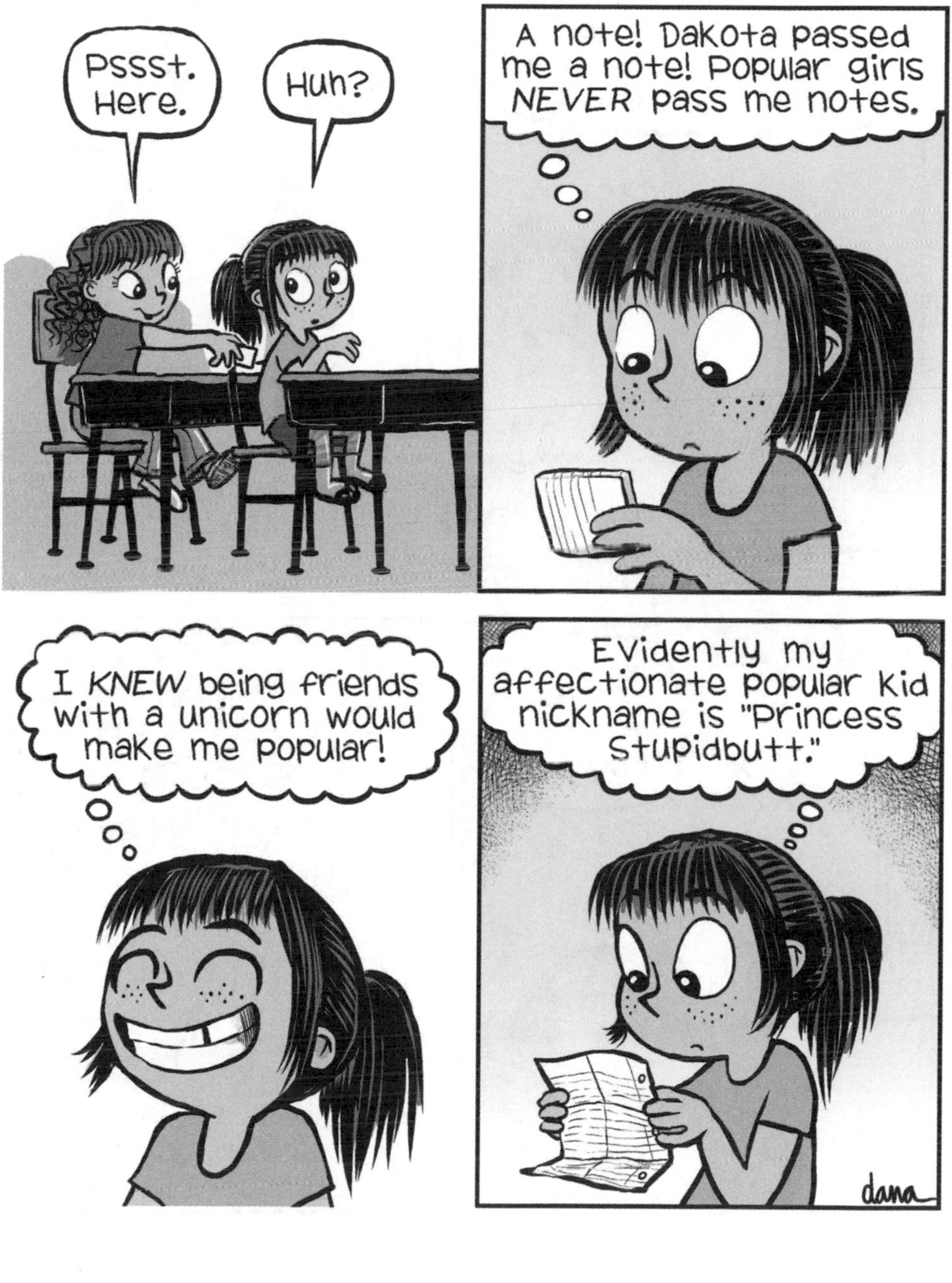
Pssst. Here.
Huh?
A note! Dakota passed me a note! Popular girls NEVER pass me notes.
I KNEW being friends with a unicorn would make me popular!
Evidently my affectionate popular kid nickname is "Princess Stupidbutt."
dana

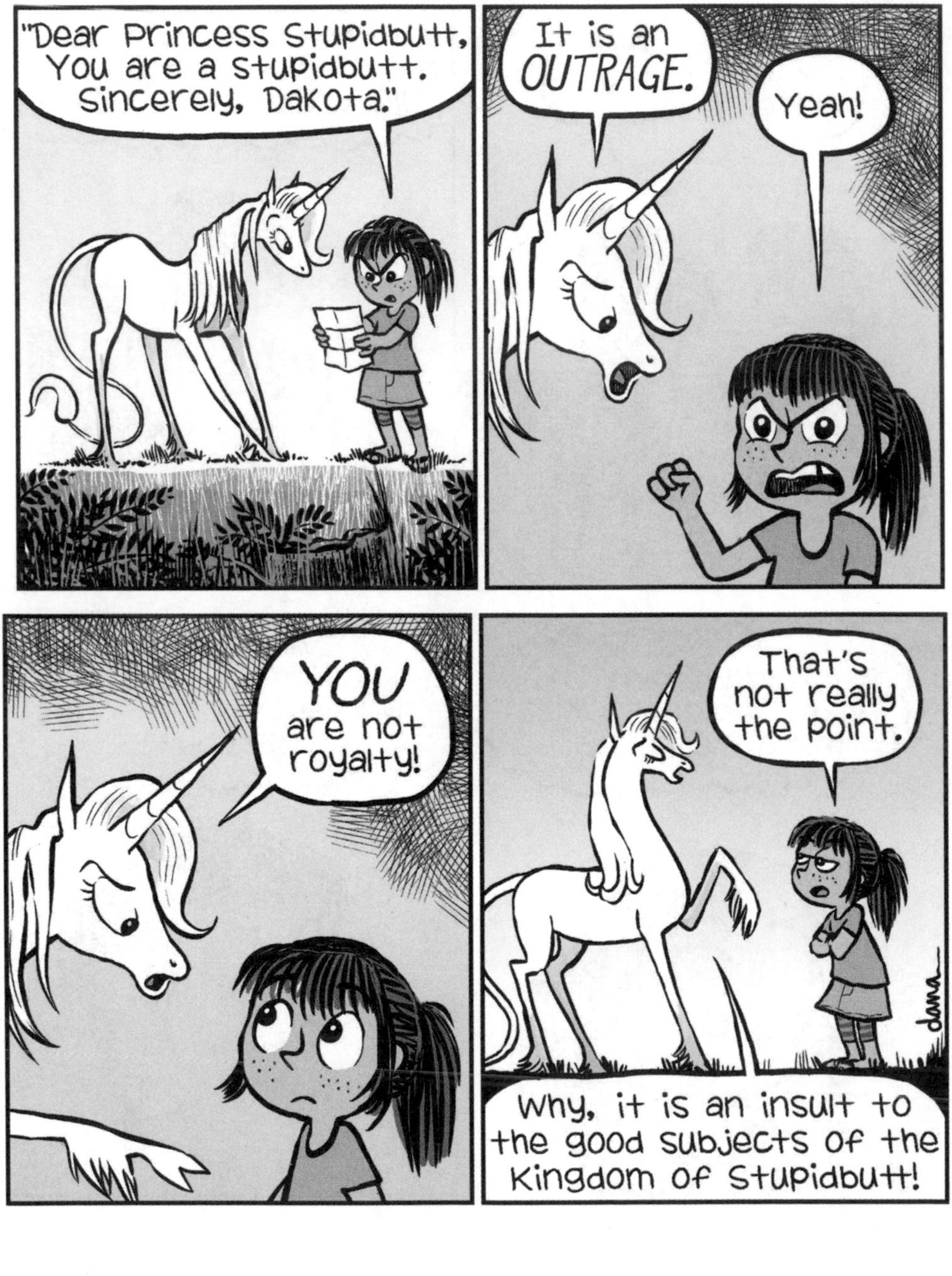
"Dear Princess Stupidbutt, You are a stupidbutt. Sincerely, Dakota."
It is an OUTRAGE.
Yeah!
YOU are not royalty!
That's not really the point.
Why, it is an insult to the good subjects of the Kingdom of Stupidbutt!
dana

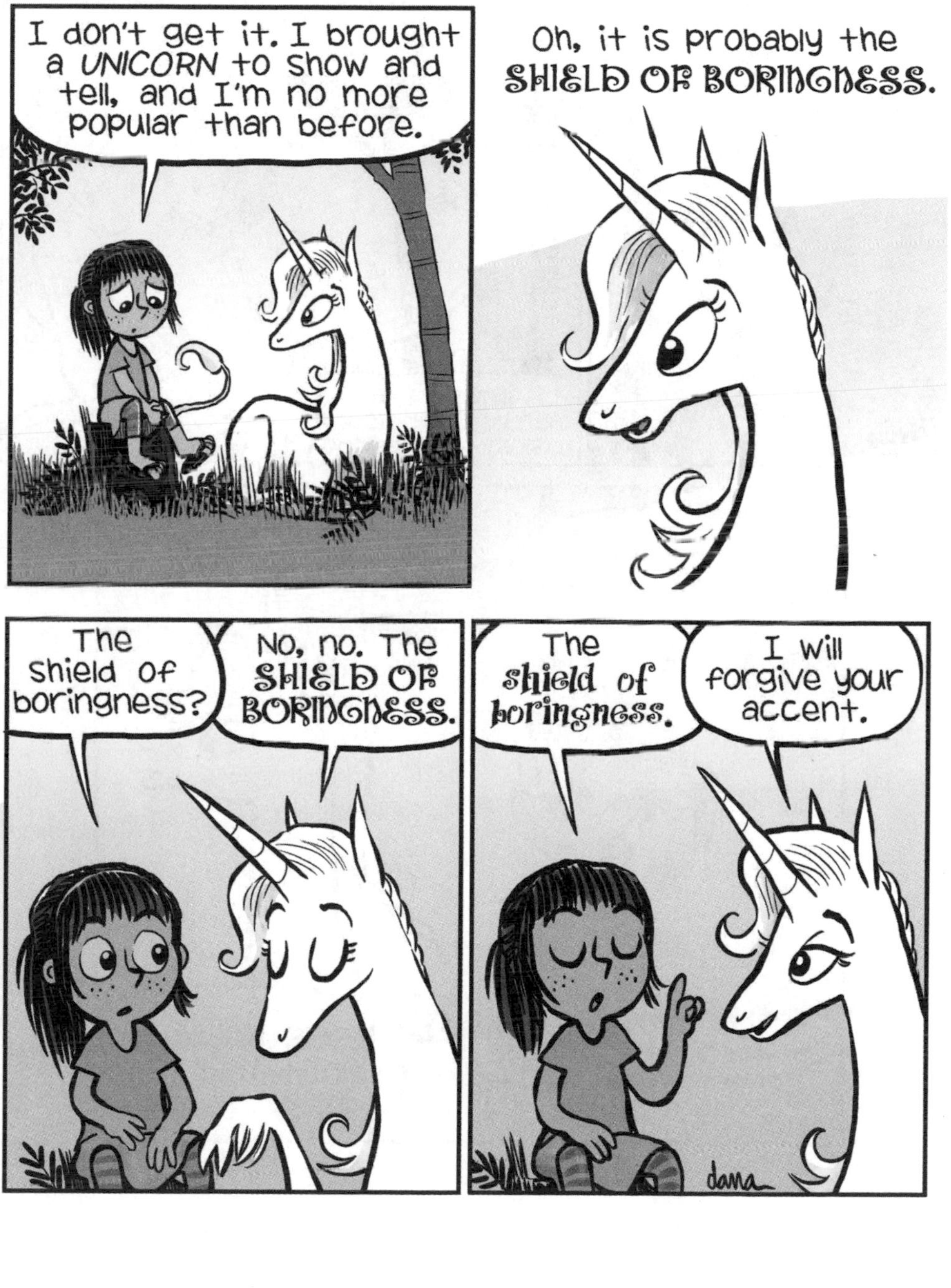
I don't get it. I brought a *UNICORN* to show and tell, and I'm no more popular than before.
Oh, it is probably the SHIELD OF BORINGNESS.
The shield of boringness?
No, no. The SHIELD OF BORINGNESS.
The shield of boringness.
I will forgive your accent.
dana

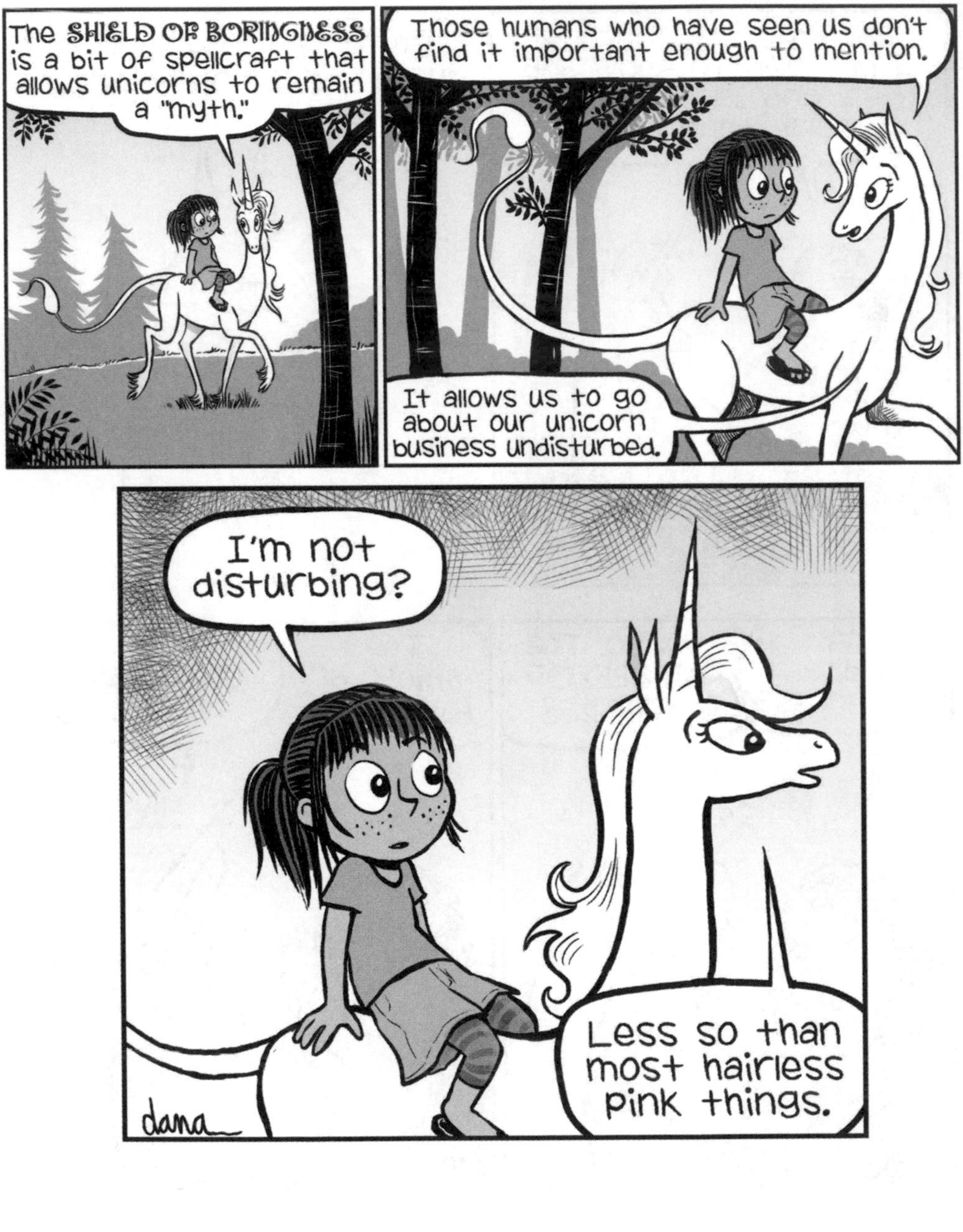
The SHIELD OF BORINGNESS is a bit of spellcraft that allows unicorns to remain a "myth."
Those humans who have seen us don't find it important enough to mention.
It allows us to go about our unicorn business undisturbed.
I'm not disturbing?
Less so than most hairless pink things.
dana

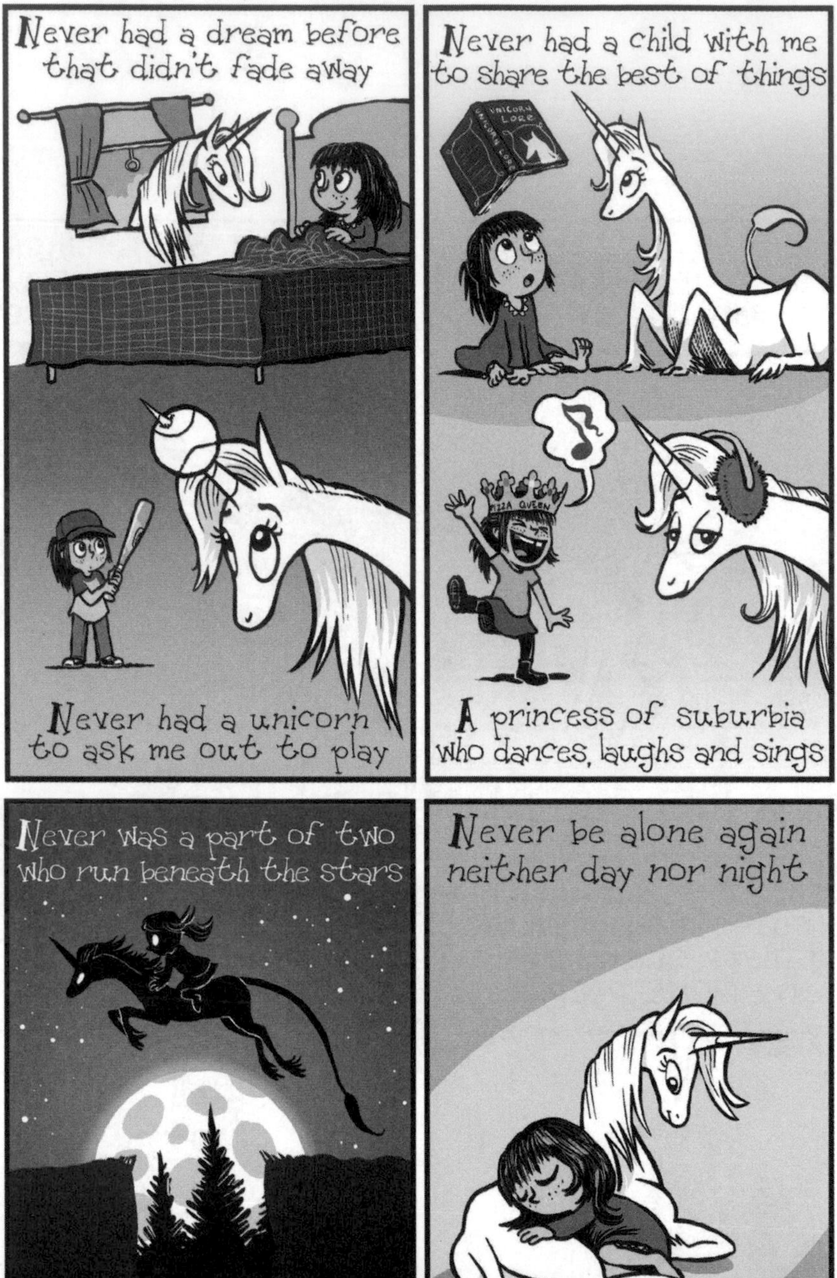
Never had a dream before that didn't fade away
Never had a unicorn to ask me out to play
Never had a child with me to share the best of things
UNICORN LORE
PIZZA QUEEN
A princess of suburbia who dances, laughs and sings
Never was a part of two who run beneath the stars
Never had a someone who could tell me "THIS IS OURS."
Never be alone again neither day nor night
A princess and a unicorn have finally got it right.

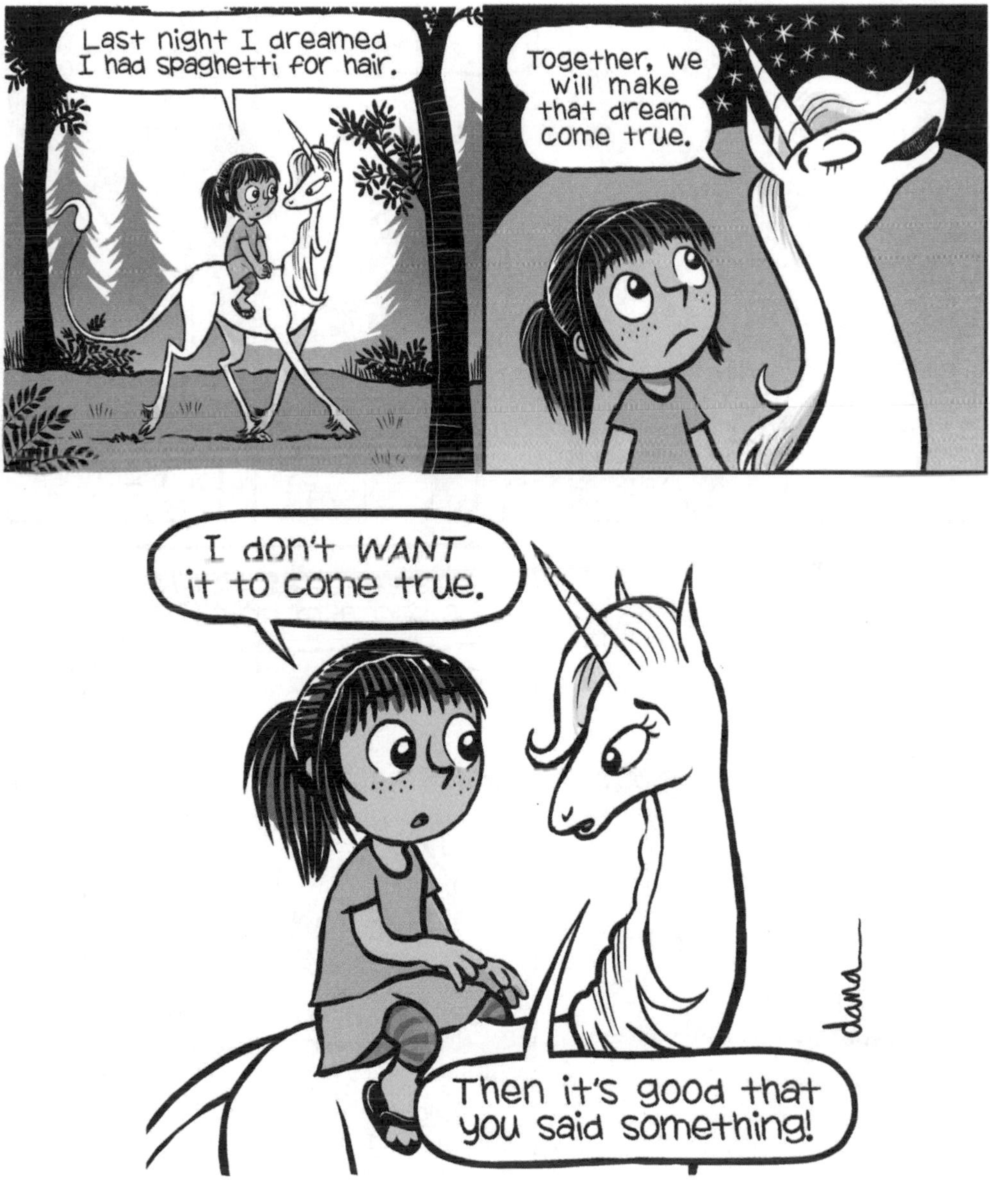
Last night I dreamed I had spaghetti for hair.
Together, we will make that dream come true.
I don't WANT it to come true.
Then it's good that you said something!
dana

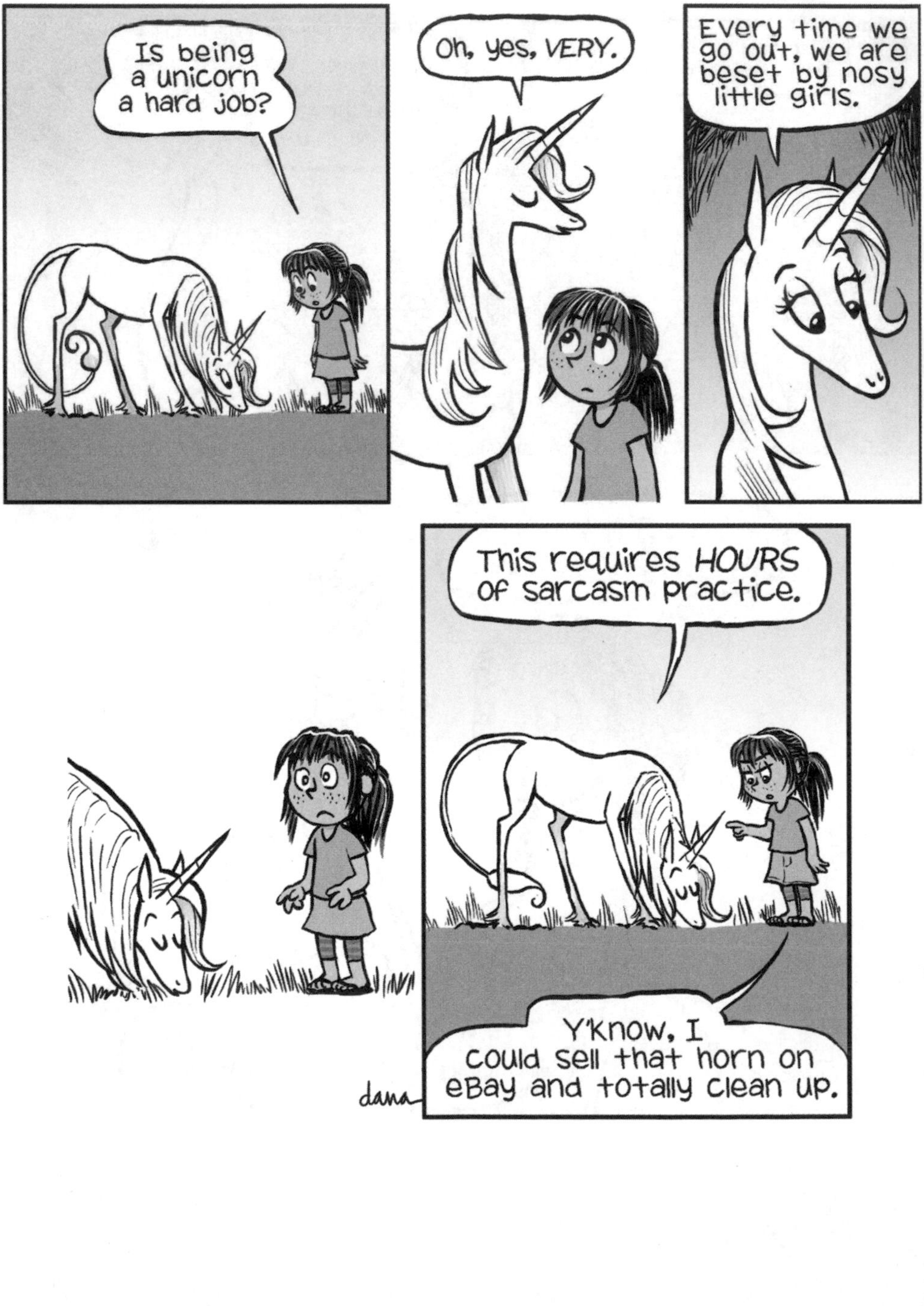
Is being a unicorn a hard job?
Oh, yes, VERY.
Every time we go out, we are beset by nosy little girls.
This requires HOURS of sarcasm practice.
Y'know, I could sell that horn on eBay and totally clean up.
dana

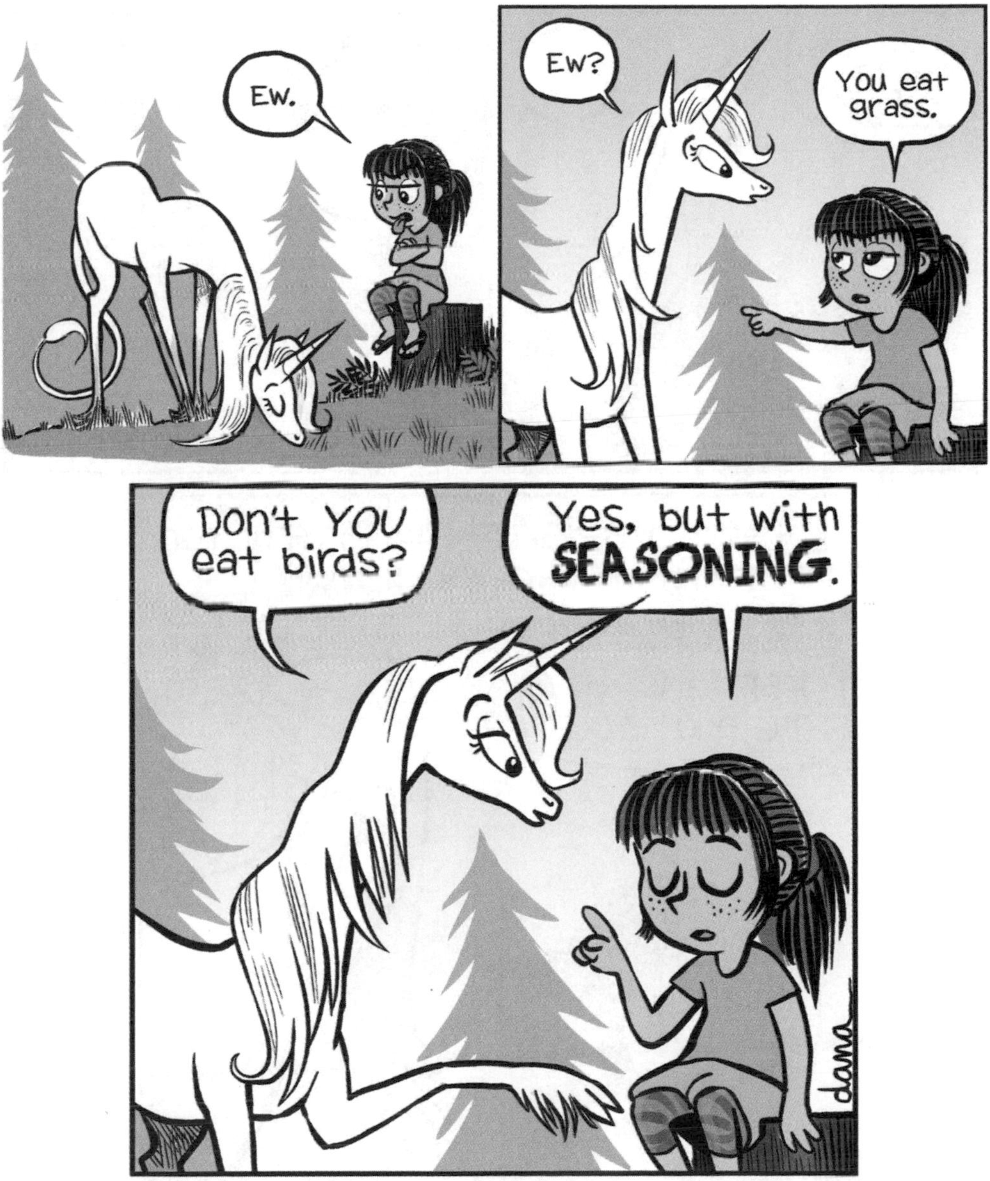
Ew.
Ew?
You eat grass.
Don't YOU eat birds?
Yes, but with SEASONING.
dana

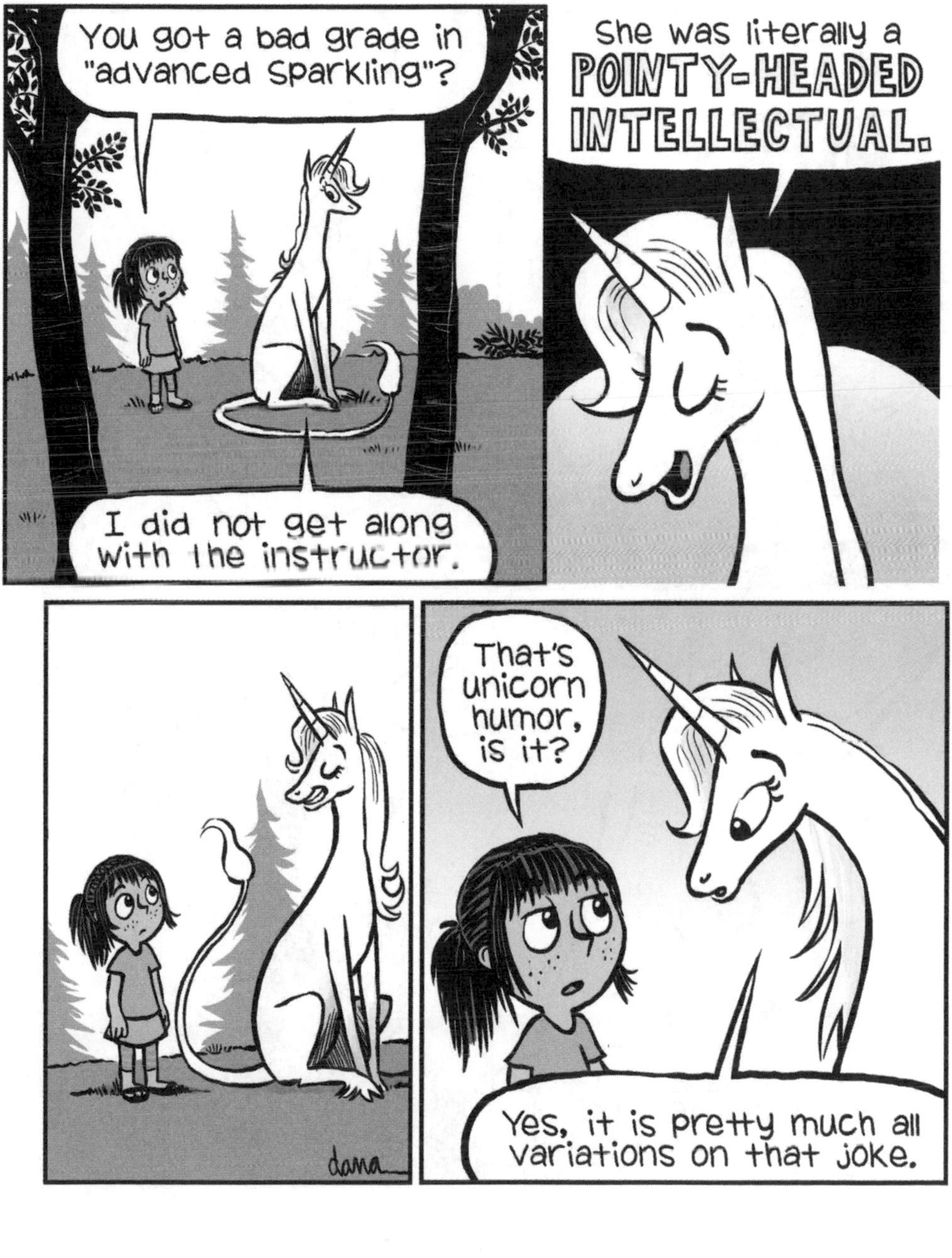
You got a bad grade in "advanced Sparkling"?
I did not get along with the instructor.
She was literally a POINTY-HEADED INTELLECTUAL.
That's unicorn humor, is it?
Yes, it is pretty much all variations on that joke.
dana

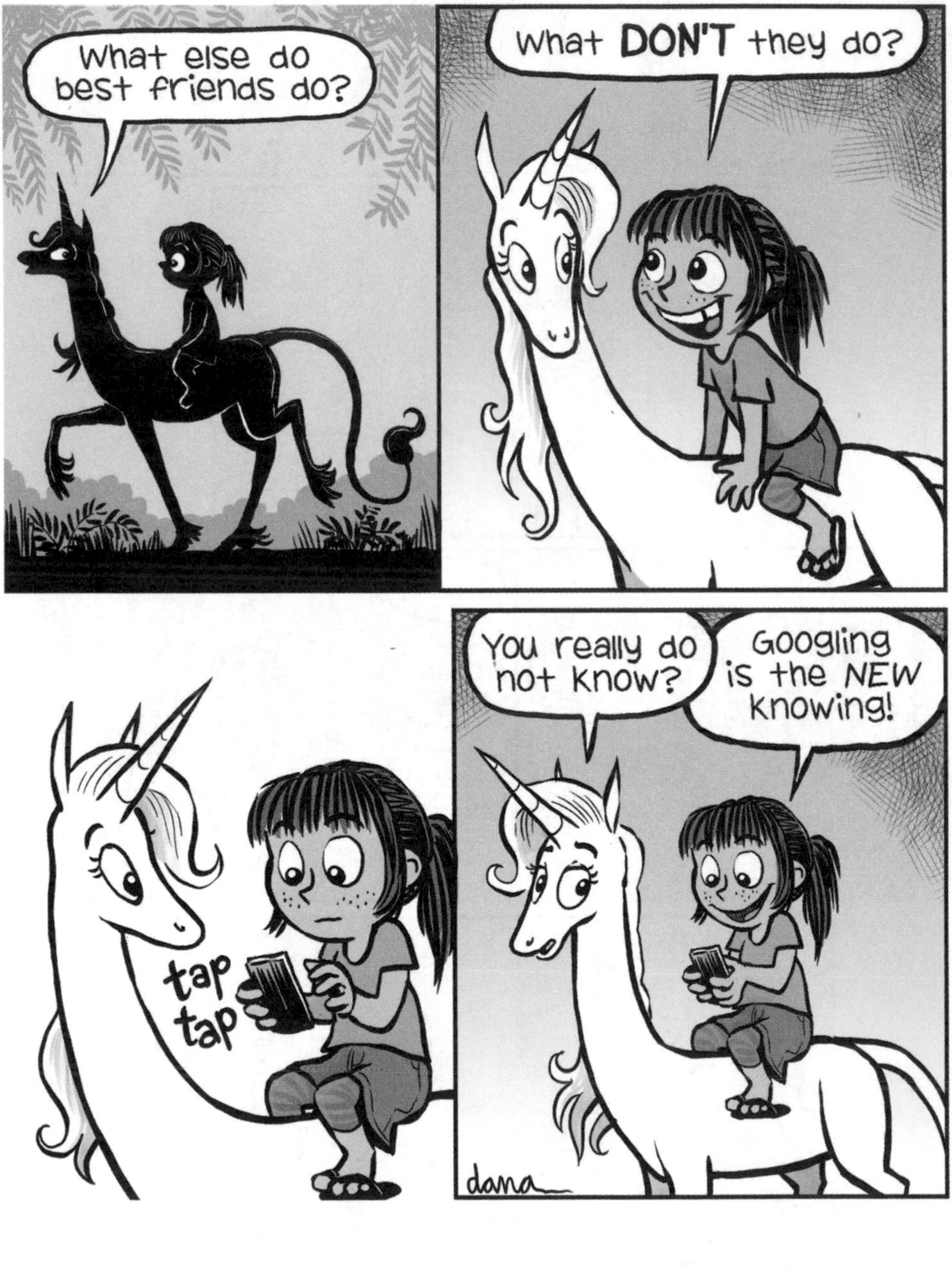
What else do best friends do?
What DON'T they do?
tap tap
You really do not know?
Googling is the NEW knowing!
dana

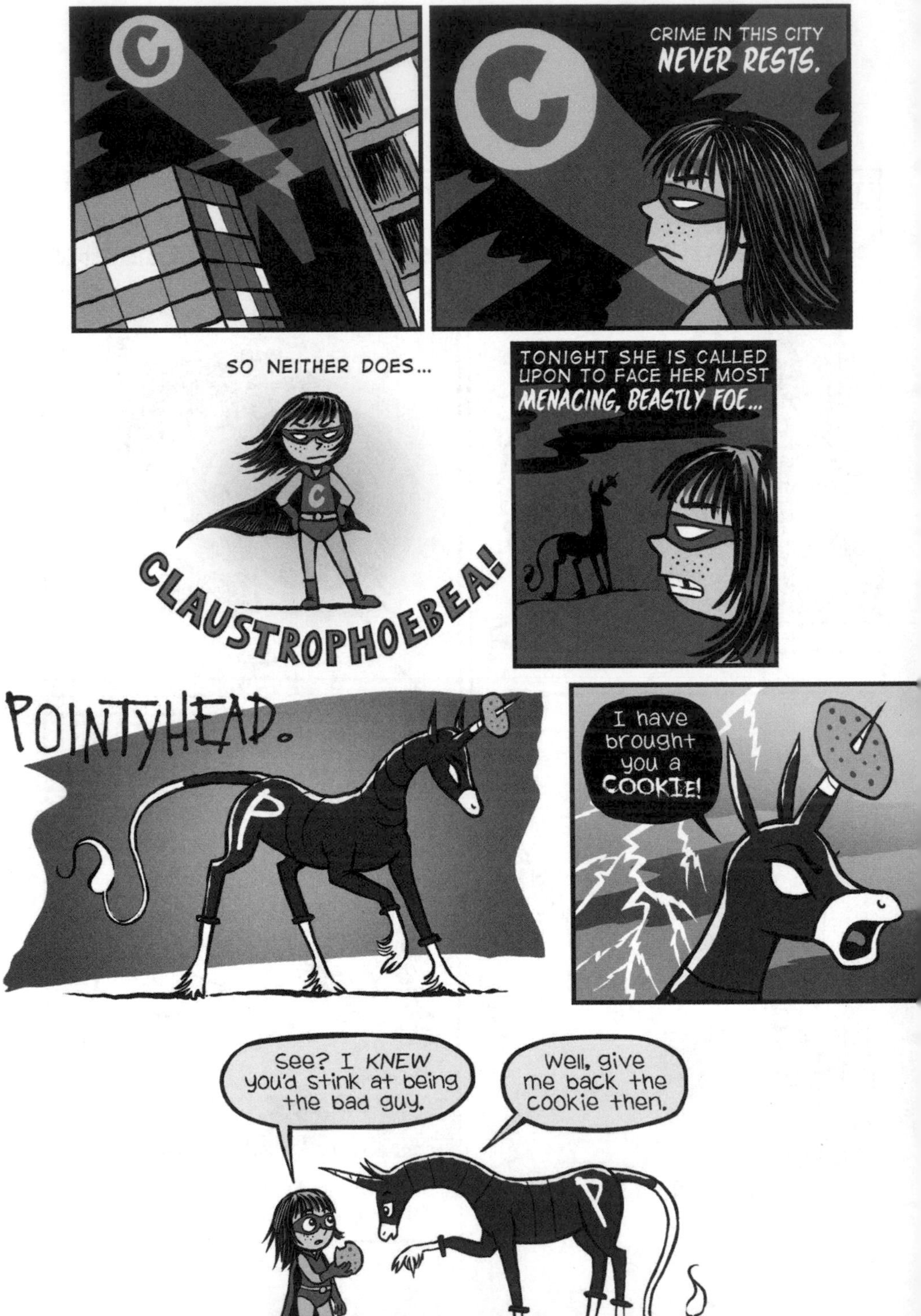
CRIME IN THIS CITY NEVER RESTS.
SO NEITHER DOES...
CLAUSTROPHOEBEA!
TONIGHT SHE IS CALLED UPON TO FACE HER MOST MENACING, BEASTLY FOE...
POINTYHEAD.
I have brought you a COOKIE!
See? I KNEW you'd stink at being the bad guy.
Well, give me back the cookie then.

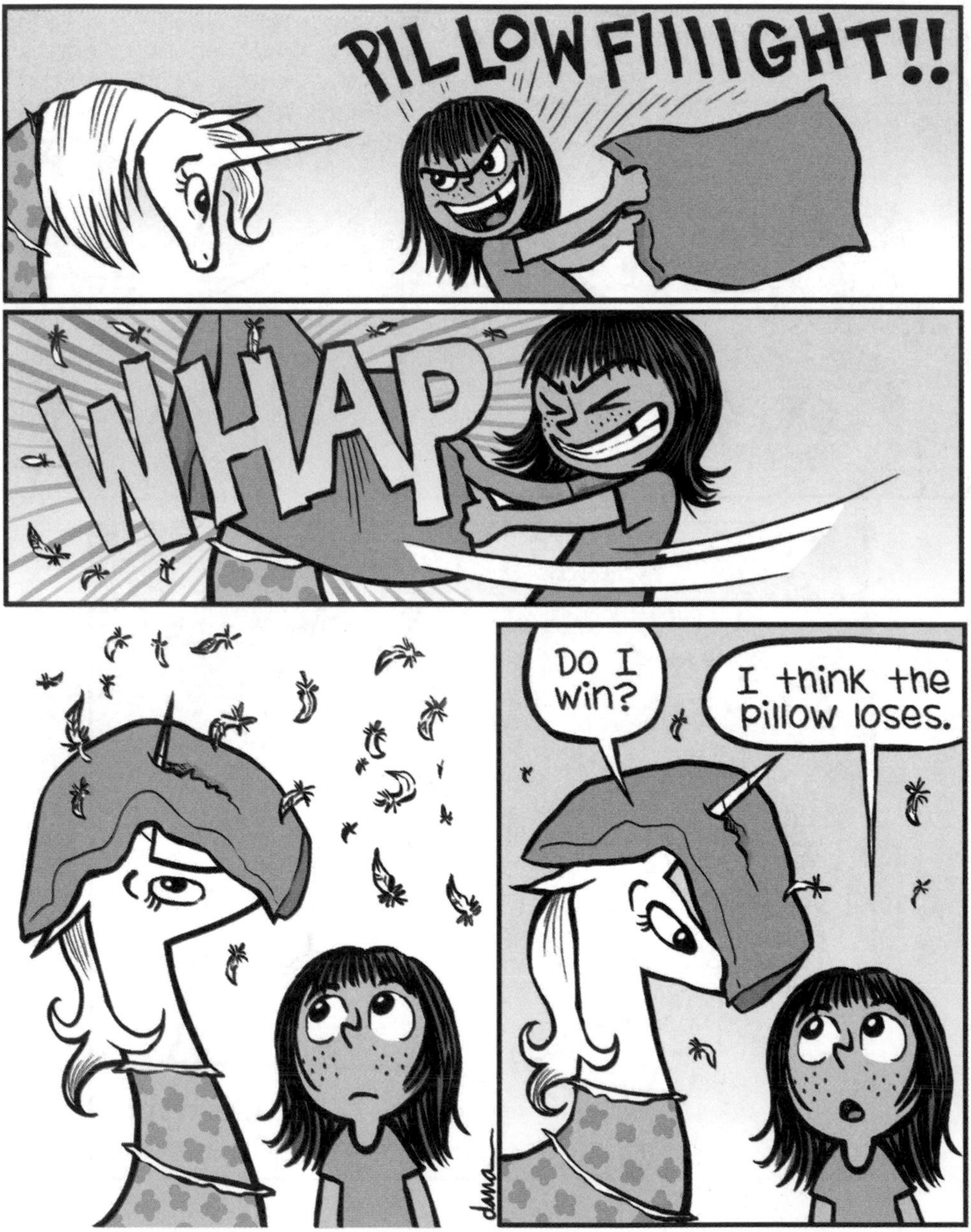
PILLOWFIIIIGHT!!
WHAP
Do I win?
I think the pillow loses.
dana

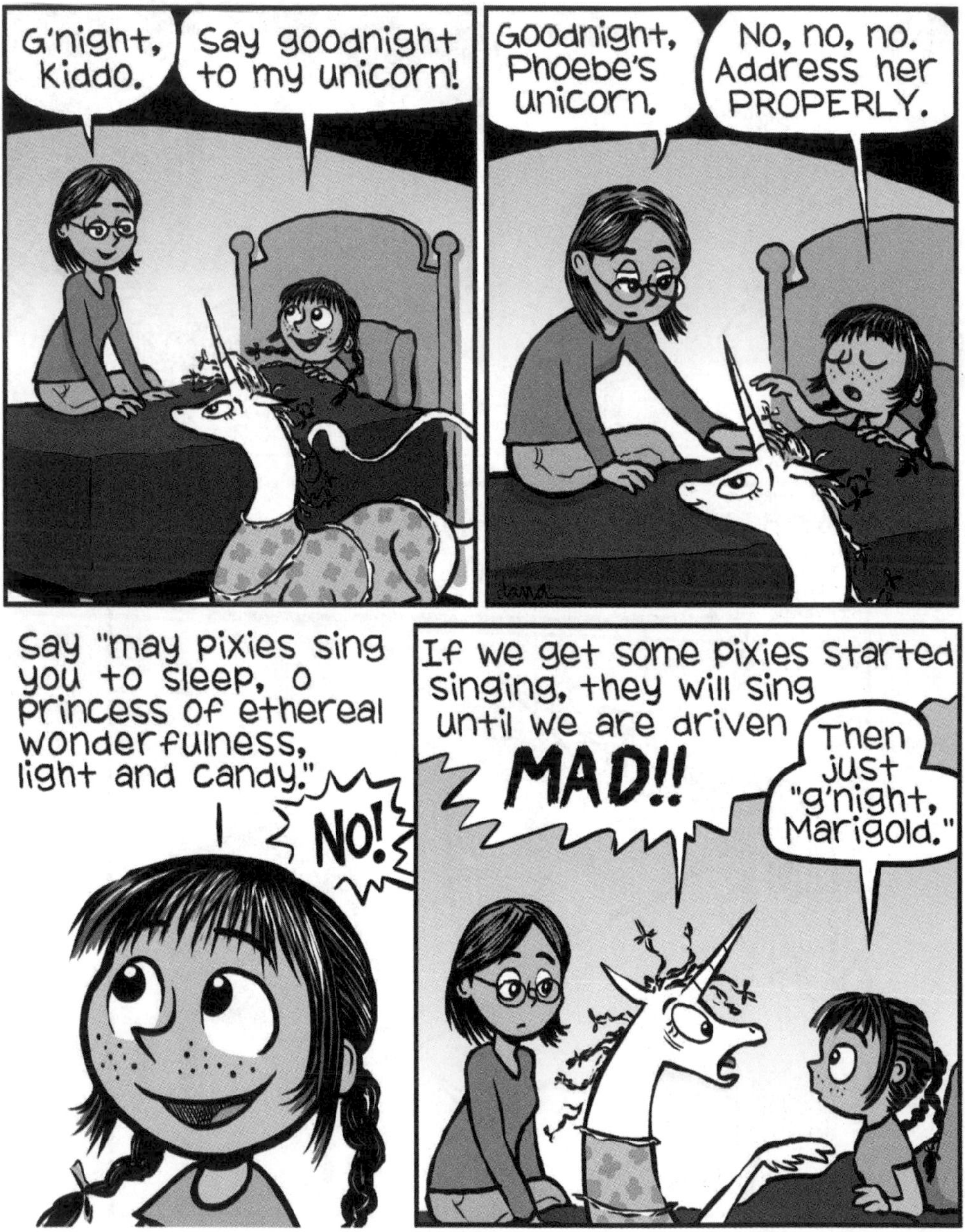
G'night, Kiddo.
Say goodnight to my unicorn!
Goodnight, Phoebe's unicorn.
No, no, no. Address her PROPERLY.
Say "may pixies sing you to sleep, O princess of ethereal wonderfulness, light and candy."
I
NO!
If we get some pixies started singing, they will sing until we are driven MAD!!
Then just "g'night, Marigold."

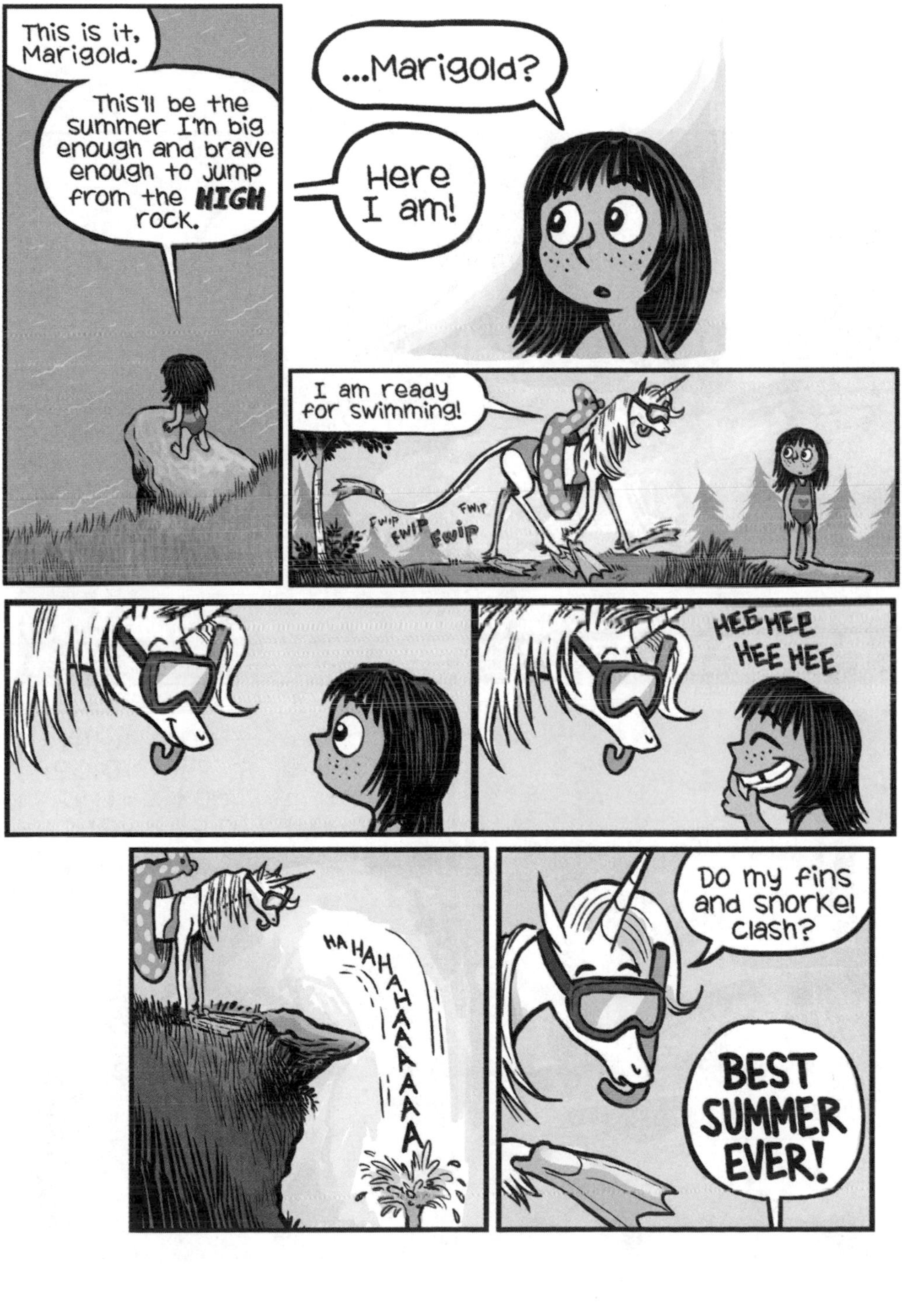

This is it, Marigold.
This'll be the summer I'm big enough and brave enough to jump from the HIGH rock.
...Marigold?
Here I am!
I am ready for swimming!
FWIP FWIP FWIP FWIP
HEE HEE HEE HEE
HA HA HAHAAAAAAA
Do my fins and snorkel clash?
BEST SUMMER EVER!

Mom says they were called "Sugar Kabooms" when she was a kid, but now people have to delude themselves into thinking everything's healthy.

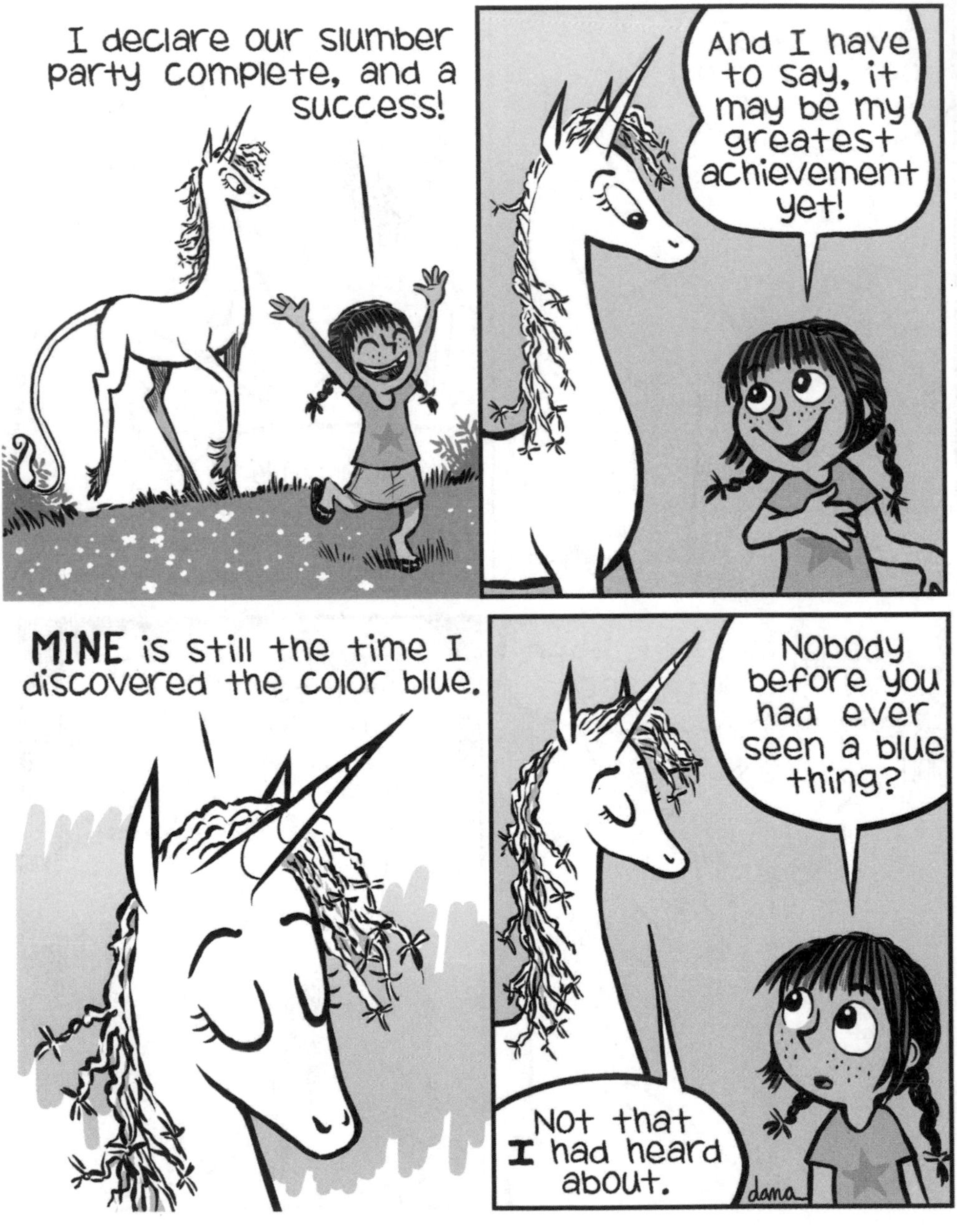
I declare our slumber party complete, and a success!
And I have to say, it may be my greatest achievement yet!
MINE is still the time I discovered the color blue.
Nobody before you had ever seen a blue thing?
Not that I had heard about.
dana

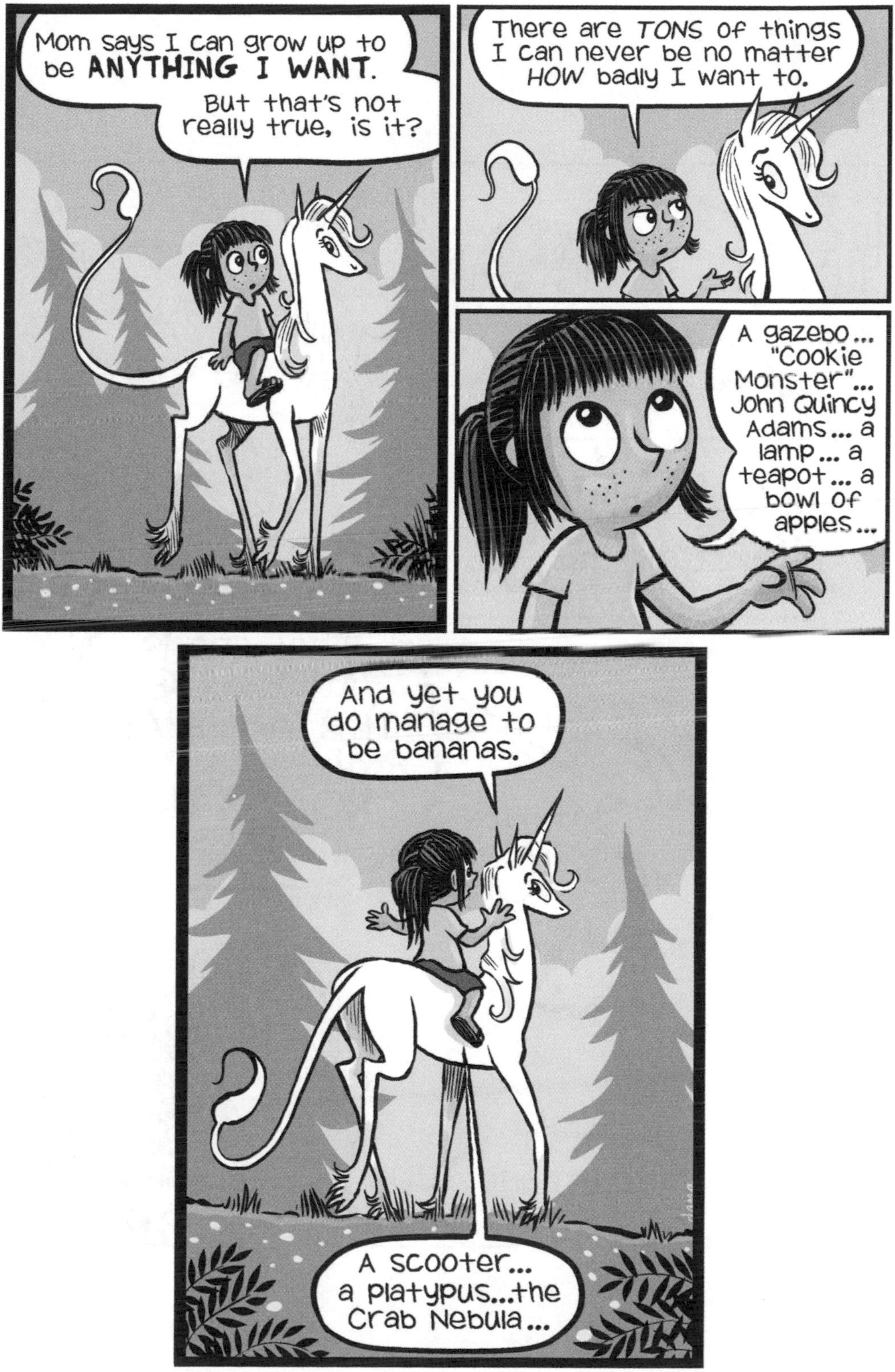
Mom says I can grow up to be **ANYTHING I WANT**.
But that's not really true, is it?
There are *TONS* of things I can never be no matter *HOW* badly I want to.
A gazebo... "Cookie Monster"... John Quincy Adams... a lamp... a teapot... a bowl of apples...
And yet you do manage to be bananas.
A scooter... a platypus...the Crab Nebula...

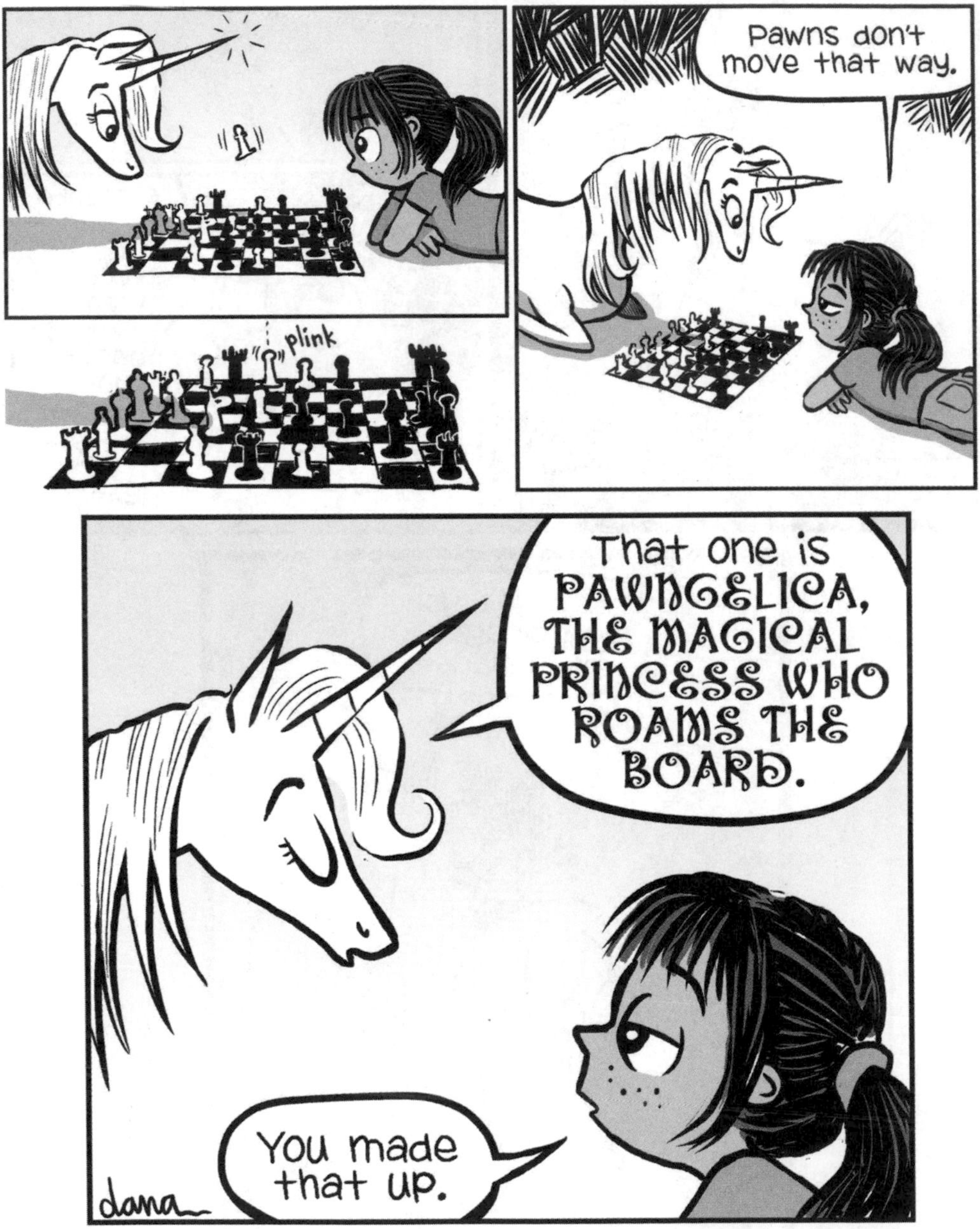
plink
Pawns don't move that way.
That one is PAWNGELICA, THE MAGICAL PRINCESS WHO ROAMS THE BOARD.
You made that up.
dana

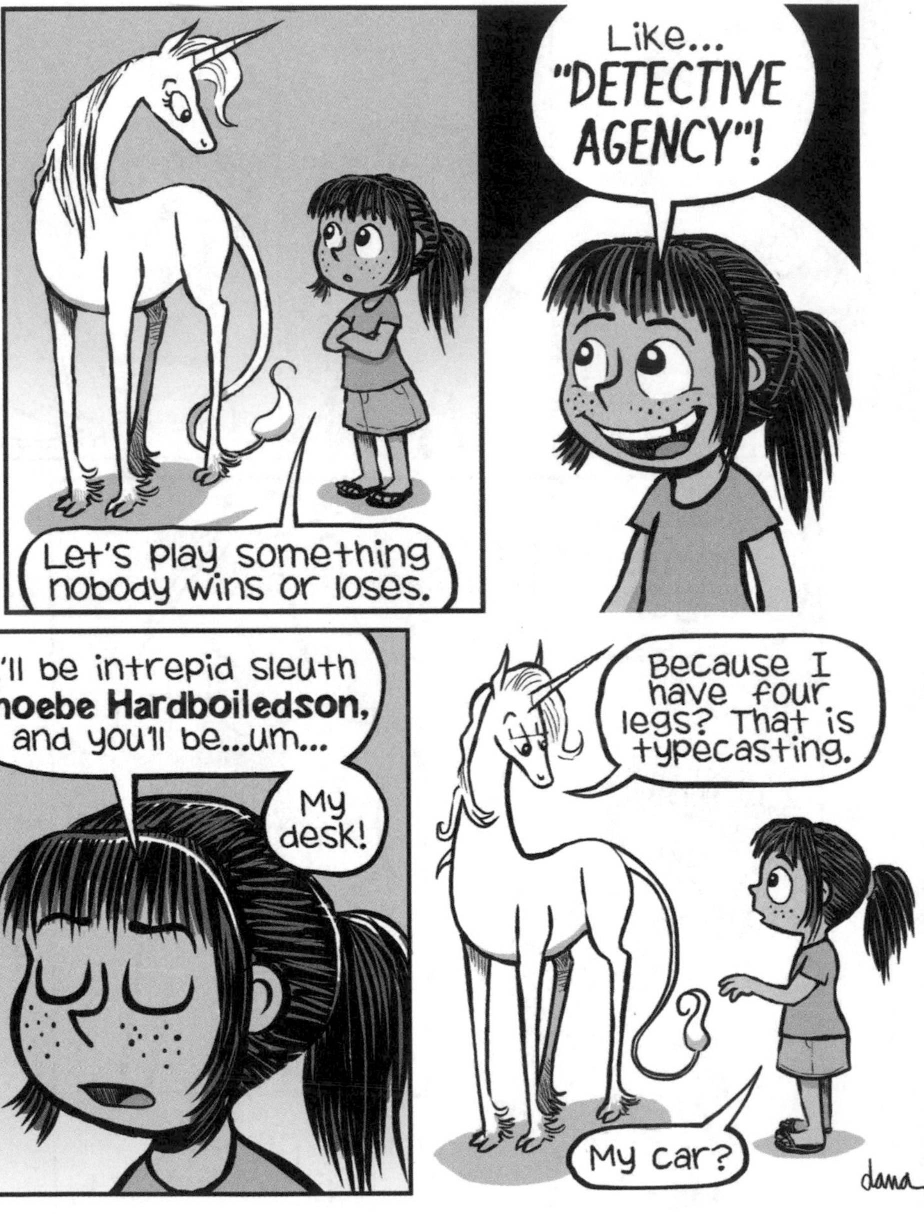

Let's play something nobody wins or loses.
Like... "DETECTIVE AGENCY"!
I'll be intrepid sleuth **Phoebe Hardboiledson,** and you'll be...um...
My desk!
Because I have four legs? That is typecasting.
My car?
dana

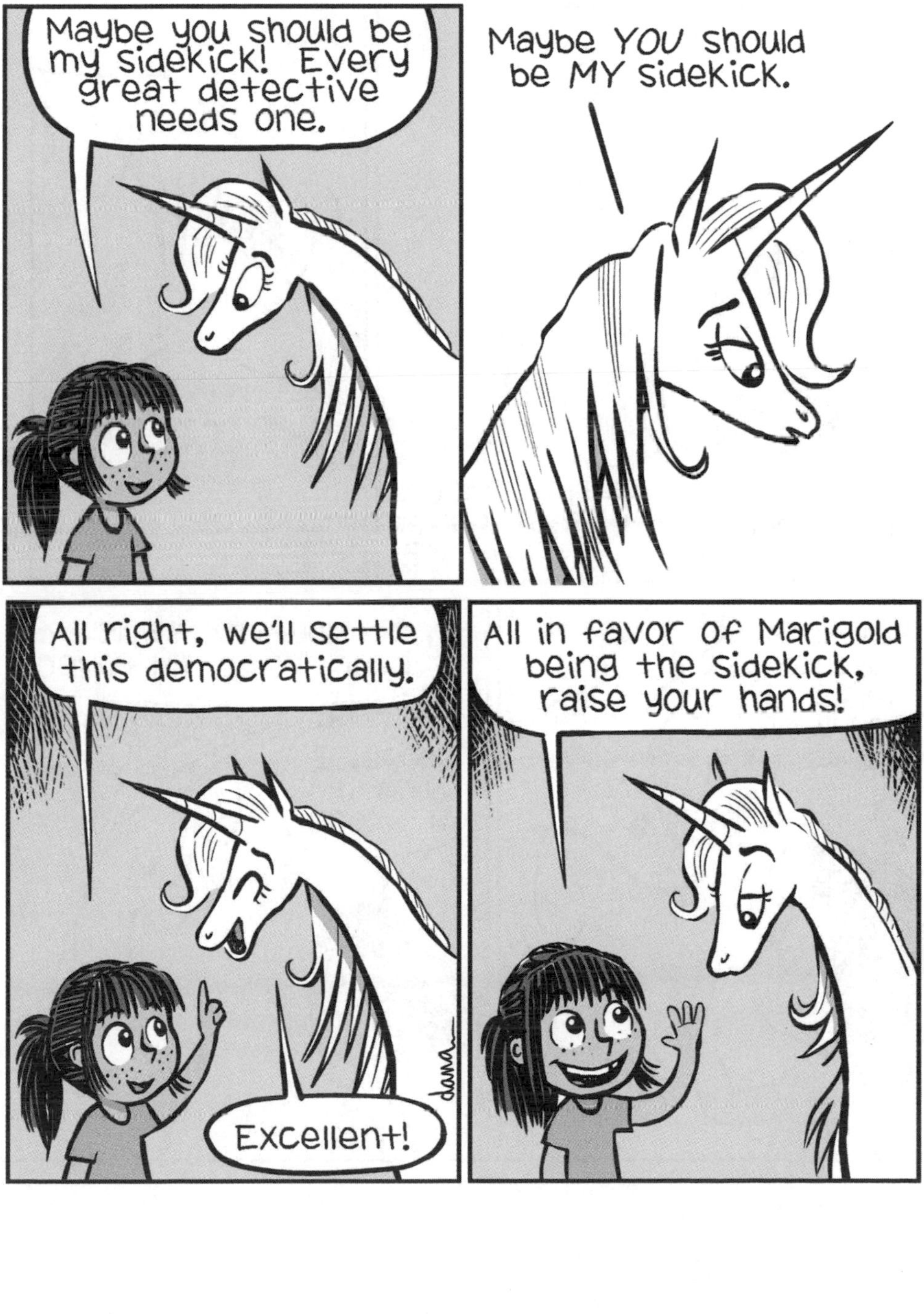
Maybe you should be my sidekick! Every great detective needs one.
Maybe YOU should be MY sidekick.
All right, we'll settle this democratically.
Excellent!
dana
All in favor of Marigold being the sidekick, raise your hands!

How about "rock paper scissors"?

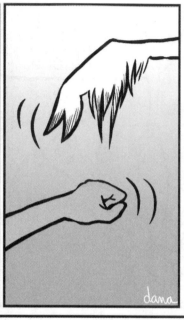

dana

Scissors beats paper! You win!

Did you just switch to cheating in my favor?

Nope, I just did it wrong.

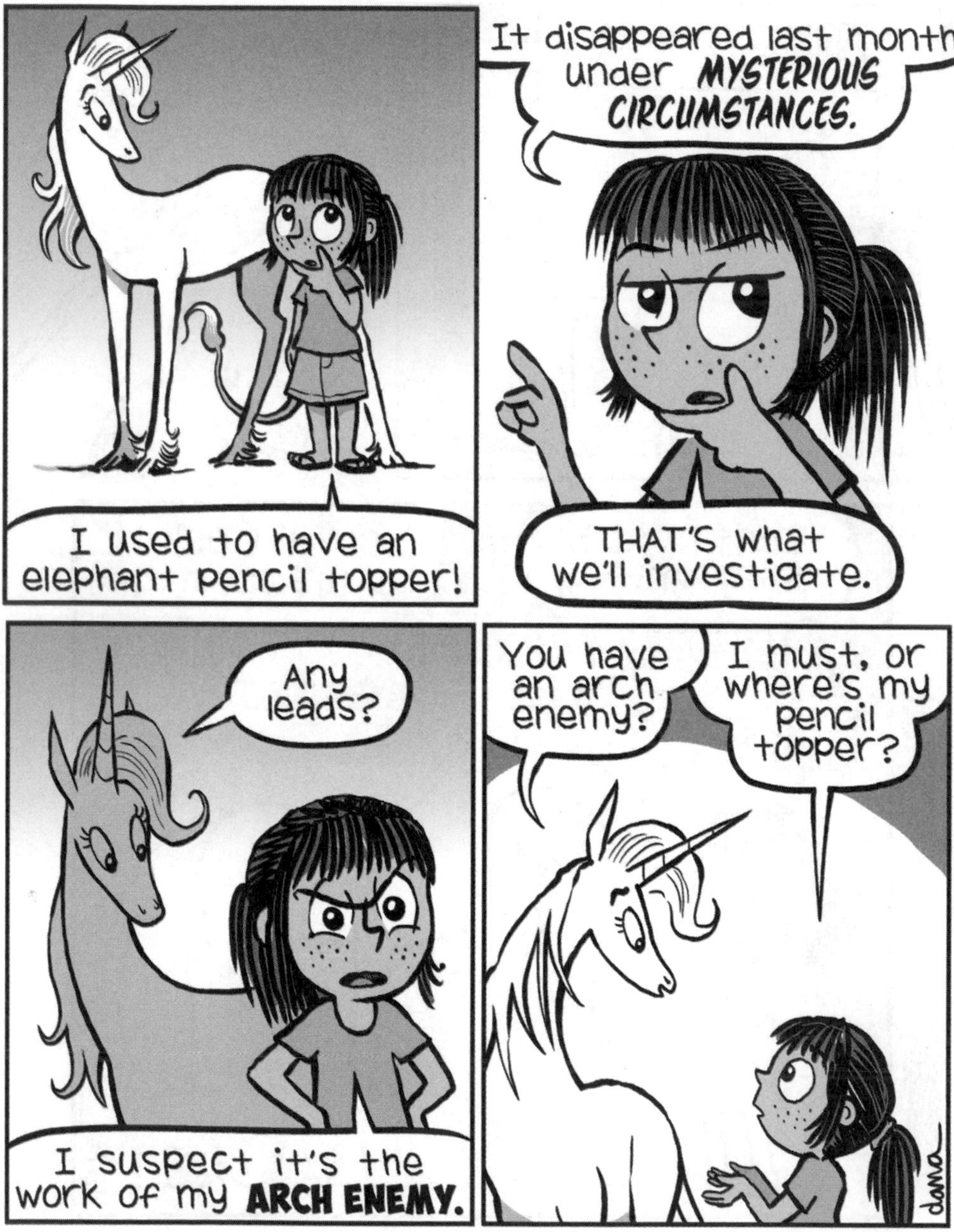
I used to have an elephant pencil topper!
It disappeared last month under MYSTERIOUS CIRCUMSTANCES.
THAT'S what we'll investigate.
Any leads?
I suspect it's the work of my ARCH ENEMY.
You have an arch enemy?
I must, or where's my pencil topper?
dana

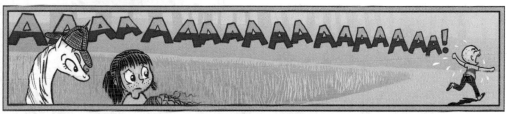

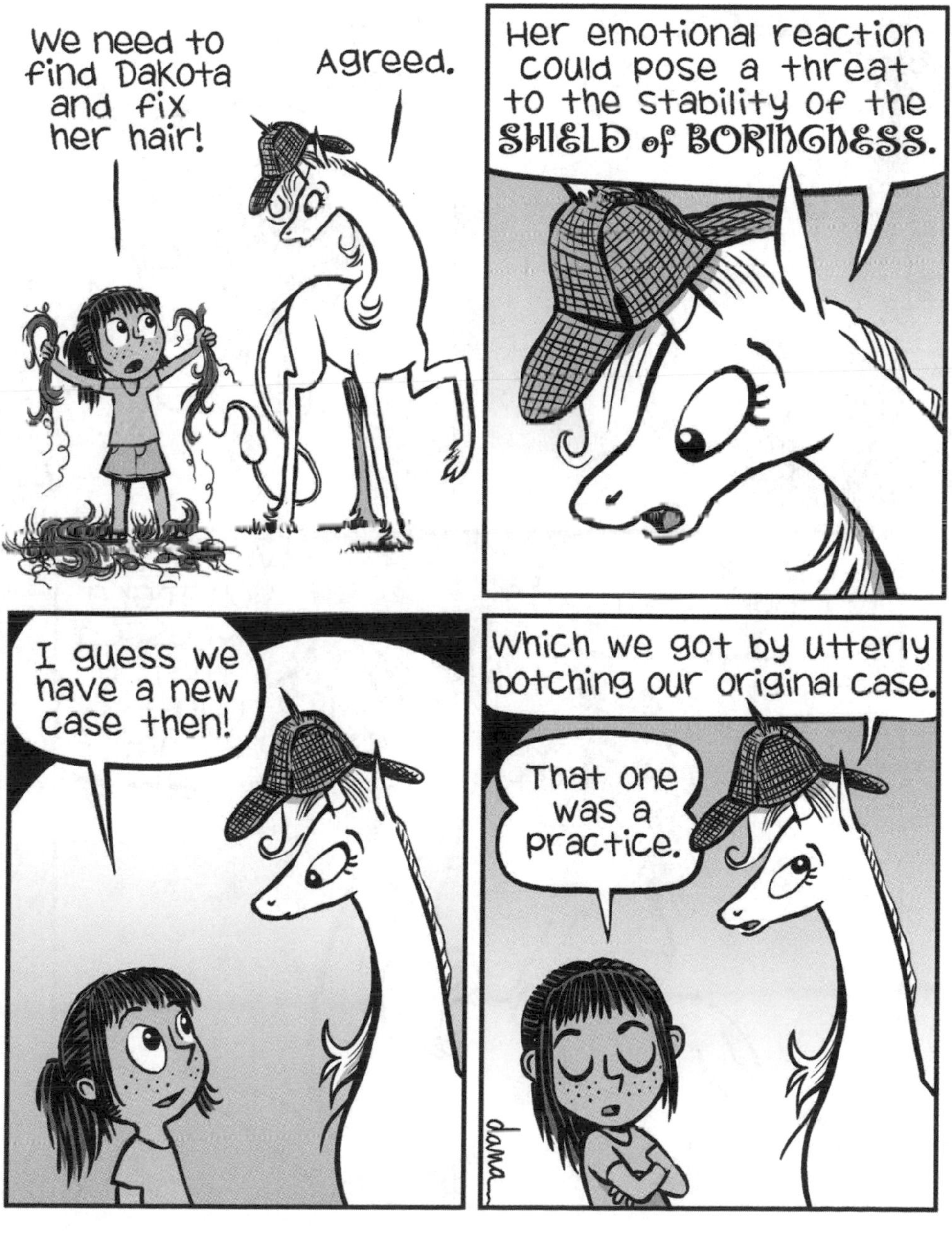
We need to find Dakota and fix her hair!
Agreed.
Her emotional reaction could pose a threat to the stability of the SHIELD of BORINGNESS.
I guess we have a new case then!
Which we got by utterly botching our original case.
That one was a practice.
dana

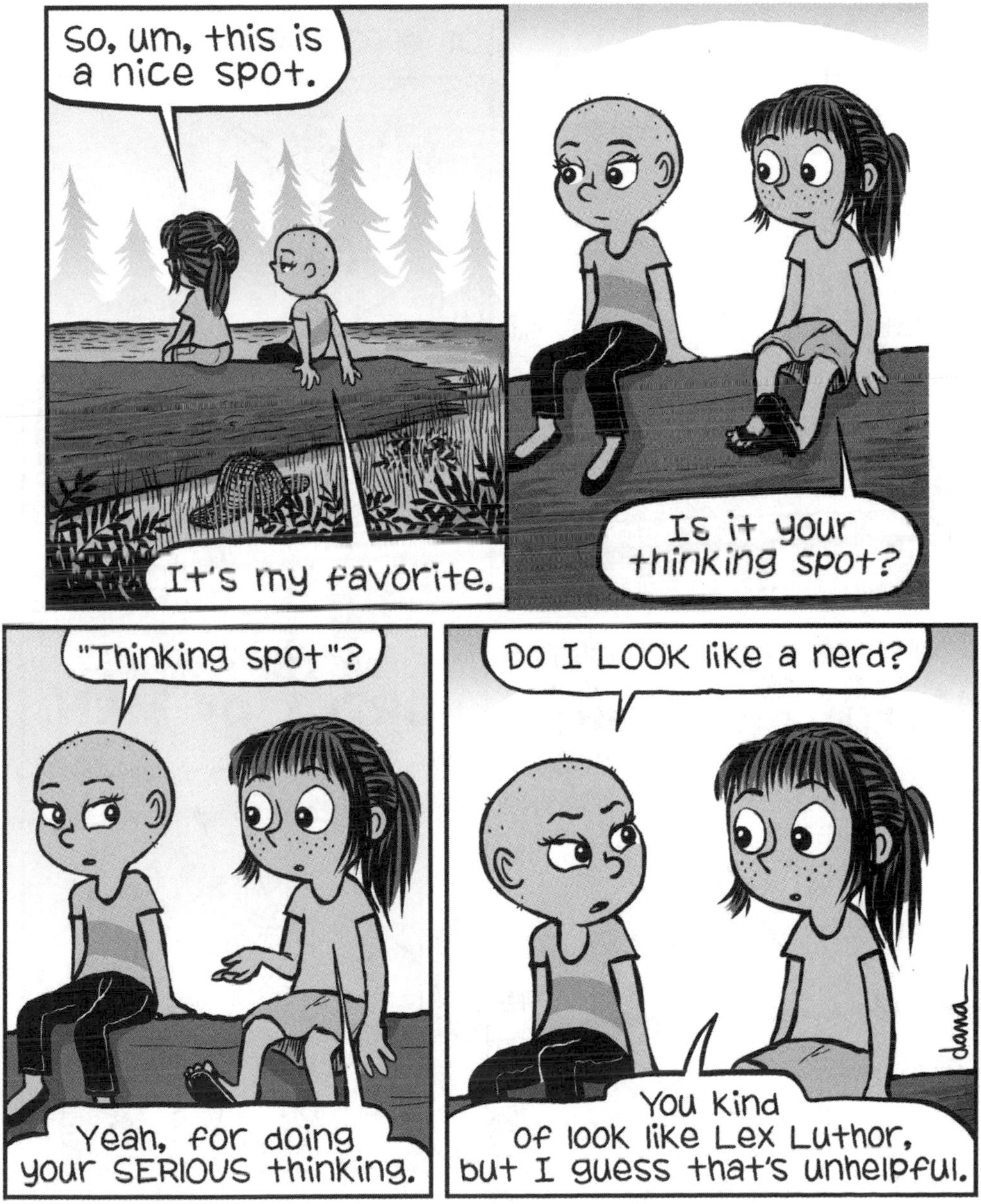
So, um, this is a nice spot.
It's my favorite.
Is it your thinking spot?
"Thinking spot"?
Yeah, for doing your SERIOUS thinking.
Do I LOOK like a nerd?
You kind of look like Lex Luthor, but I guess that's unhelpful.
dana

Dakota's shock at losing her hair has distorted the SHIELD of BORINGNESS into something FAR worse...

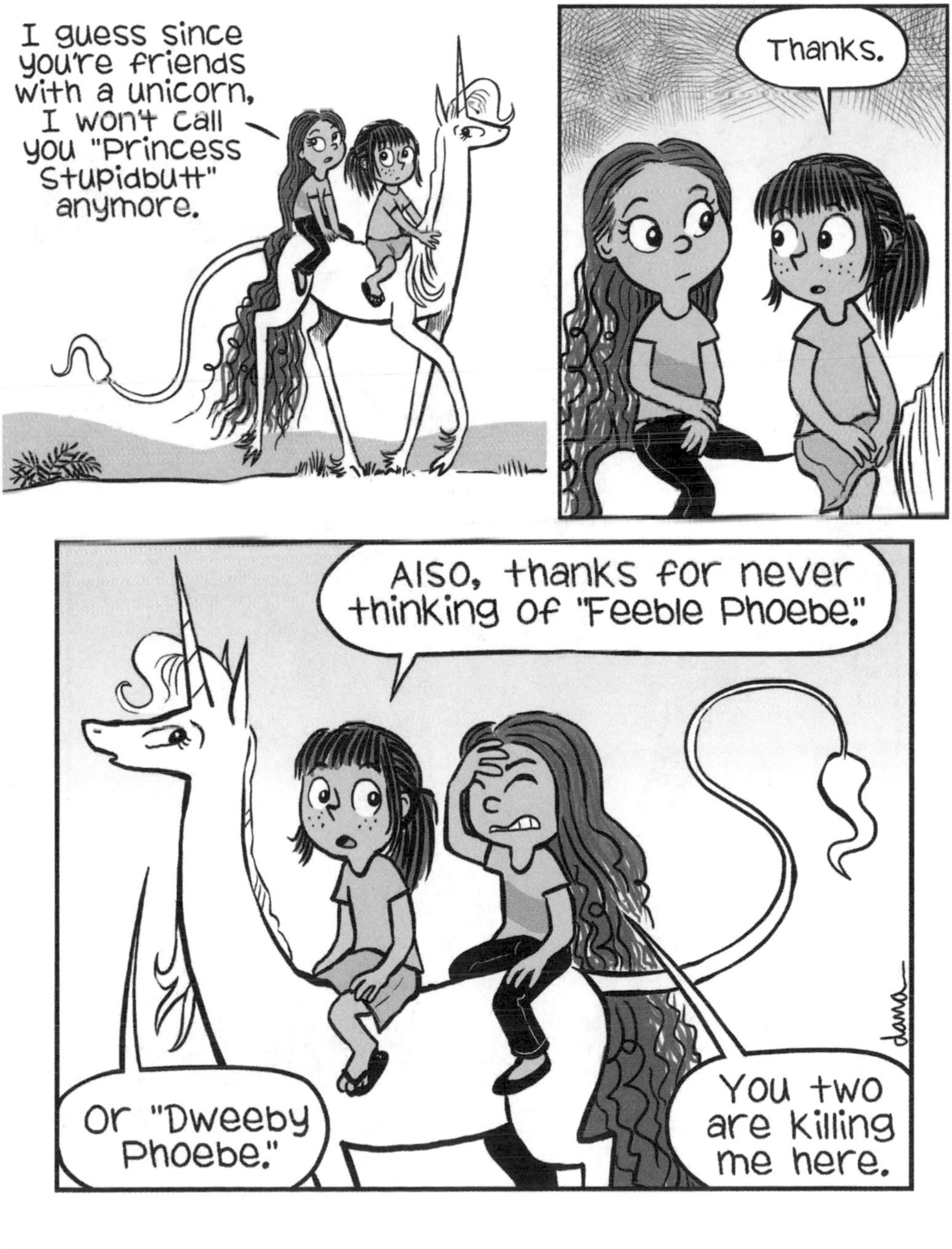
I guess since you're friends with a unicorn, I won't call you "Princess Stupidbutt" anymore.
Thanks.
Also, thanks for never thinking of "Feeble Phoebe."
Or "Dweeby Phoebe."
You two are killing me here.
dana

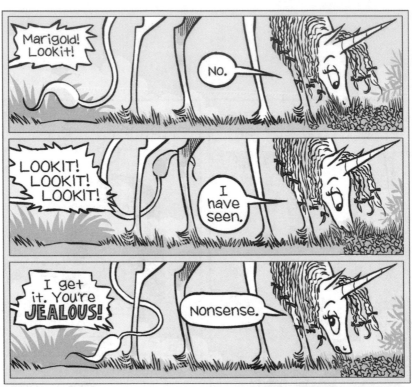

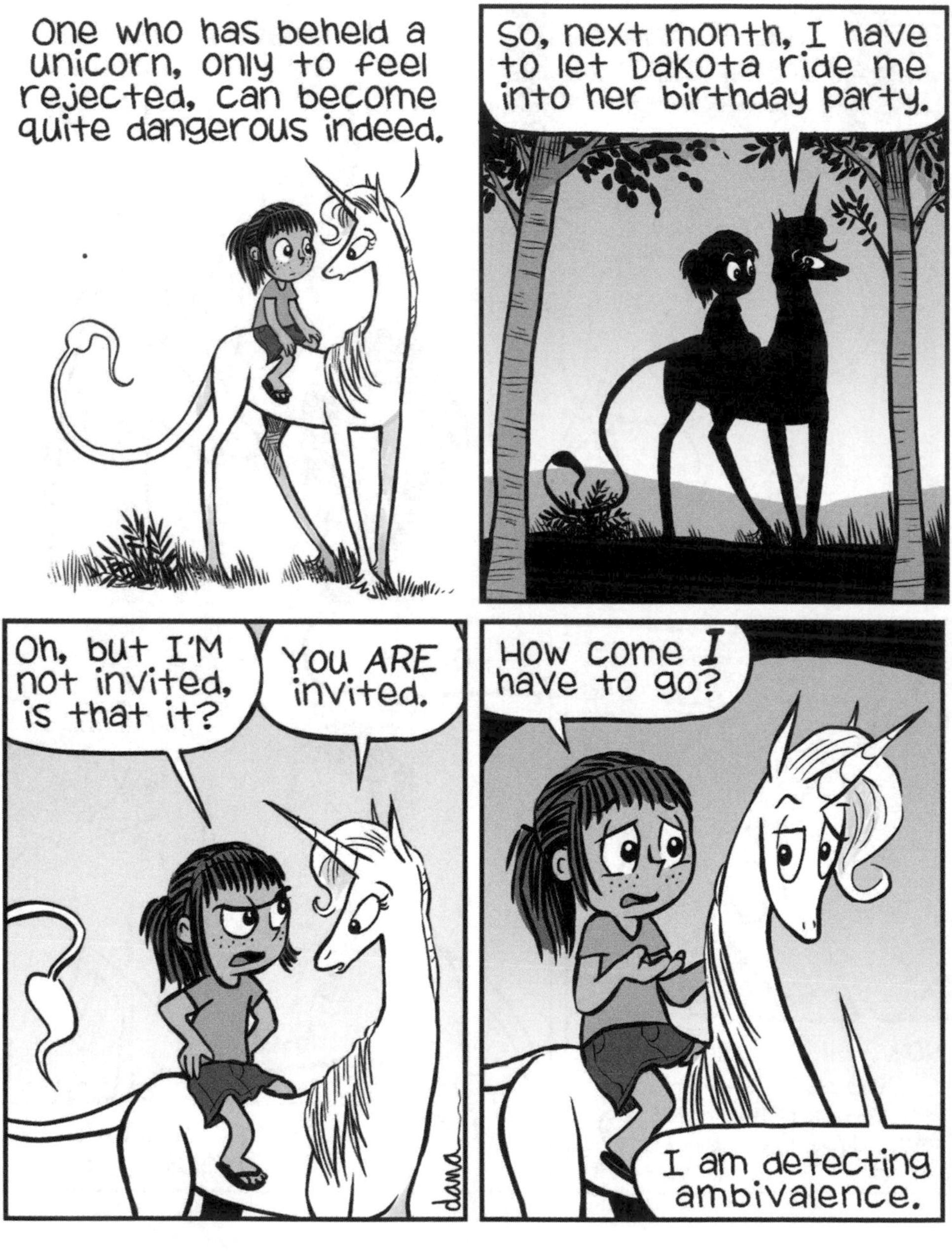
One who has beheld a unicorn, only to feel rejected, can become quite dangerous indeed.
So, next month, I have to let Dakota ride me into her birthday party.
Oh, but I'M not invited, is that it?
You ARE invited.
dana
How come I have to go?
I am detecting ambivalence.

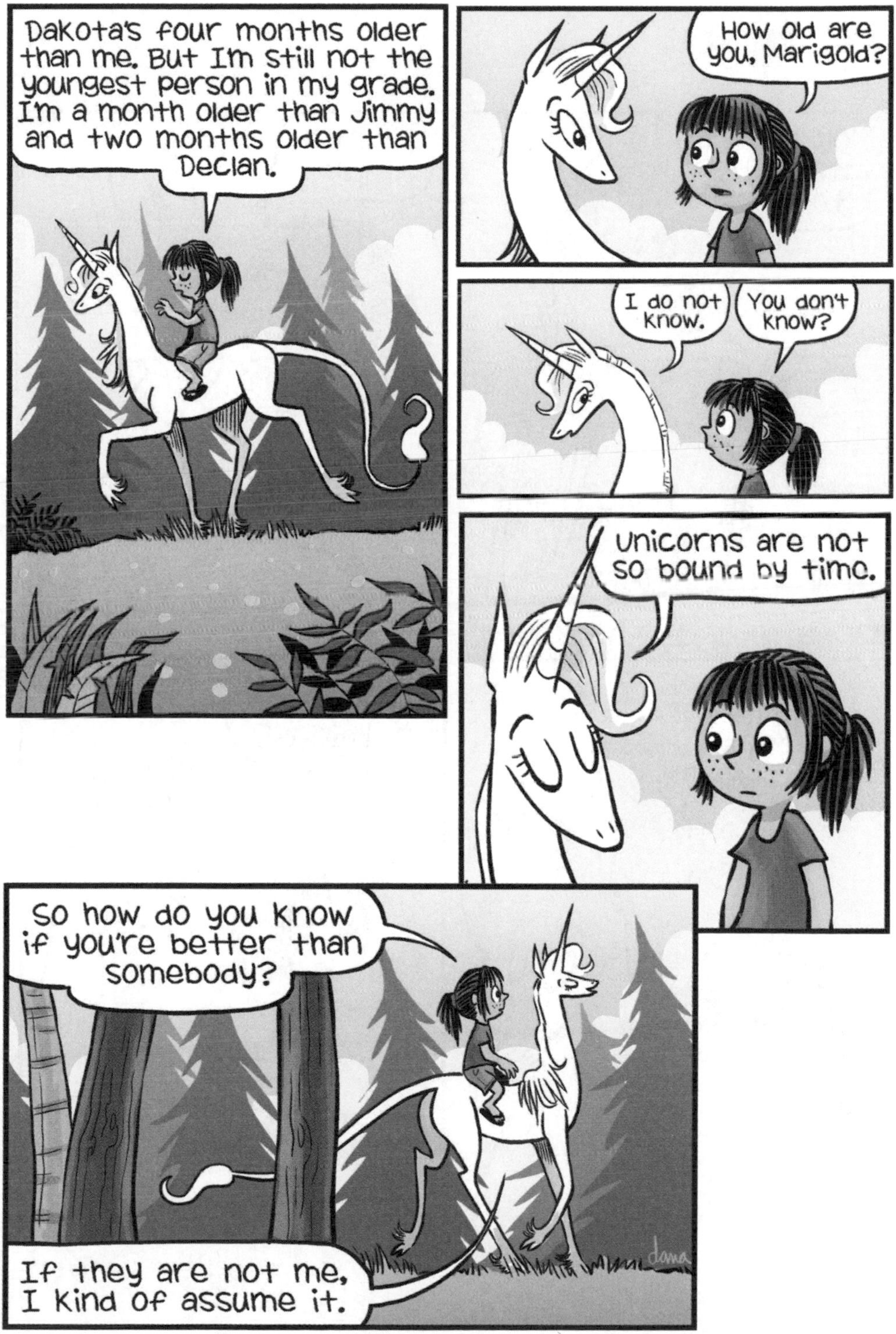
Dakota's four months older than me. But I'm still not the youngest person in my grade. I'm a month older than Jimmy and two months older than Declan.
How old are you, Marigold?
I do not know.
You don't know?
Unicorns are not so bound by time.
So how do you know if you're better than somebody?
If they are not me, I kind of assume it.

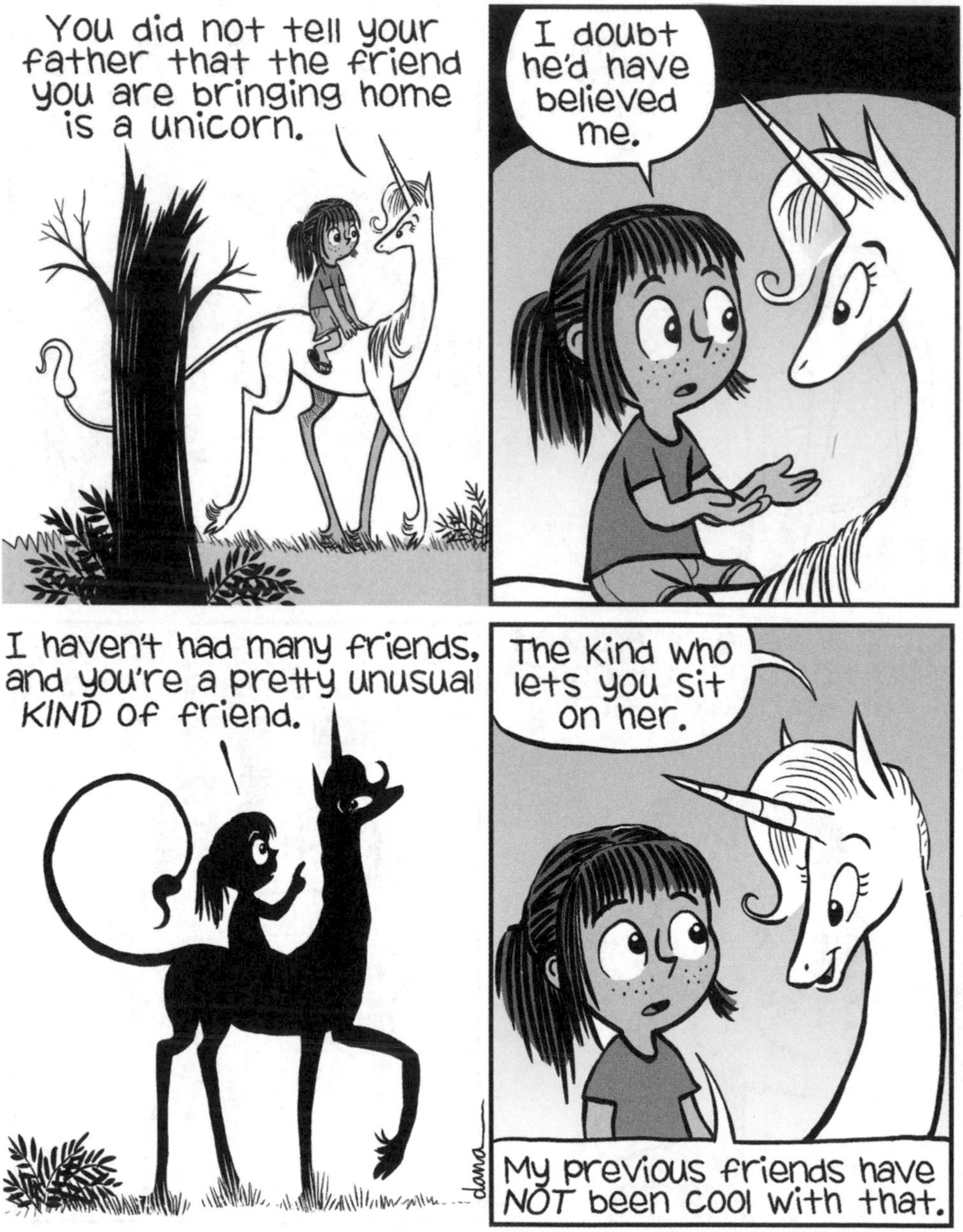

You did not tell your father that the friend you are bringing home is a unicorn.
I doubt he'd have believed me.
I haven't had many friends, and you're a pretty unusual *KIND* of friend.
The kind who lets you sit on her.
My previous friends have *NOT* been cool with that.
dana

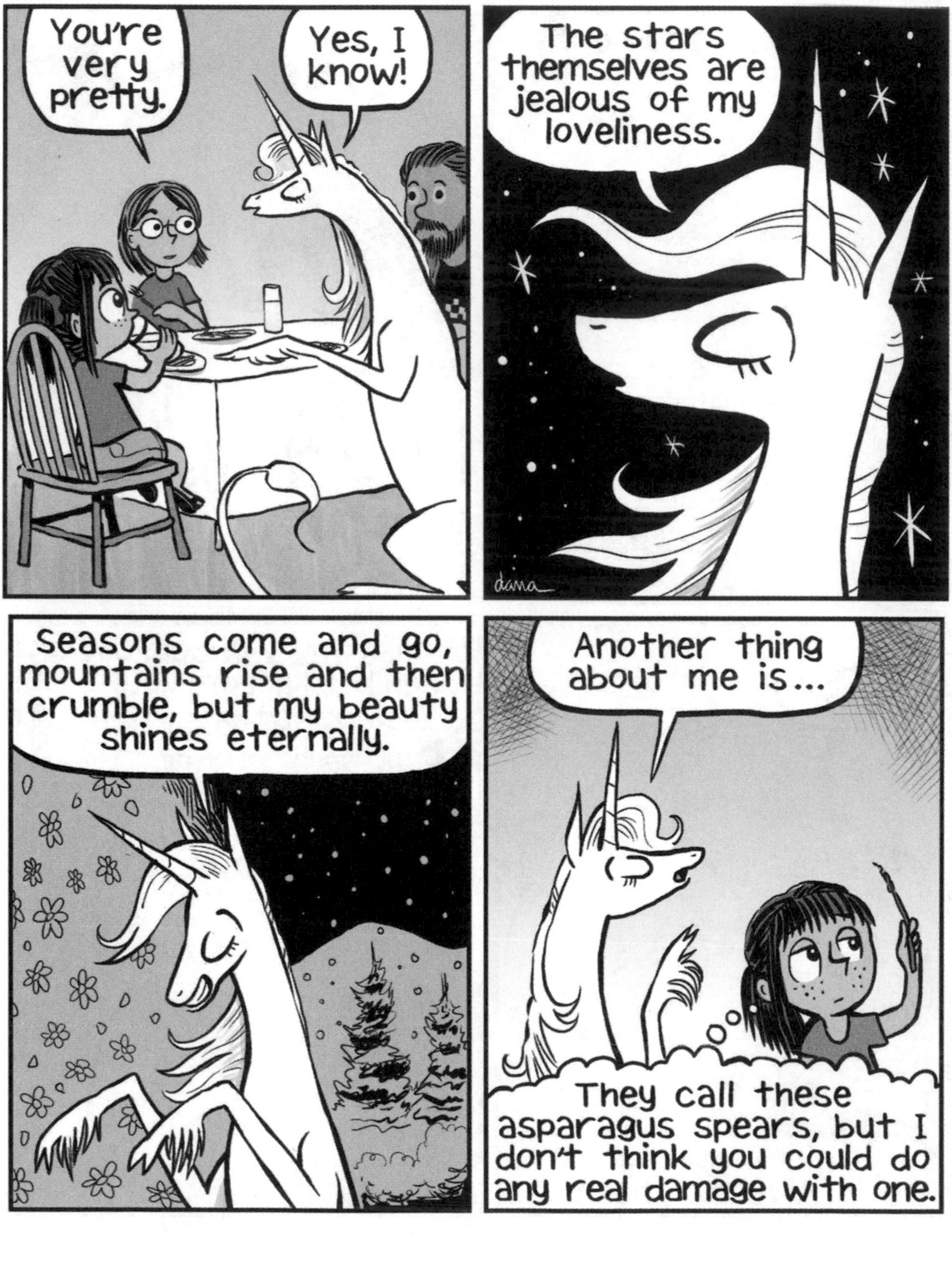
You're very pretty.
Yes, I know!
The stars themselves are jealous of my loveliness.
dana
Seasons come and go, mountains rise and then crumble, but my beauty shines eternally.
Another thing about me is...
They call these asparagus spears, but I don't think you could do any real damage with one.

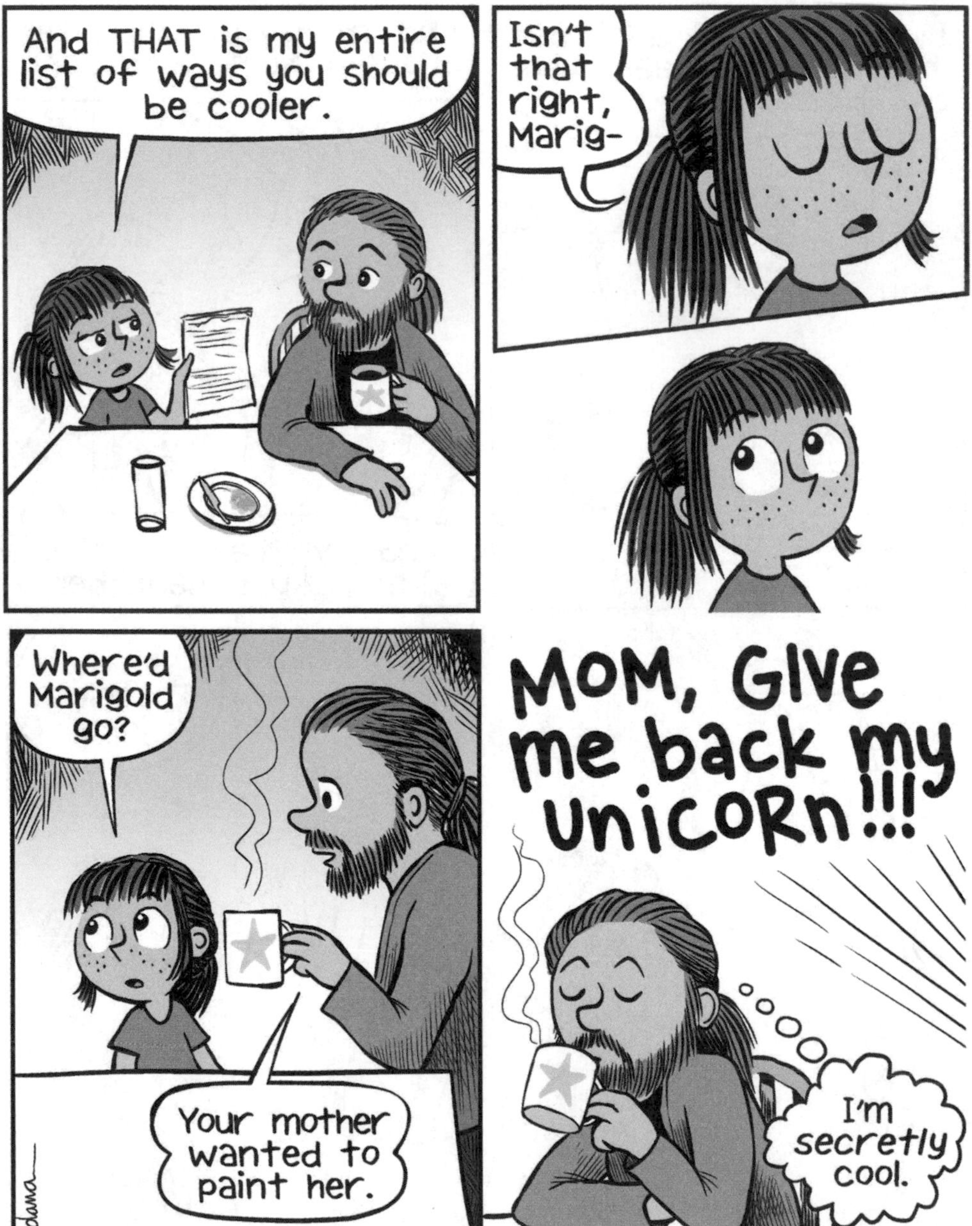
And THAT is my entire list of ways you should be cooler.
Isn't that right, Marig-
Where'd Marigold go?
Your mother wanted to paint her.
MOM, GIVE me back my UNICORN!!!
I'm secretly cool.
dana

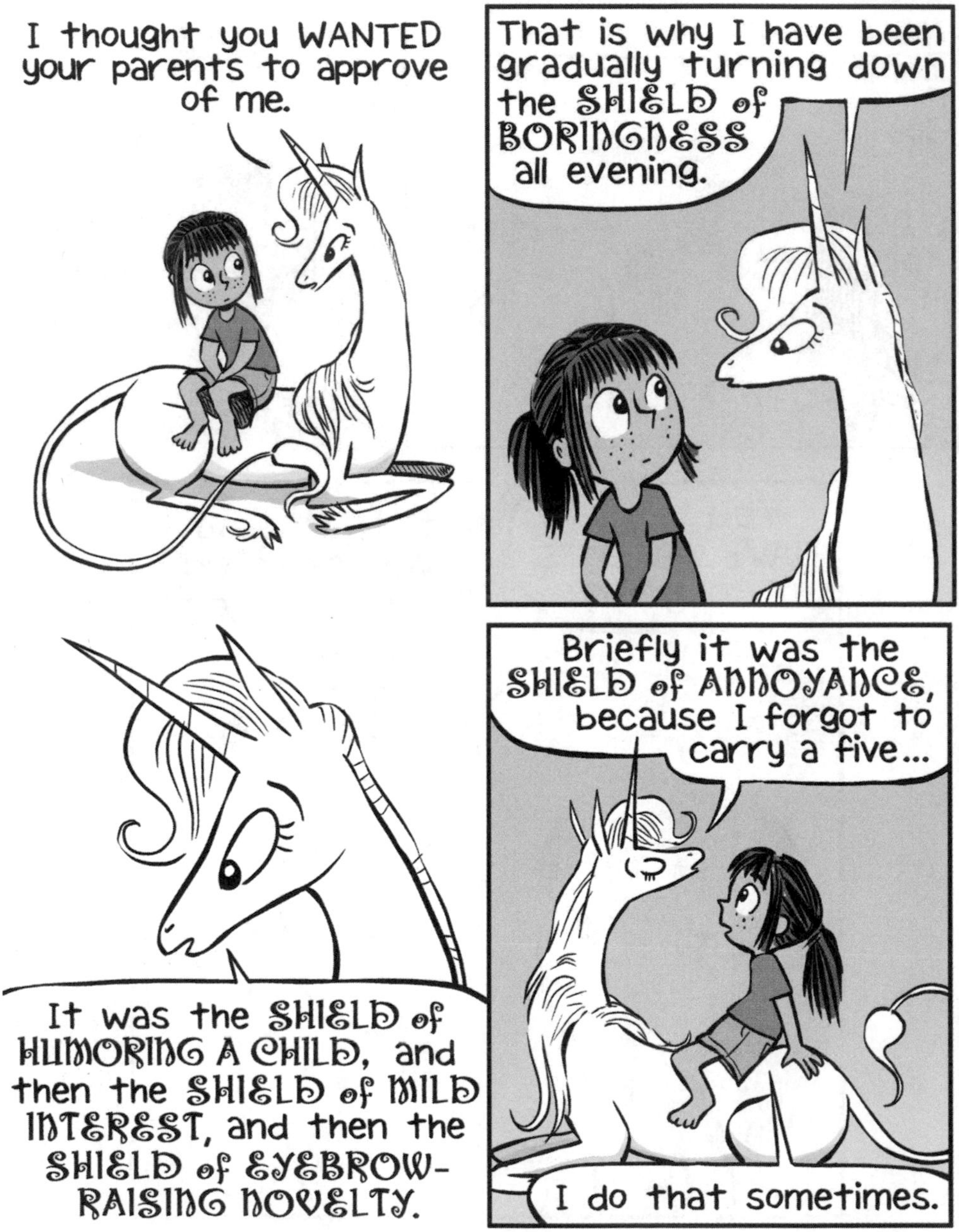
I thought you WANTED your parents to approve of me.
That is why I have been gradually turning down the SHIELD of BORINGNESS all evening.
It was the SHIELD of HUMORING A CHILD, and then the SHIELD of MILD INTEREST, and then the SHIELD of EYEBROW-RAISING NOVELTY.
Briefly it was the SHIELD of ANNOYANCE, because I forgot to carry a five...
I do that sometimes.

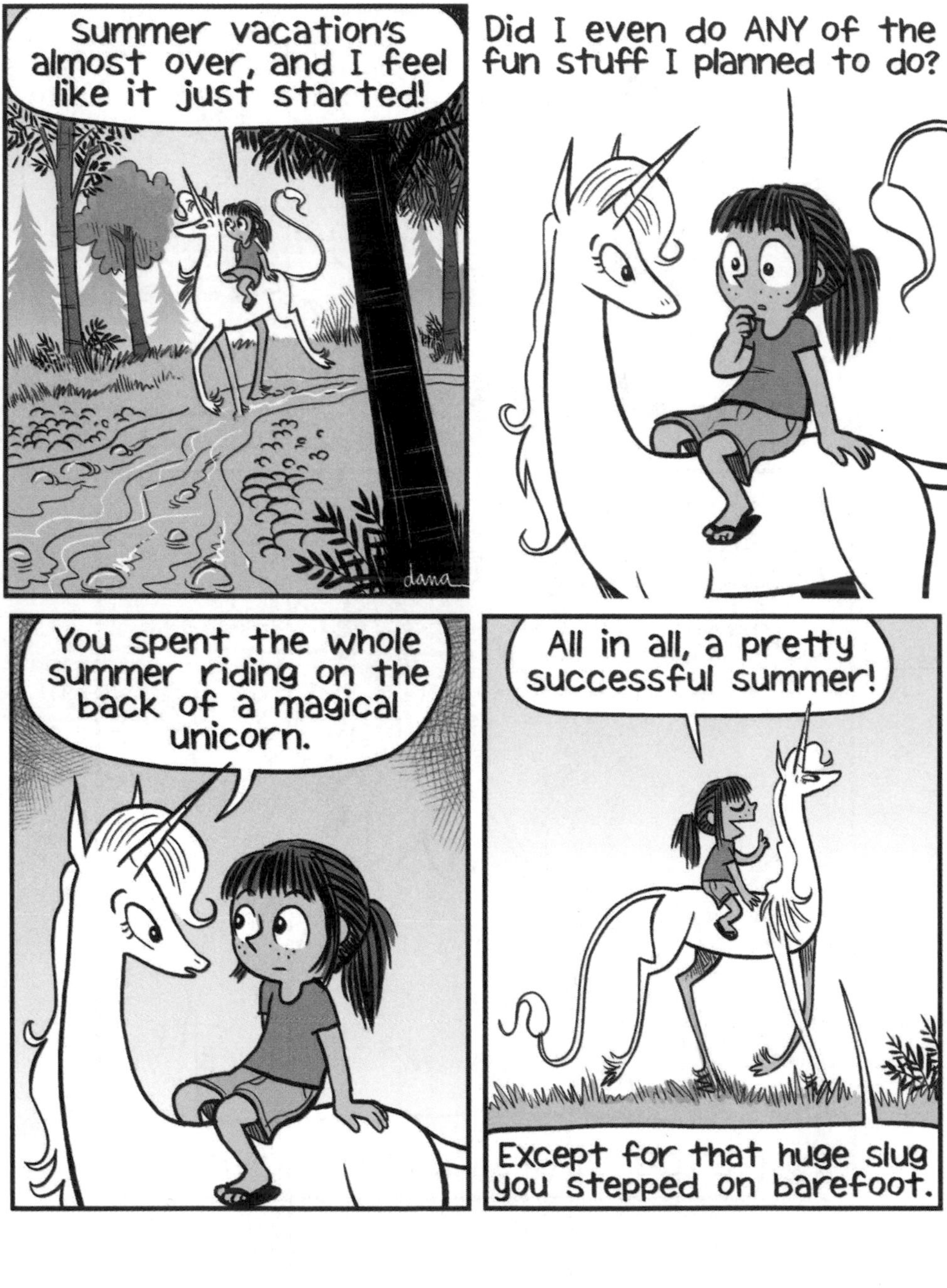
Summer vacation's almost over, and I feel like it just started!
Did I even do ANY of the fun stuff I planned to do?
You spent the whole summer riding on the back of a magical unicorn.
All in all, a pretty successful summer!
Except for that huge slug you stepped on barefoot.
dana

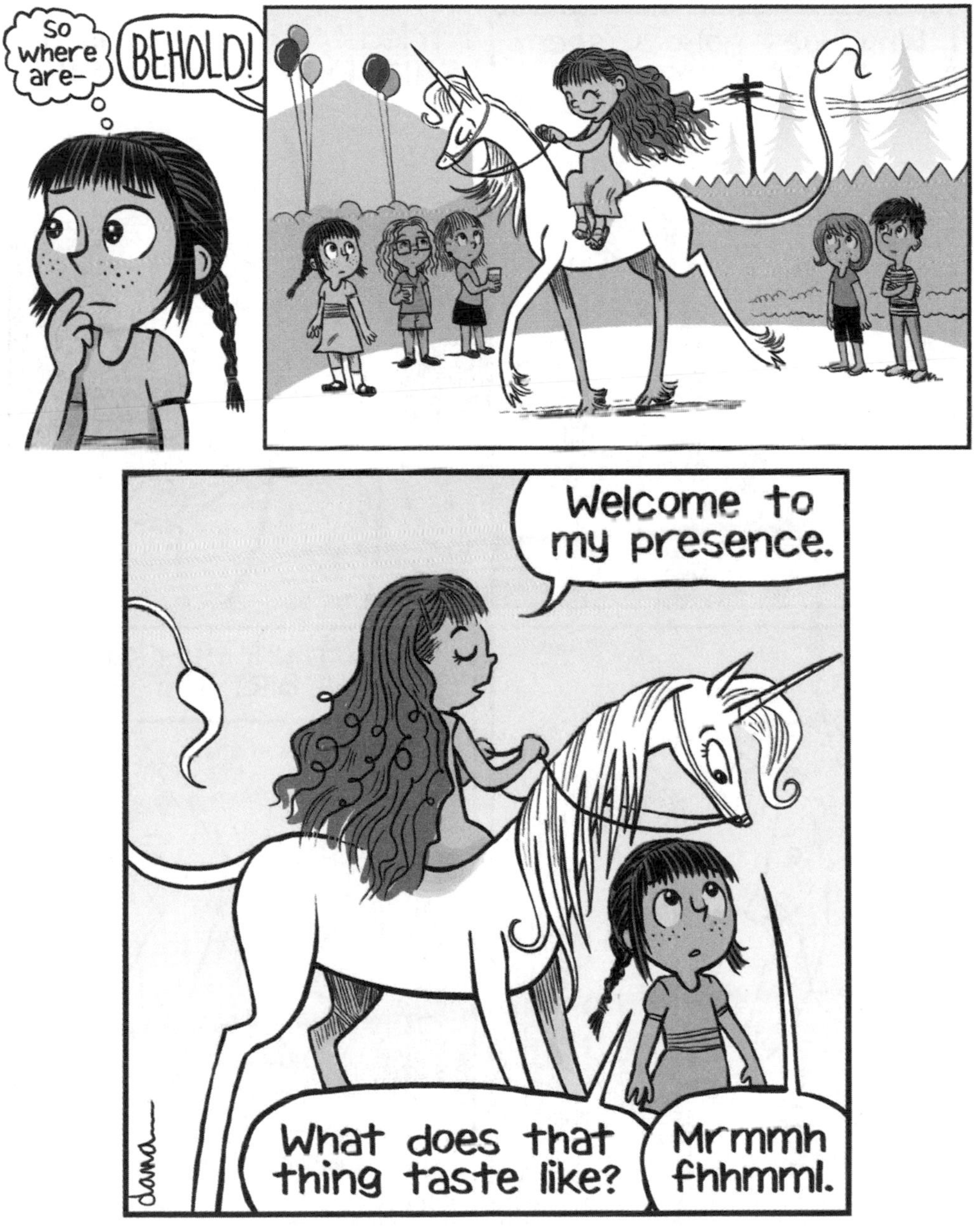
So where are-
BEHOLD!
Welcome to my presence.
What does that thing taste like?
Mrmmh fhhmml.
dana

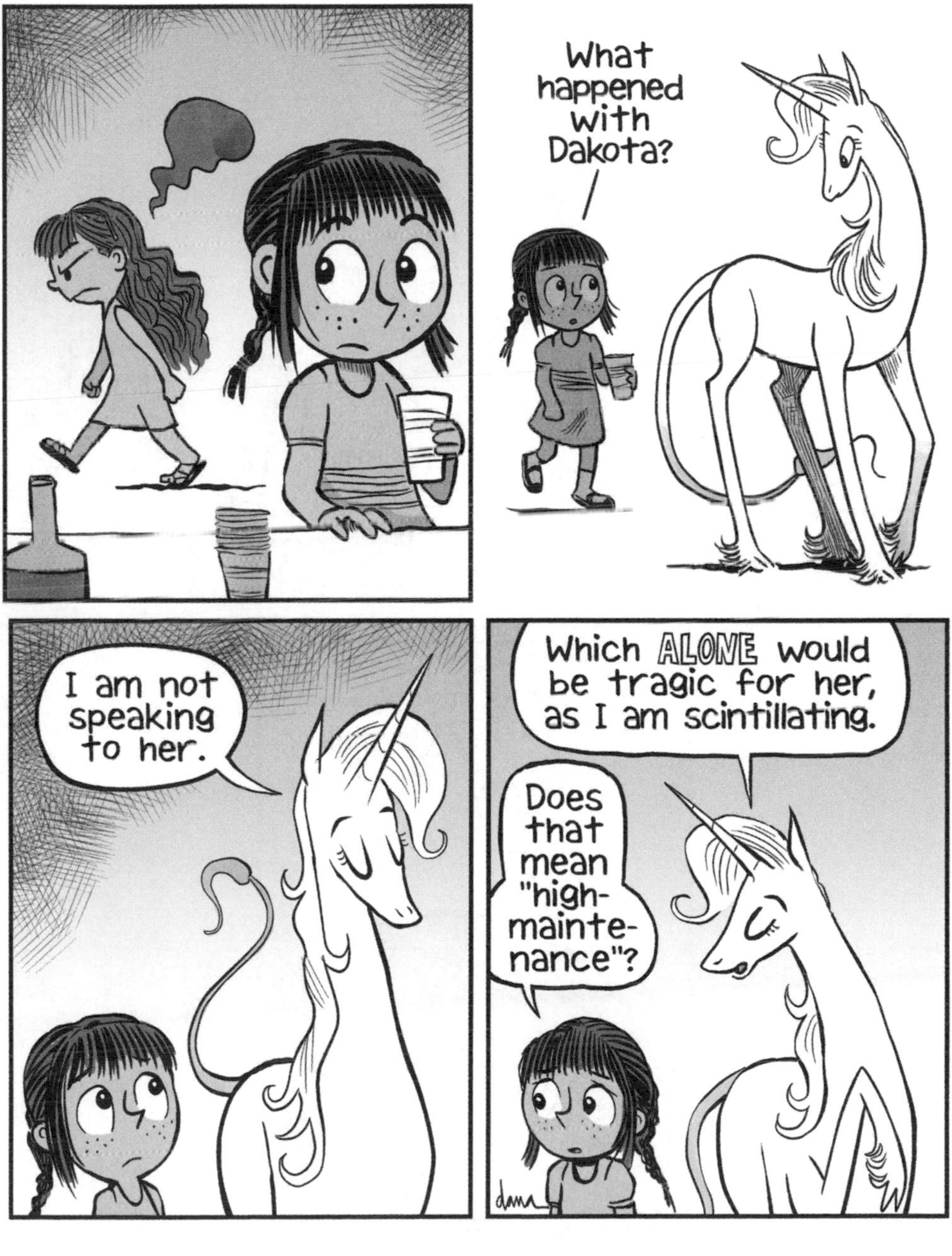
What happened with Dakota?
I am not speaking to her.
Which ALONE would be tragic for her, as I am scintillating.
Does that mean "high-maintenance"?

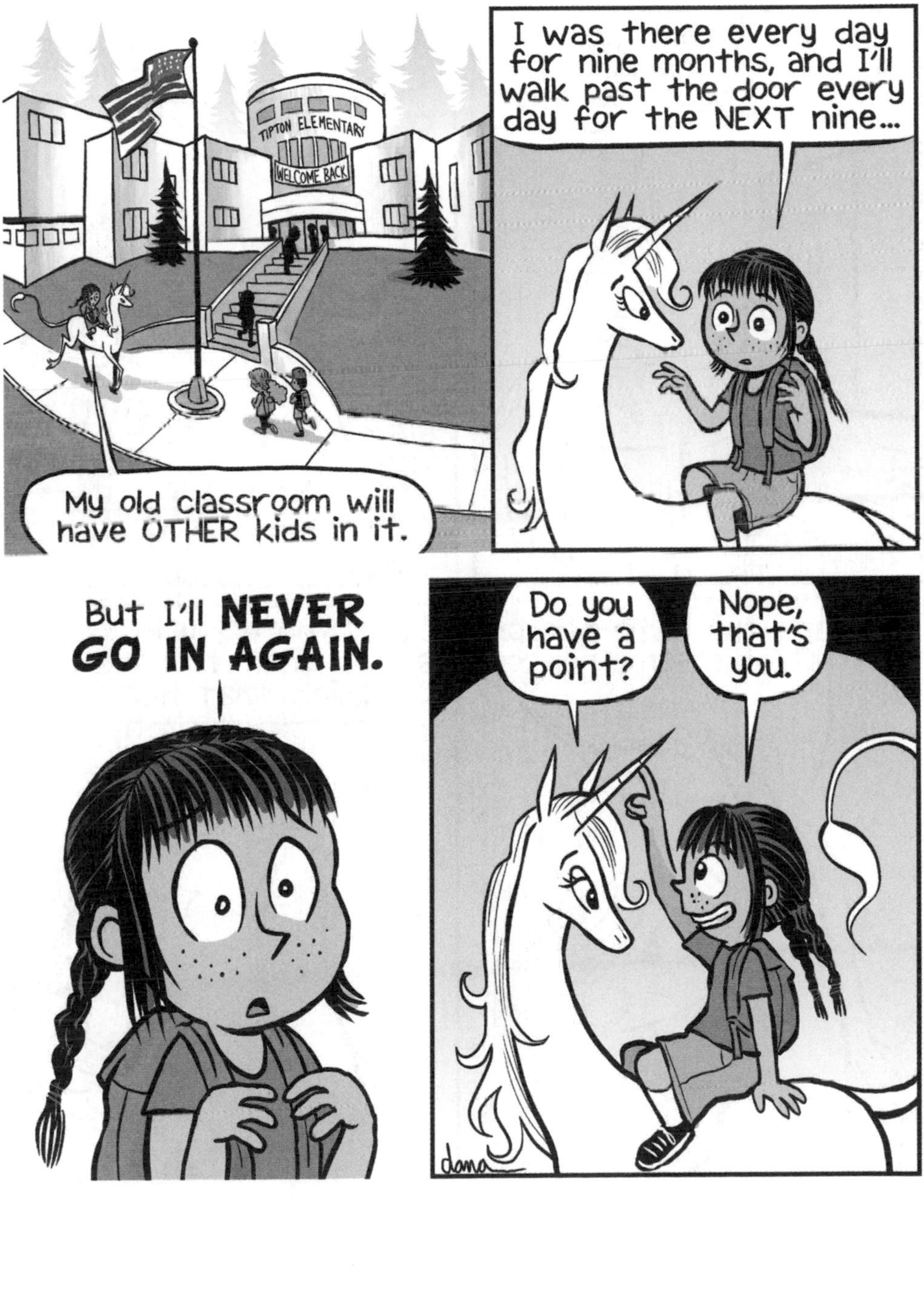
TIPTON ELEMENTARY
WELCOME BACK
My old classroom will have OTHER kids in it.
I was there every day for nine months, and I'll walk past the door every day for the NEXT nine...
But I'll **NEVER GO IN AGAIN.**
Do you have a point?
Nope, that's you.
dana

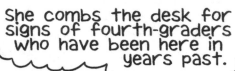

Dr. Phoebe scans for evidence of ancient civilizations.

She combs the desk for signs of fourth-graders who have been here in years past.

Signs point to a king, in the age of metal.

A ruler referred to here as OZZY.

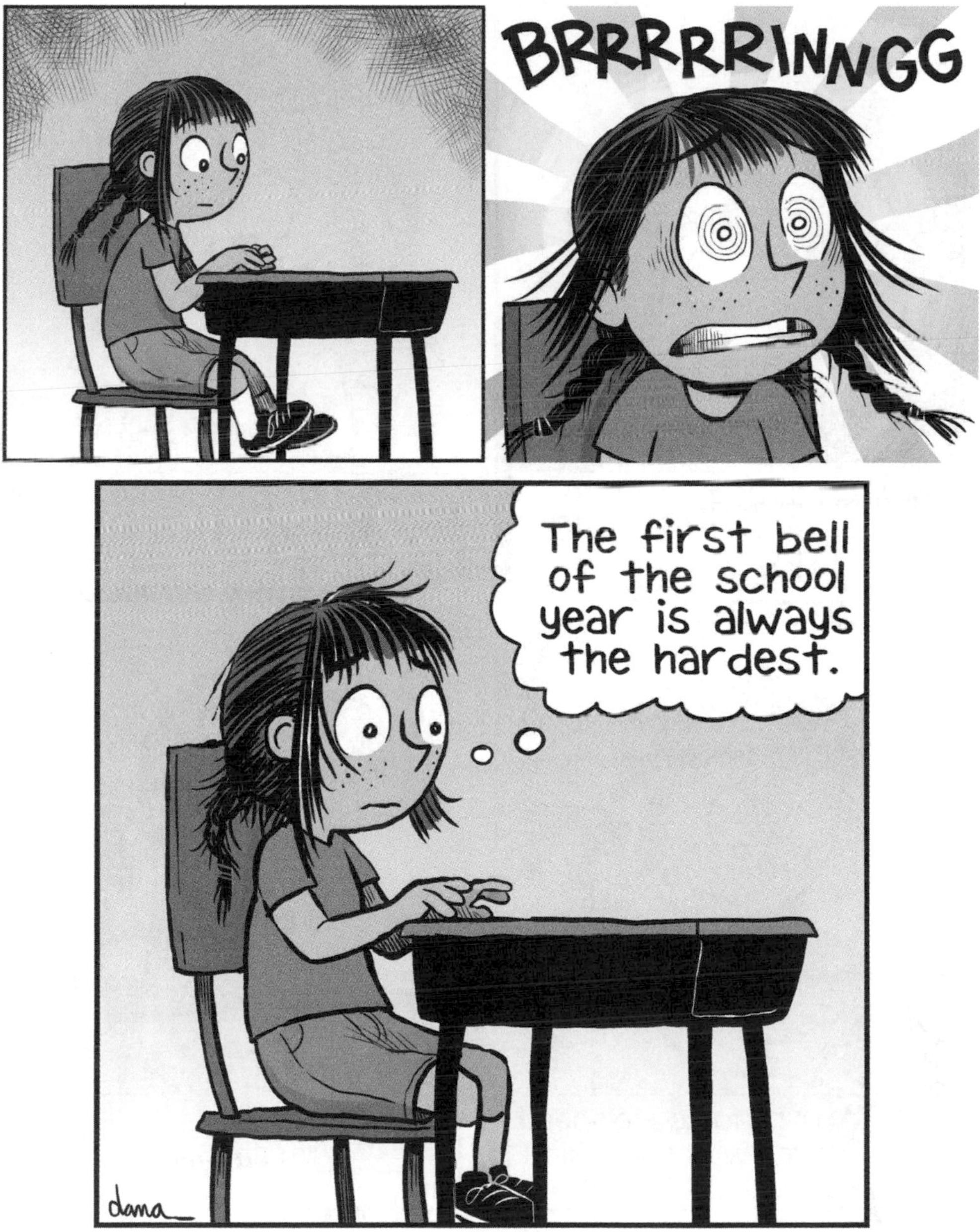
BRRRRRINNGG
The first bell of the school year is always the hardest.
dana

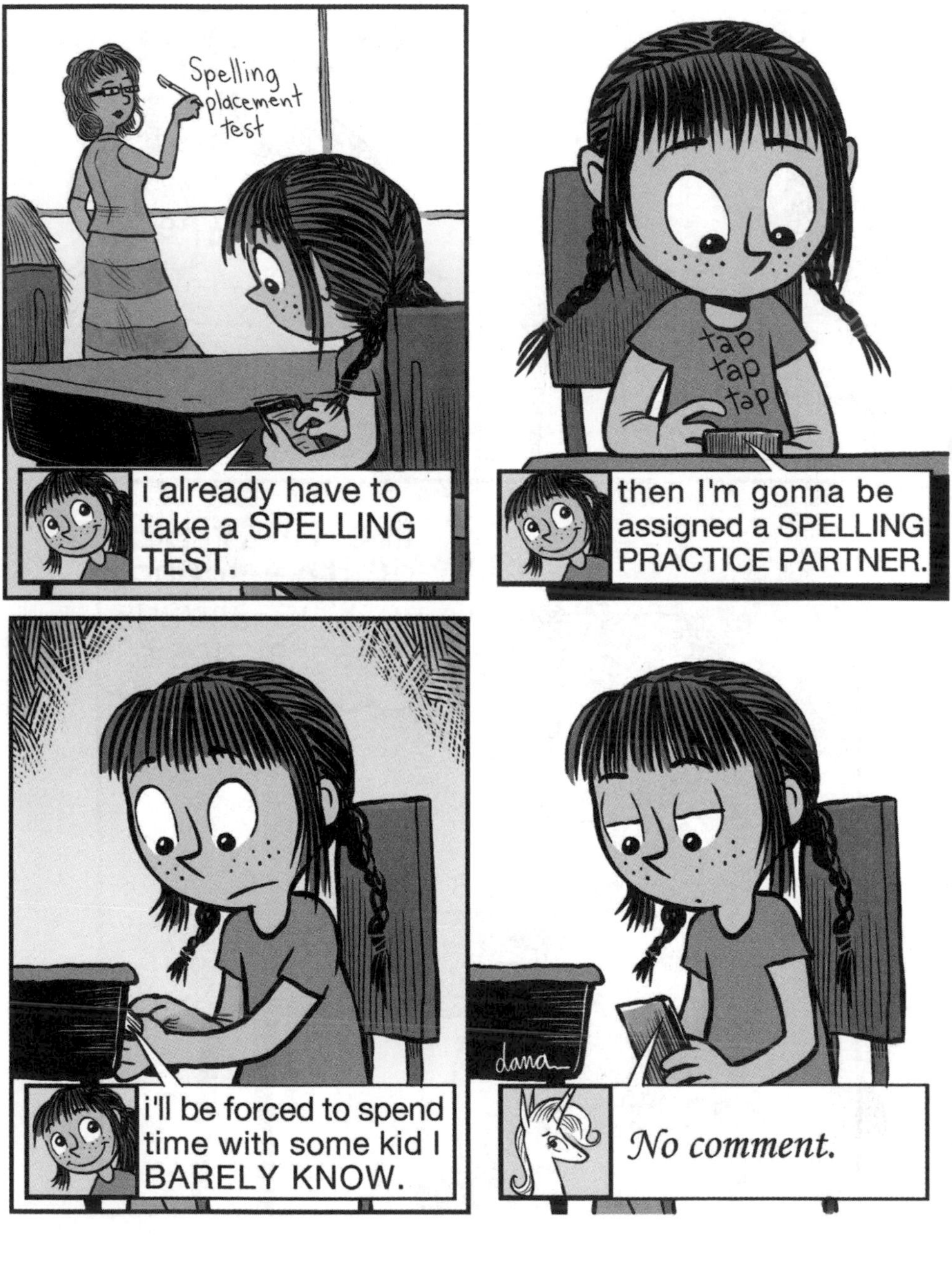
Spelling placement test
i already have to take a SPELLING TEST.
then I'm gonna be assigned a SPELLING PRACTICE PARTNER.
tap tap tap
i'll be forced to spend time with some kid I BARELY KNOW.
dana
No comment.

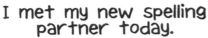

I met my new spelling partner today.

How did it go?

Great!

I...borrowed his glasses without asking, and then demanded he spell my name.

So NOT great.

Kind of dreadful, yeah.

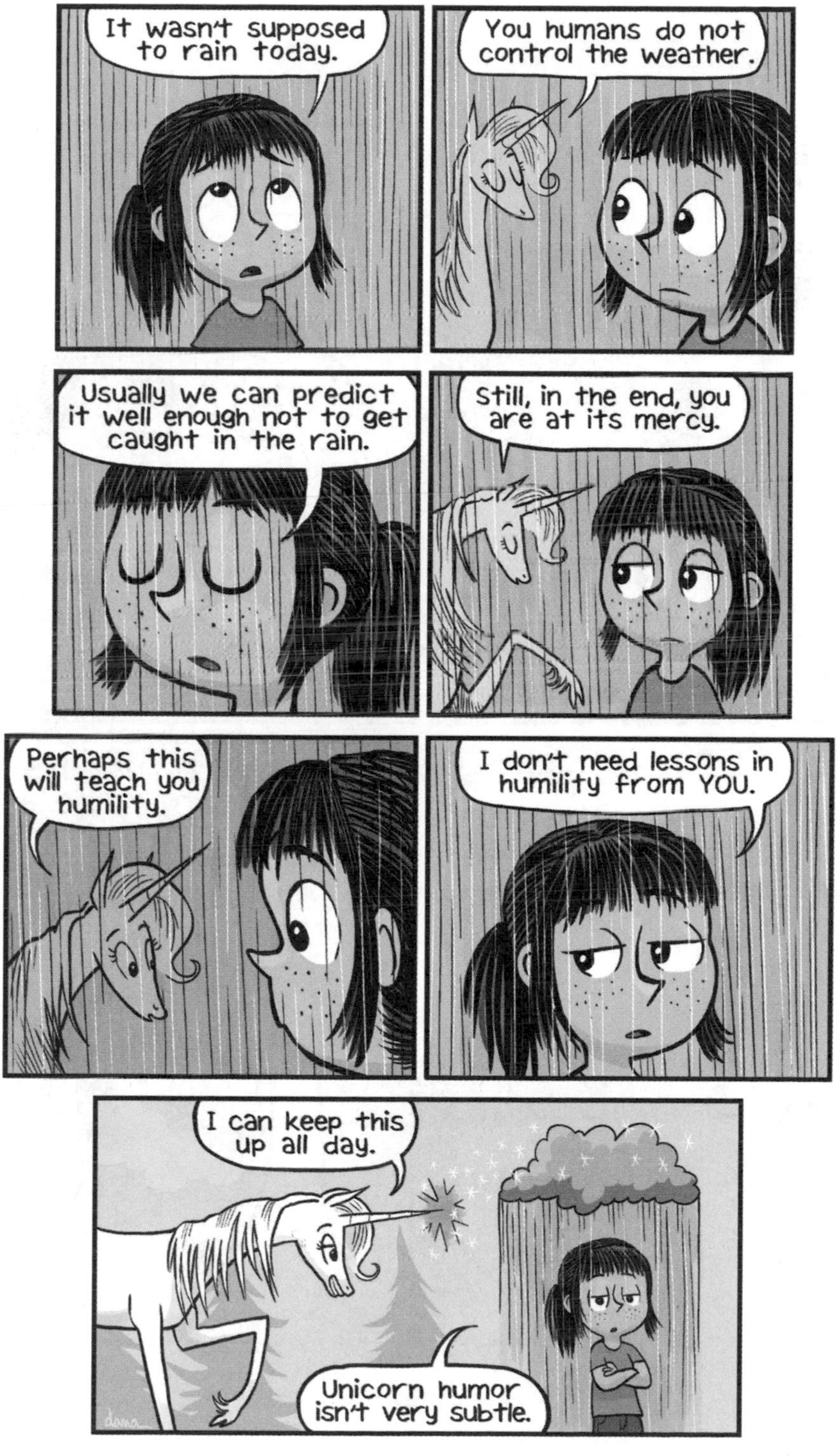
It wasn't supposed to rain today.
You humans do not control the weather.
Usually we can predict it well enough not to get caught in the rain.
Still, in the end, you are at its mercy.
Perhaps this will teach you humility.
I don't need lessons in humility from YOU.
I can keep this up all day.
Unicorn humor isn't very subtle.
dana

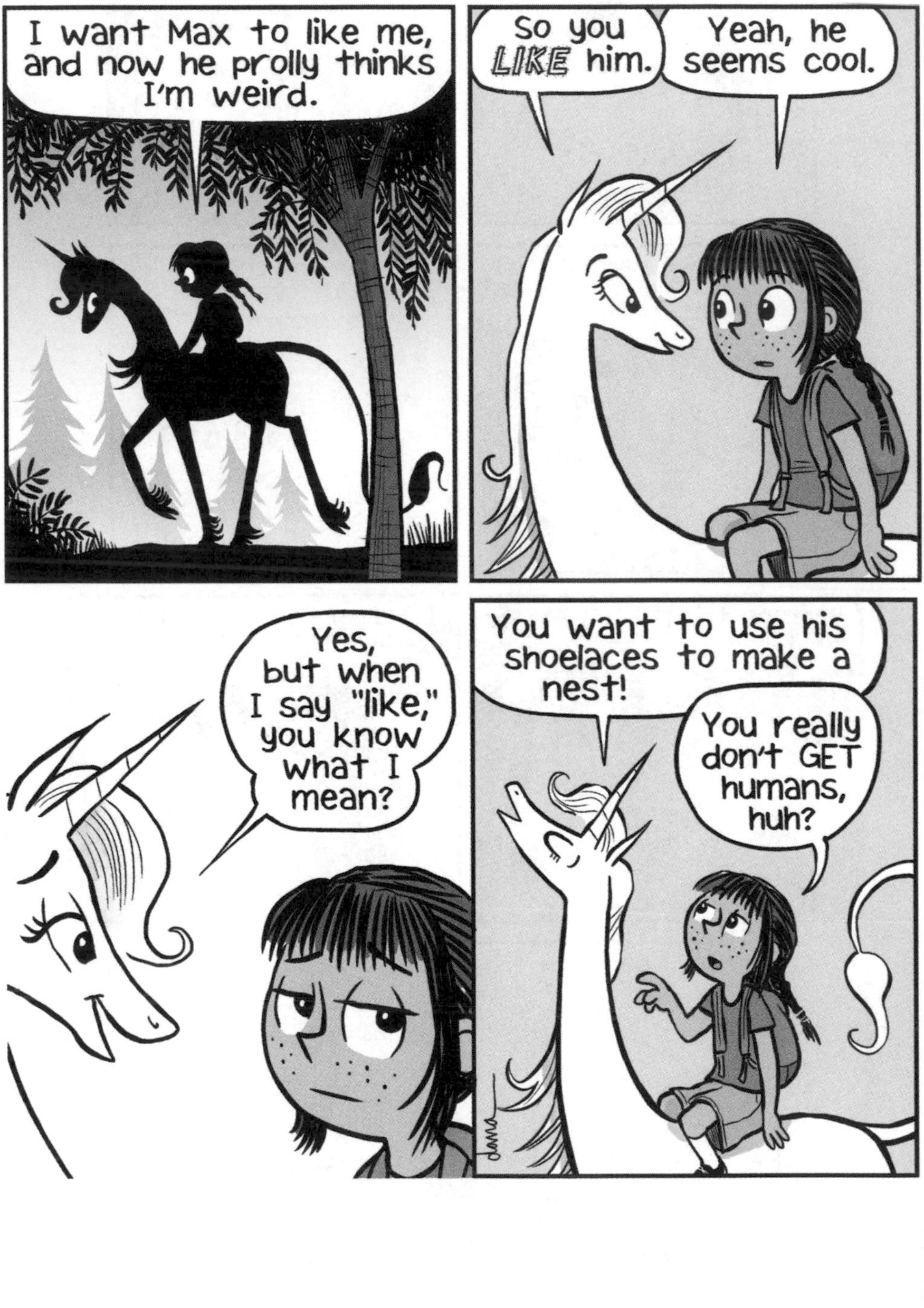
I want Max to like me, and now he prolly thinks I'm weird.
So you LIKE him.
Yeah, he seems cool.
Yes, but when I say "like," you know what I mean?
You want to use his shoelaces to make a nest!
You really don't GET humans, huh?

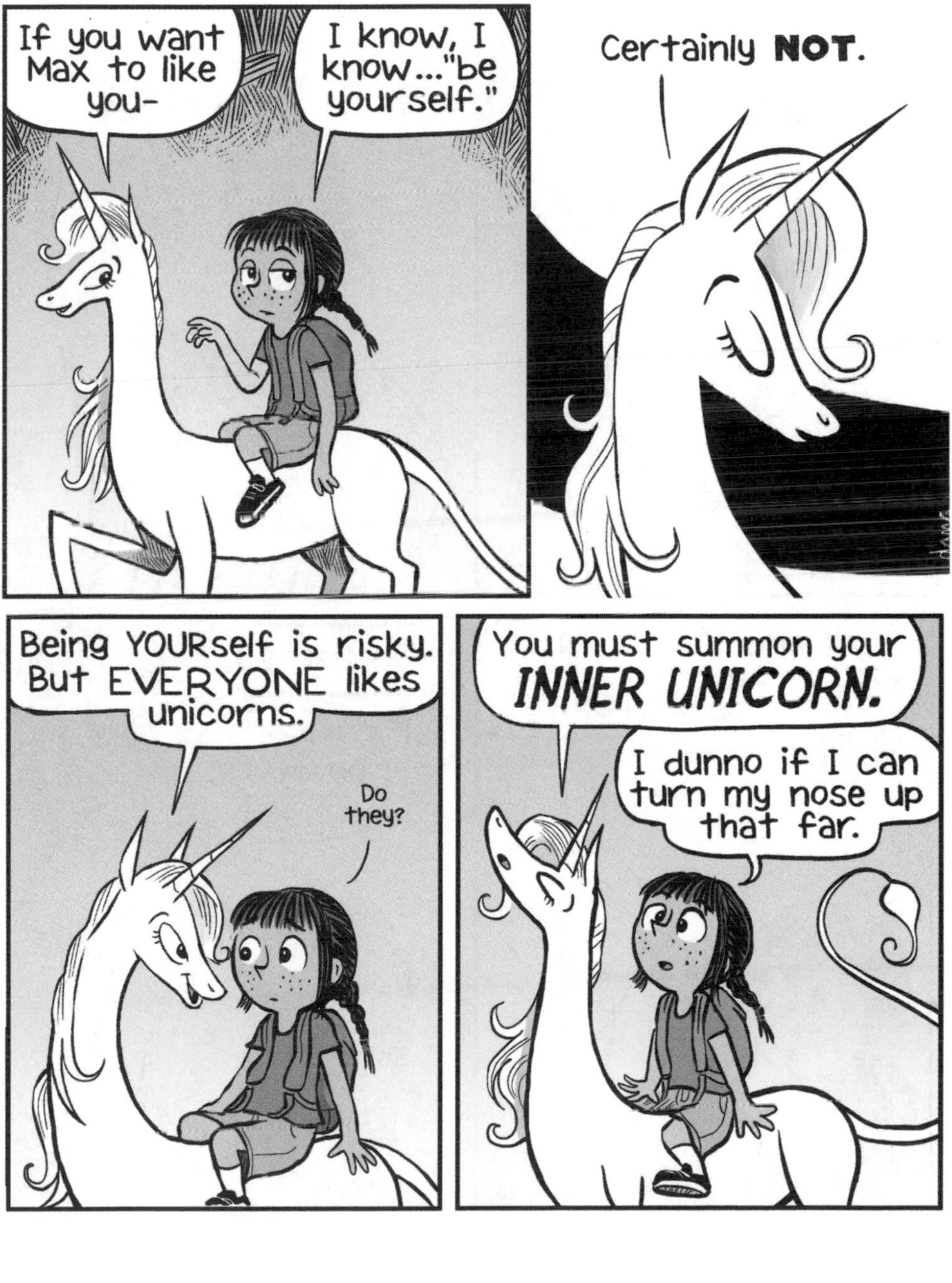
If you want Max to like you-
I know, I know..."be yourself."
Certainly **NOT**.
Being YOURself is risky. But EVERYONE likes unicorns.
Do they?
You must summon your *INNER UNICORN.*
I dunno if I can turn my nose up that far.

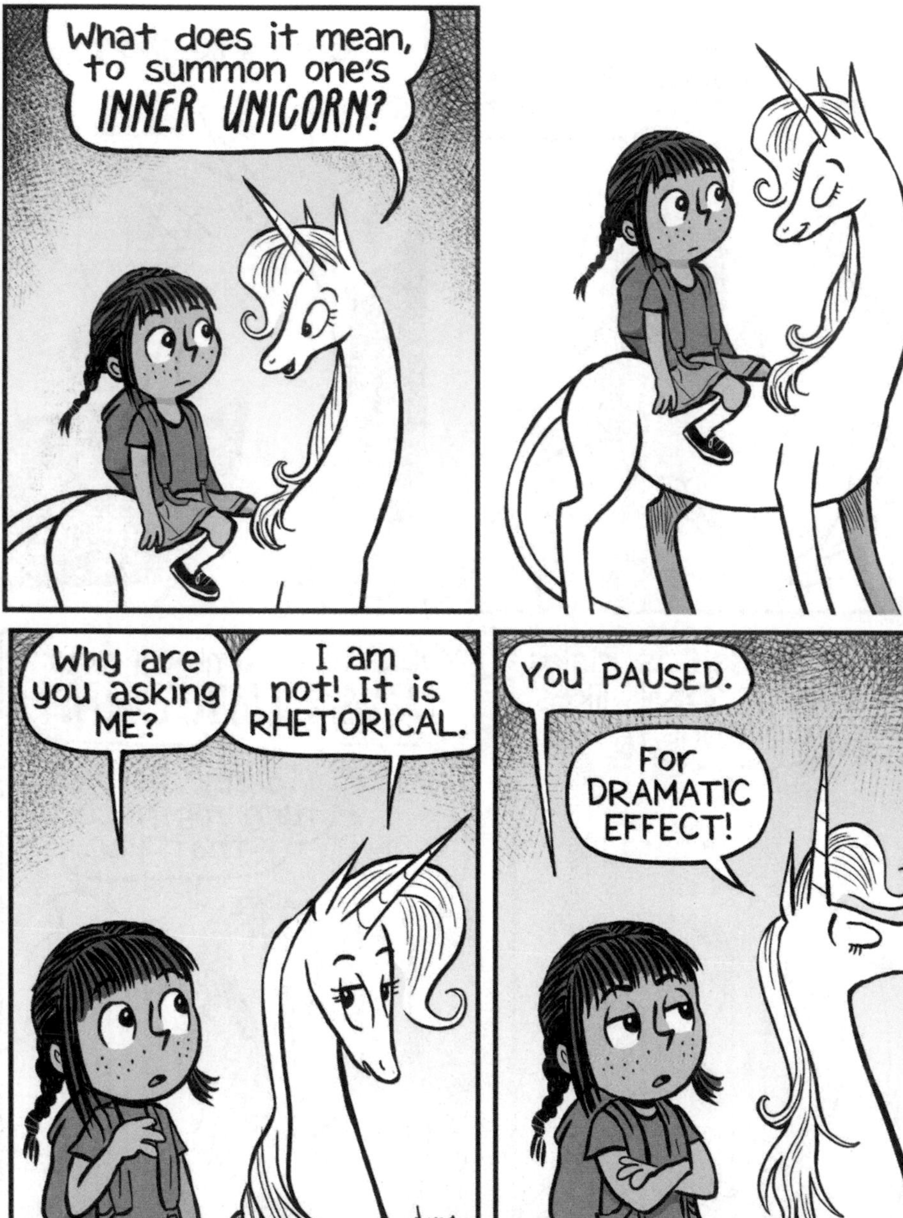
What does it mean, to summon one's INNER UNICORN?
Why are you asking ME?
I am not! It is RHETORICAL.
dana
You PAUSED.
For DRAMATIC EFFECT!

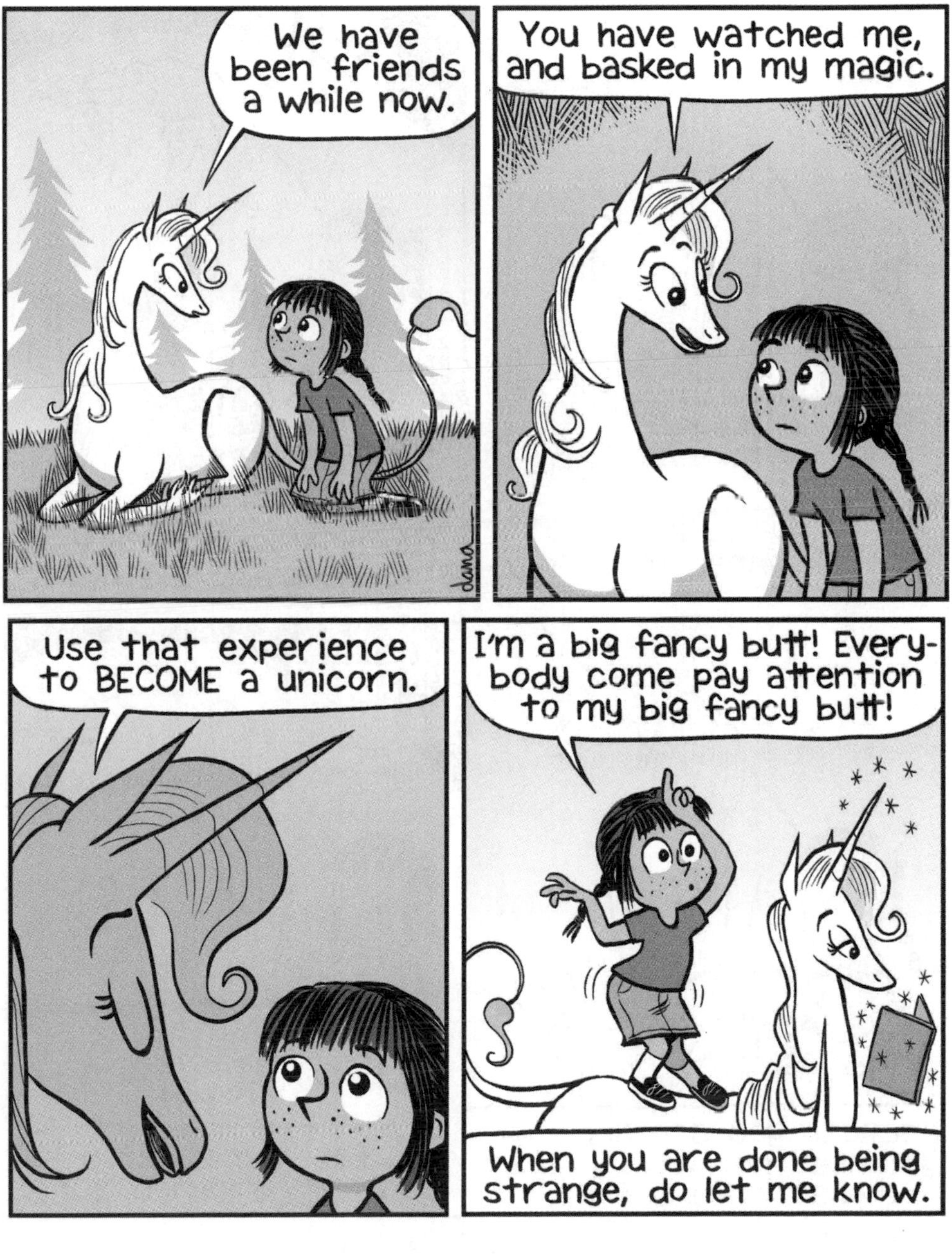
We have been friends a while now.
You have watched me, and basked in my magic.
Use that experience to BECOME a unicorn.
I'm a big fancy butt! Every-body come pay attention to my big fancy butt!
When you are done being strange, do let me know.
dana

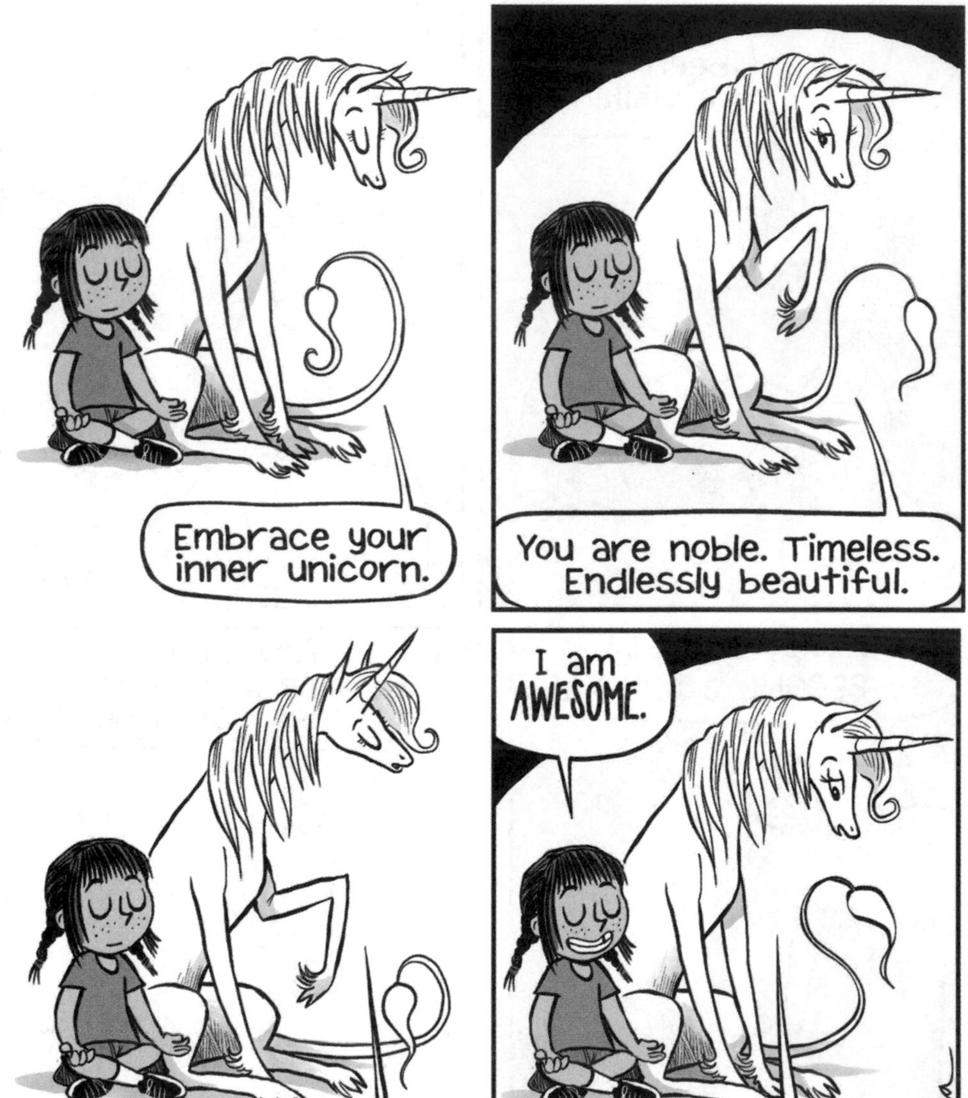
Embrace your inner unicorn.
You are noble. Timeless. Endlessly beautiful.
Because you are superior, you need not worry about what others think.
I am AWESOME.
...for the sake of this conversation, sure.
dana

166

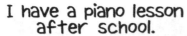

I have a piano lesson after school.

I'll be done with school, except WAIT! Instead of freedom, here's MORE school.

Just when I thought I was out, they pull me back in!

Is that a line from something?

Yeah, probably.

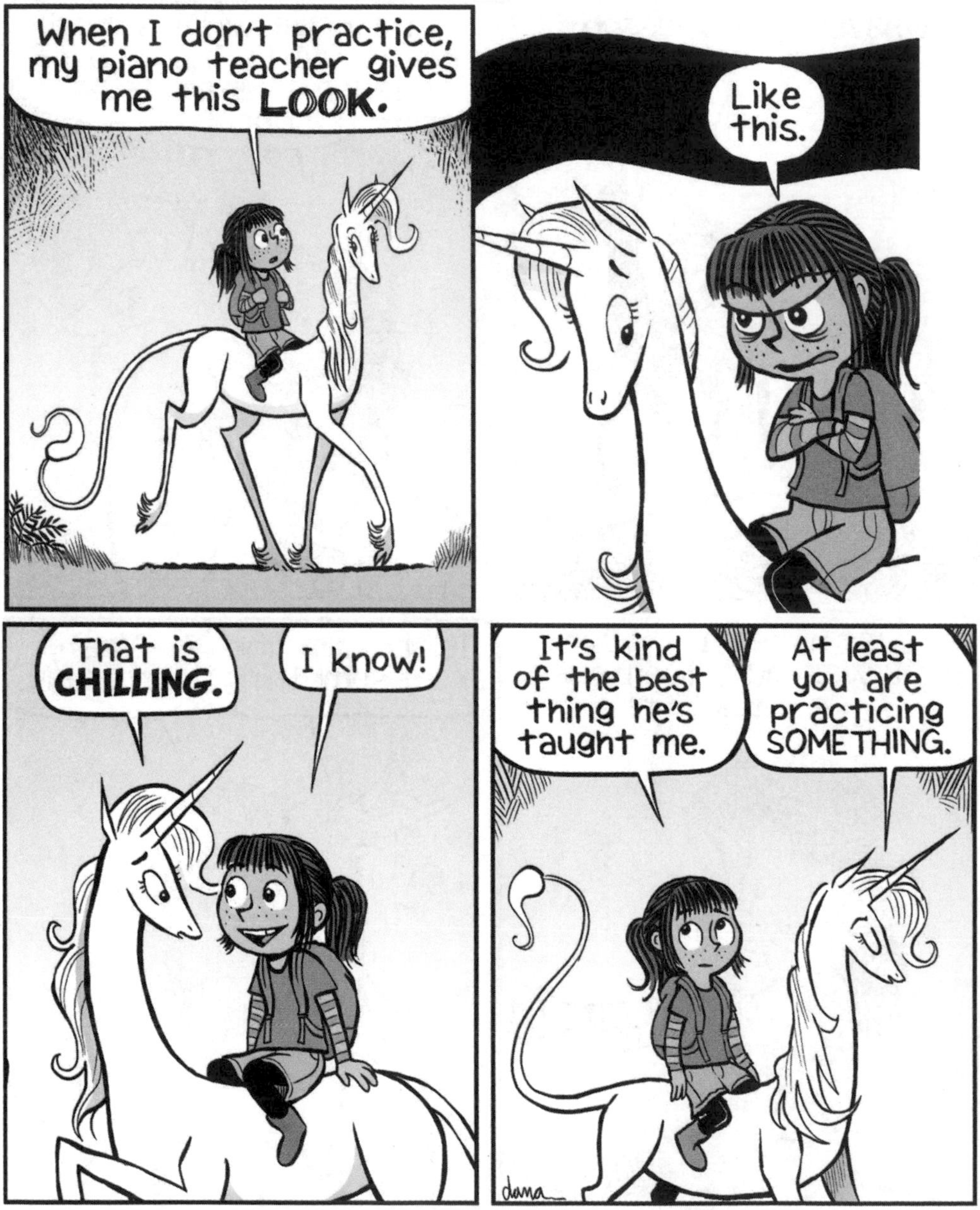

When I don't practice, my piano teacher gives me this LOOK.
Like this.
That is CHILLING.
I know!
It's kind of the best thing he's taught me.
At least you are practicing SOMETHING.
dana

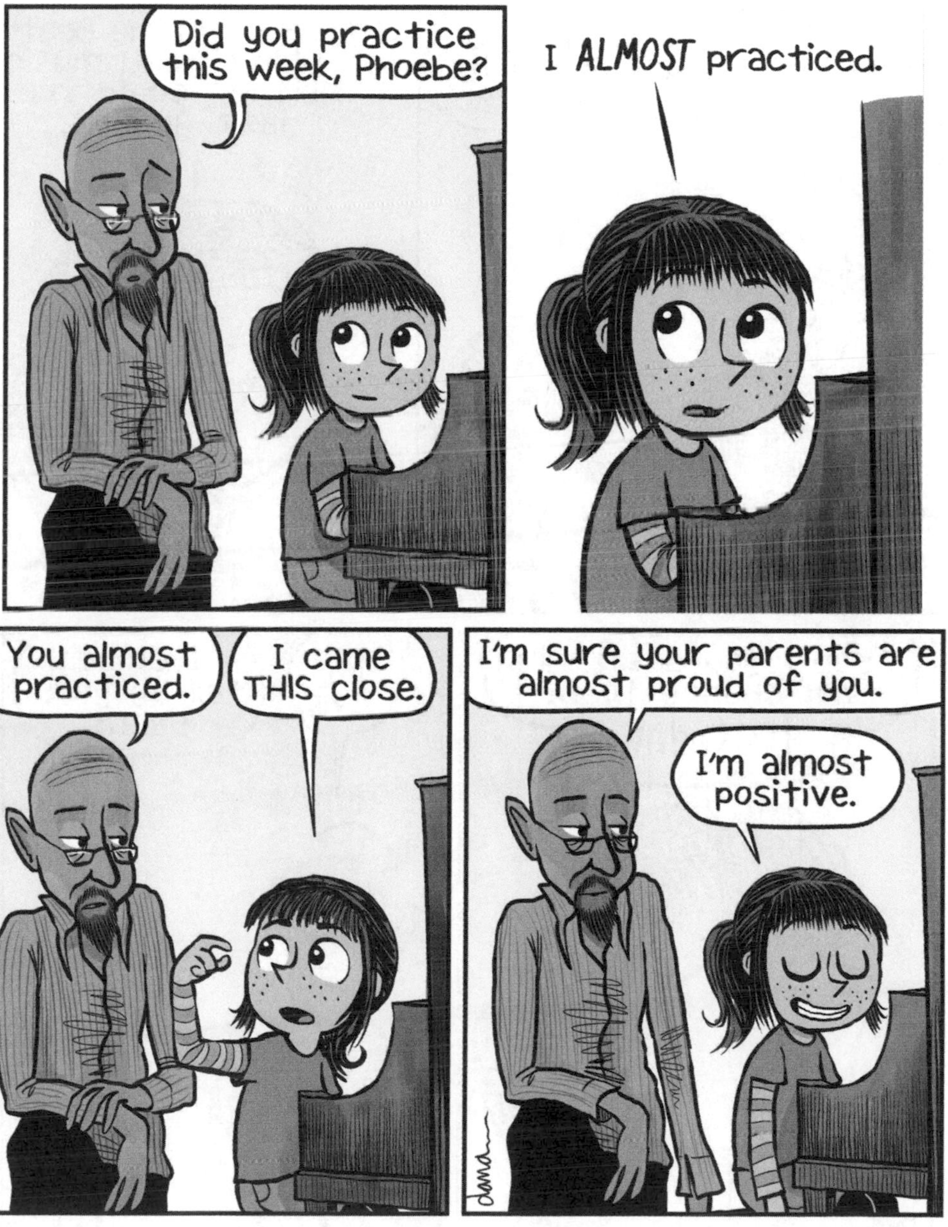
Did you practice this week, Phoebe?
I ALMOST practiced.
You almost practiced.
I came THIS close.
I'm sure your parents are almost proud of you.
I'm almost positive.
dana

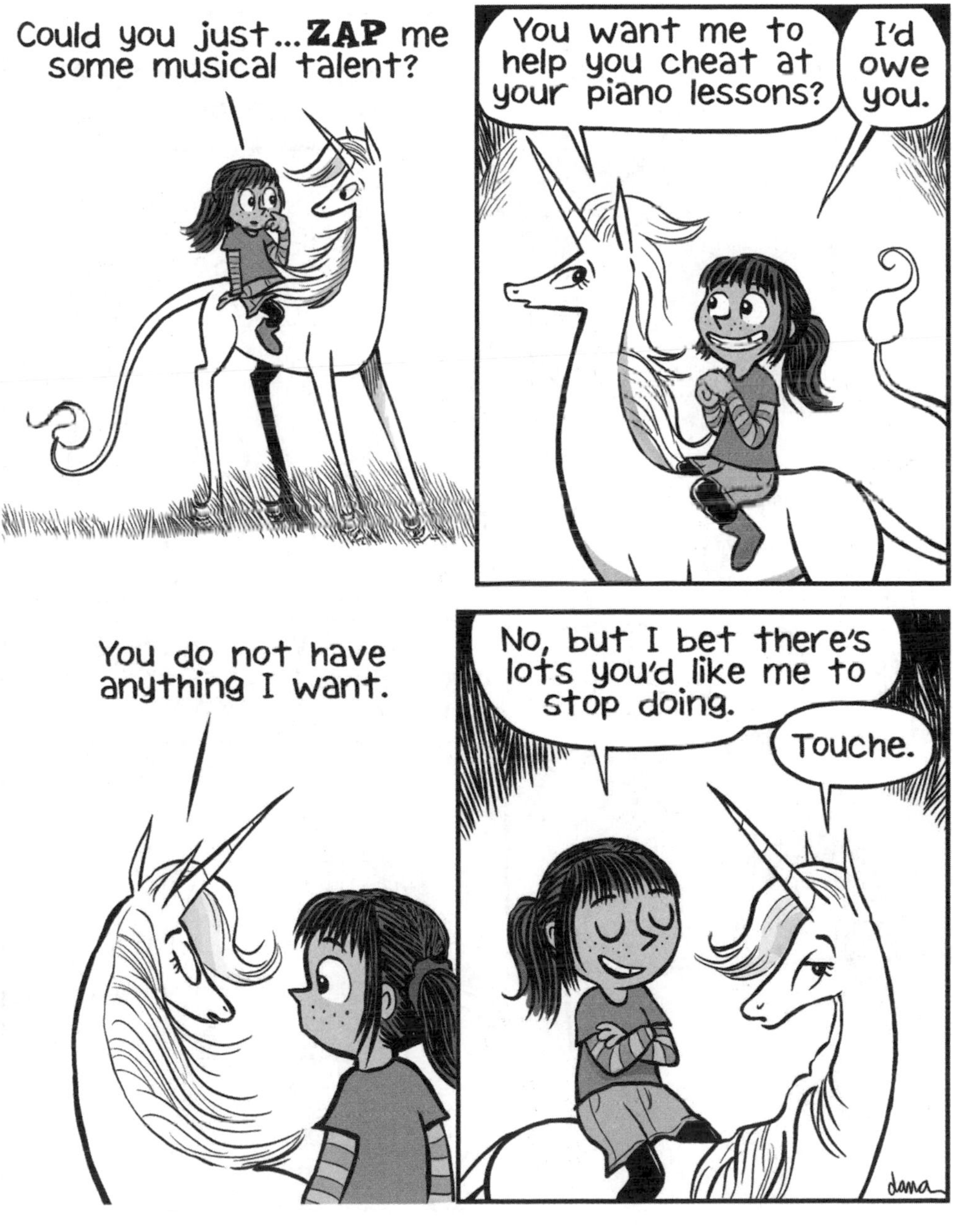
Could you just... ZAP me some musical talent?
You want me to help you cheat at your piano lessons?
I'd owe you.
You do not have anything I want.
No, but I bet there's lots you'd like me to stop doing.
Touche.
dana

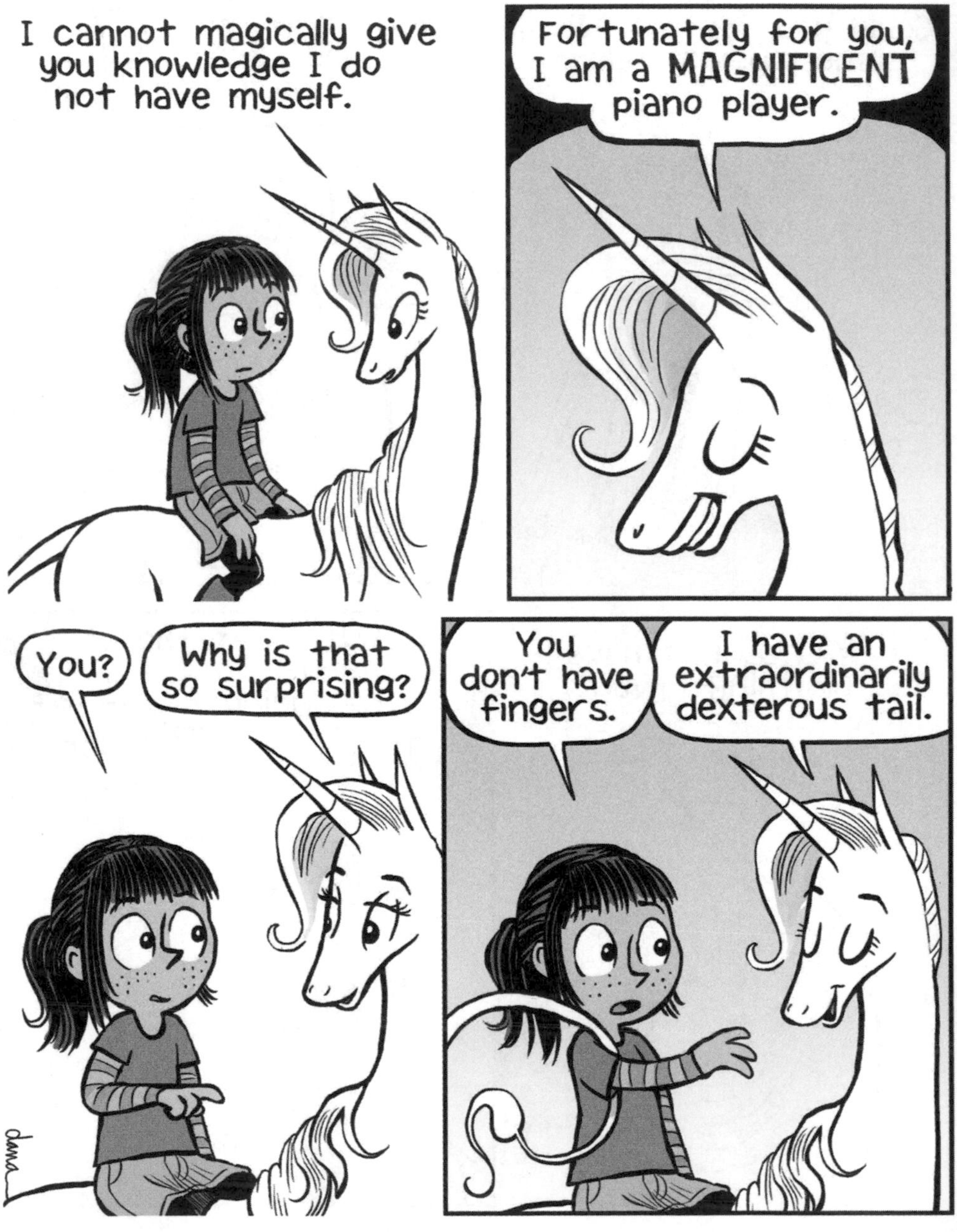
I cannot magically give you knowledge I do not have myself.
Fortunately for you, I am a MAGNIFICENT piano player.
You?
Why is that so surprising?
You don't have fingers.
I have an extraordinarily dexterous tail.

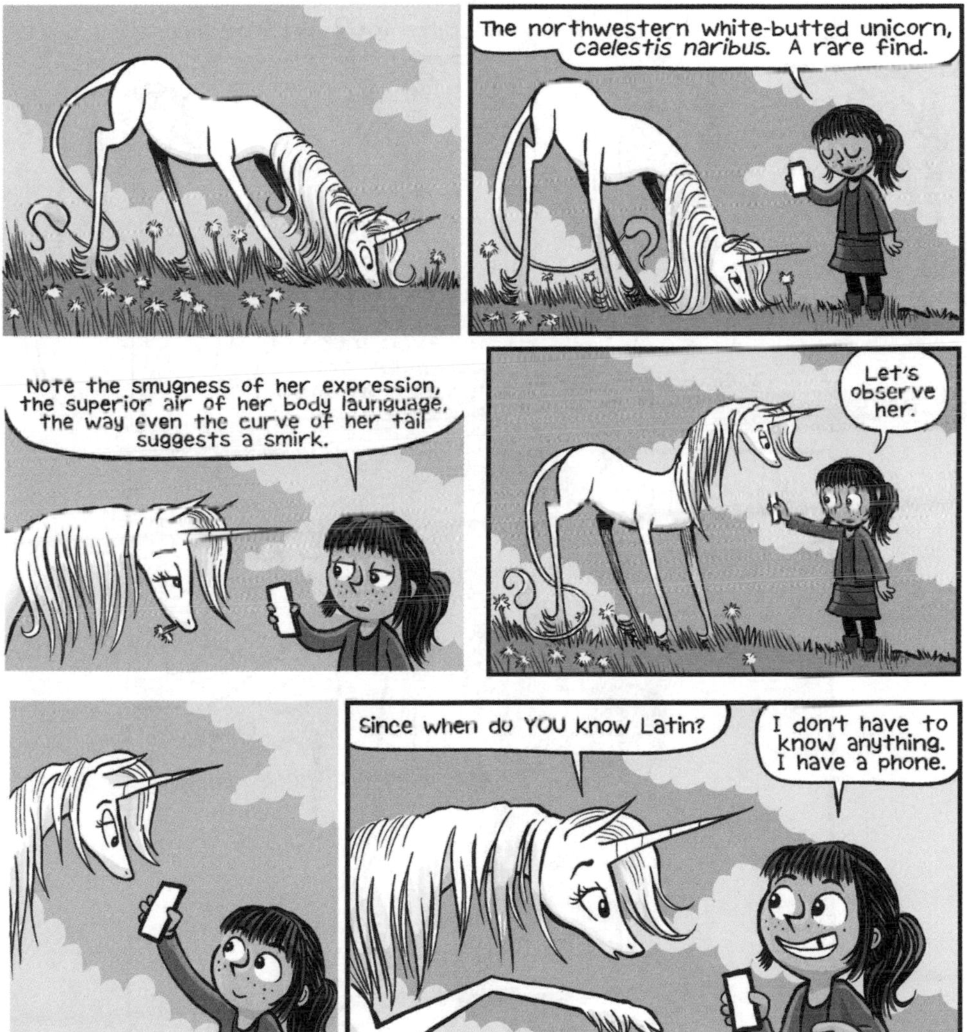
The northwestern white-butted unicorn, *caelestis naribus*. A rare find.
Note the smugness of her expression, the superior air of her body launguage, the way even the curve of her tail suggests a smirk.
Let's observe her.
Since when do YOU know Latin?
I don't have to know anything. I have a phone.

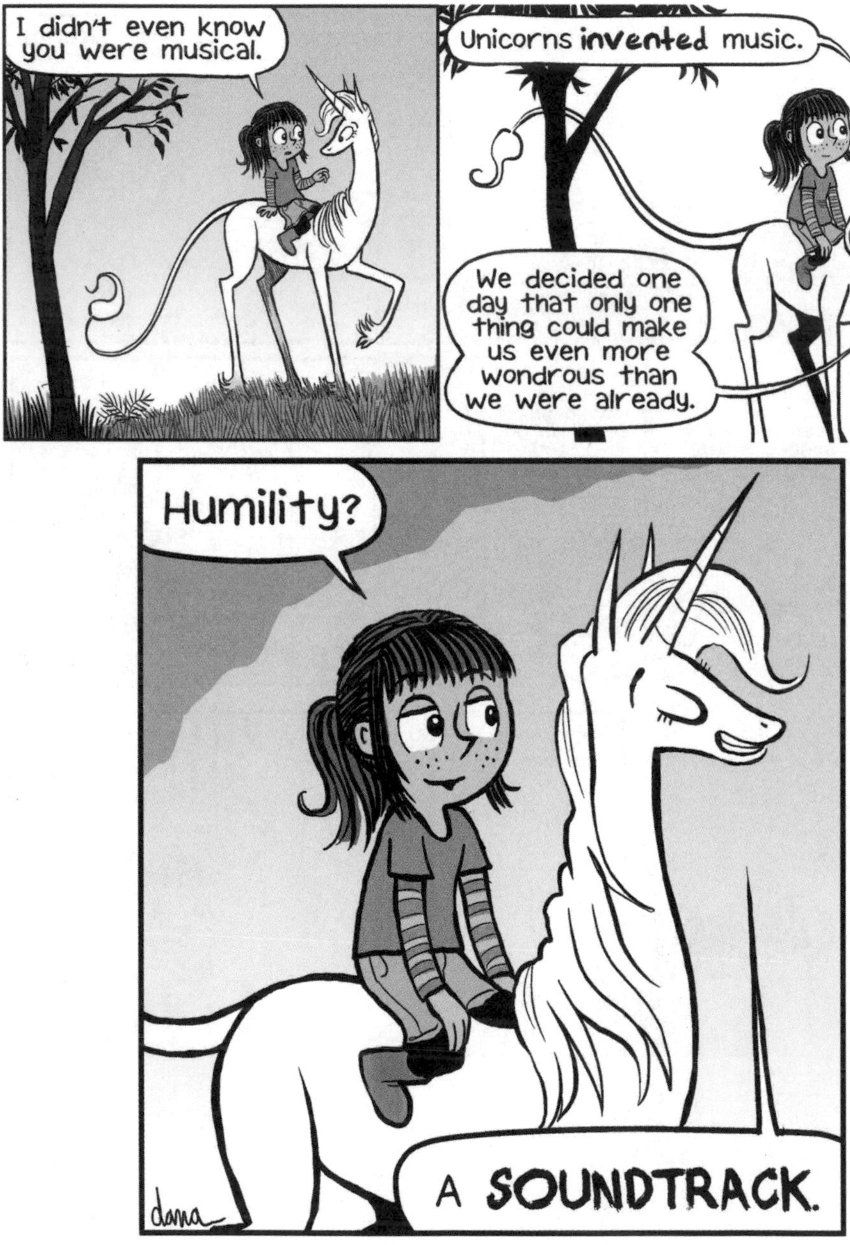
I didn't even know you were musical.
Unicorns **invented** music.
We decided one day that only one thing could make us even more wondrous than we were already.
Humility?
A **SOUNDTRACK.**
dana

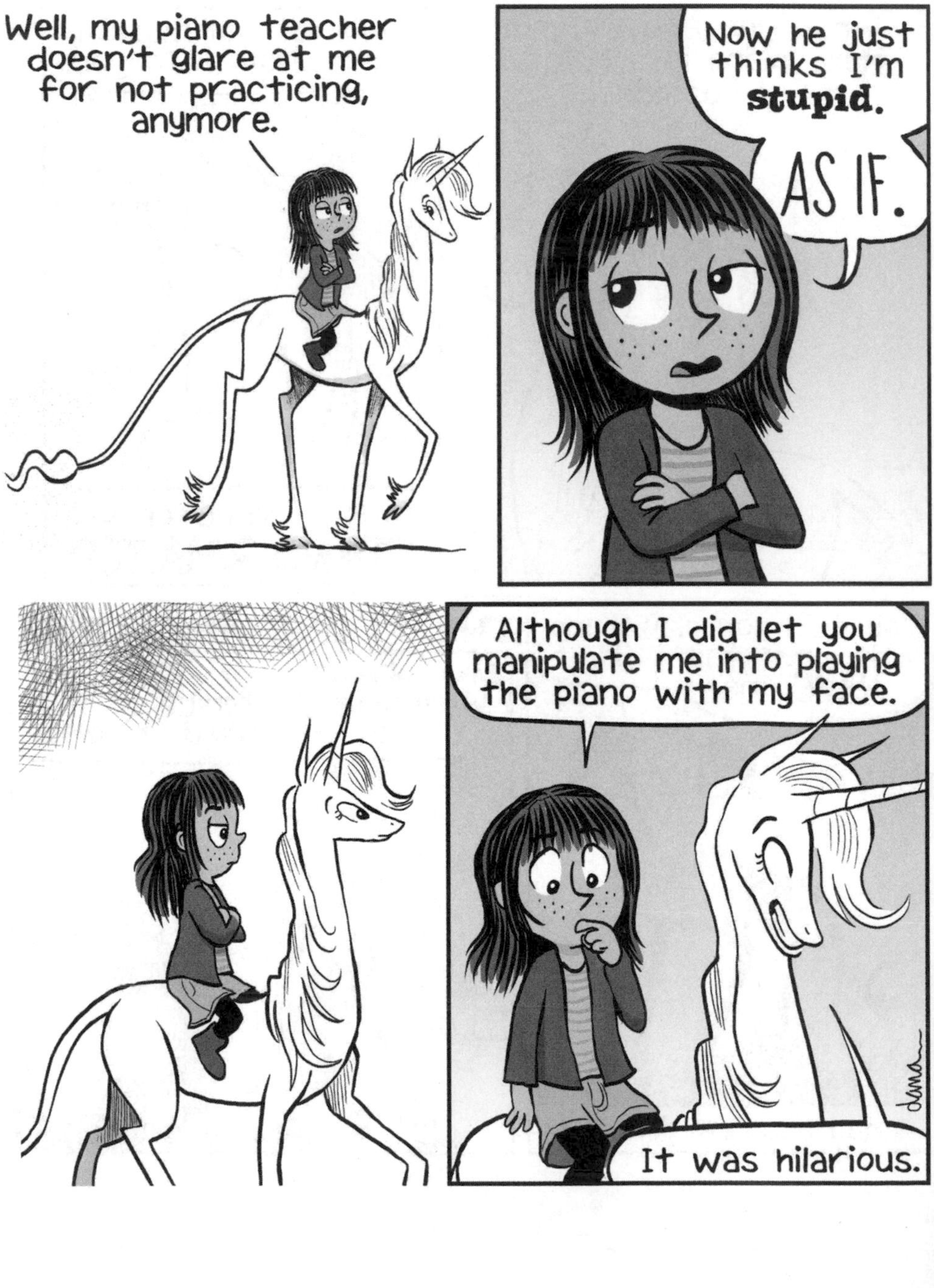
Well, my piano teacher doesn't glare at me for not practicing, anymore.
Now he just thinks I'm **stupid**.
AS IF.
Although I did let you manipulate me into playing the piano with my face.
It was hilarious.
dana

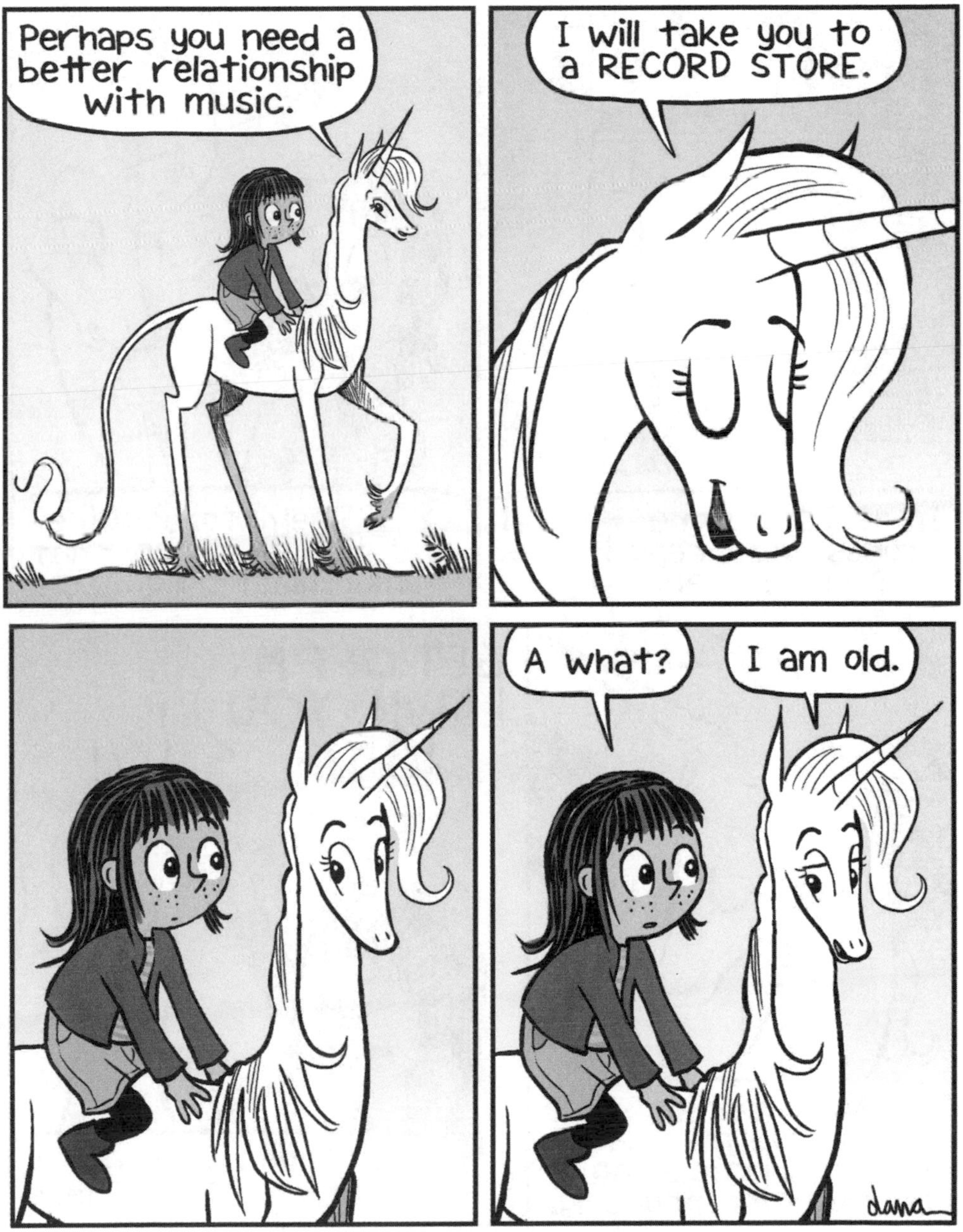
Perhaps you need a better relationship with music.
I will take you to a RECORD STORE.
A what?
I am old.
dana

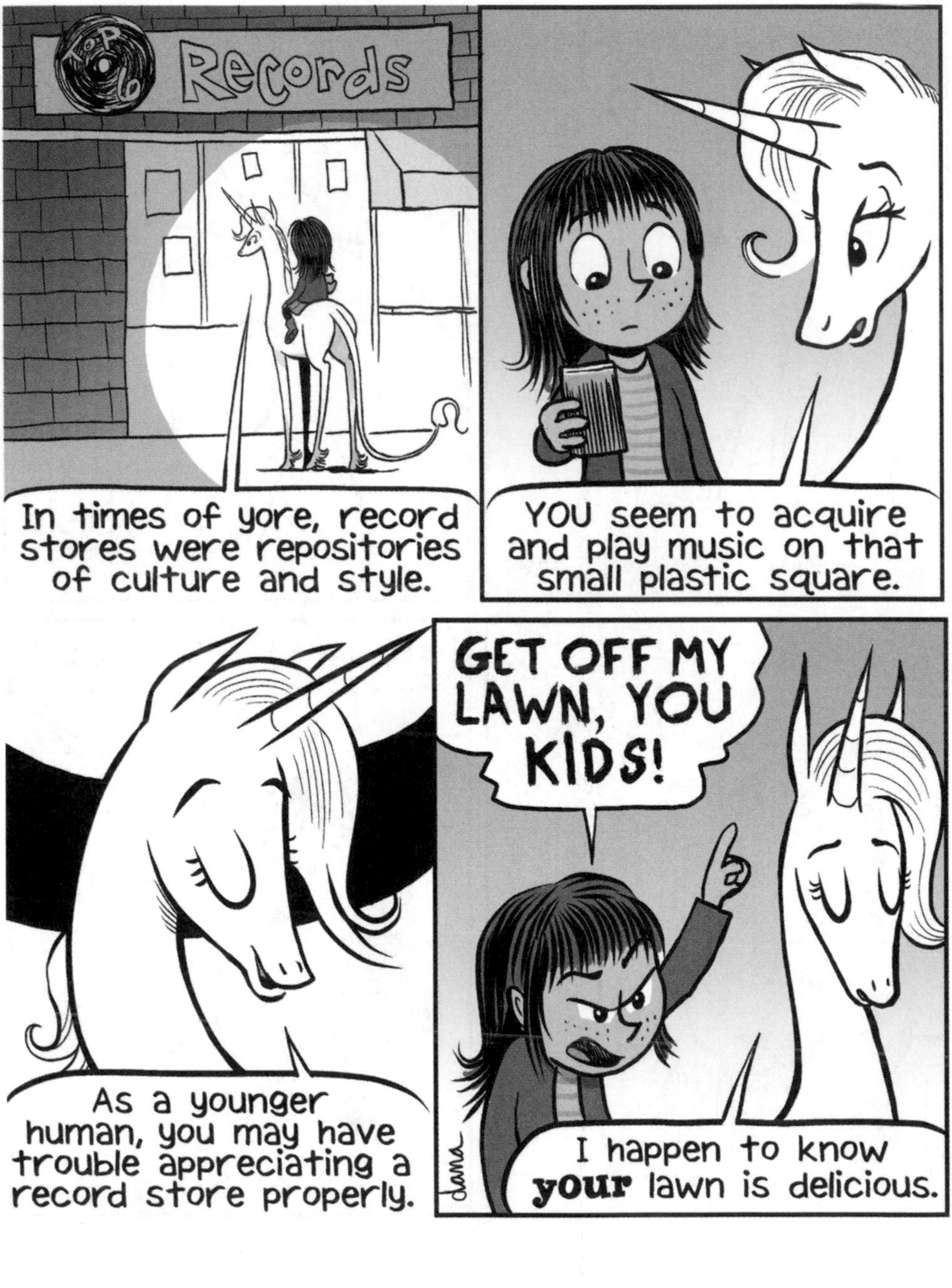

Records
In times of yore, record stores were repositories of culture and style.
YOU seem to acquire and play music on that small plastic square.
As a younger human, you may have trouble appreciating a record store properly.
GET OFF MY LAWN, YOU KIDS!
I happen to know **your** lawn is delicious.
dana

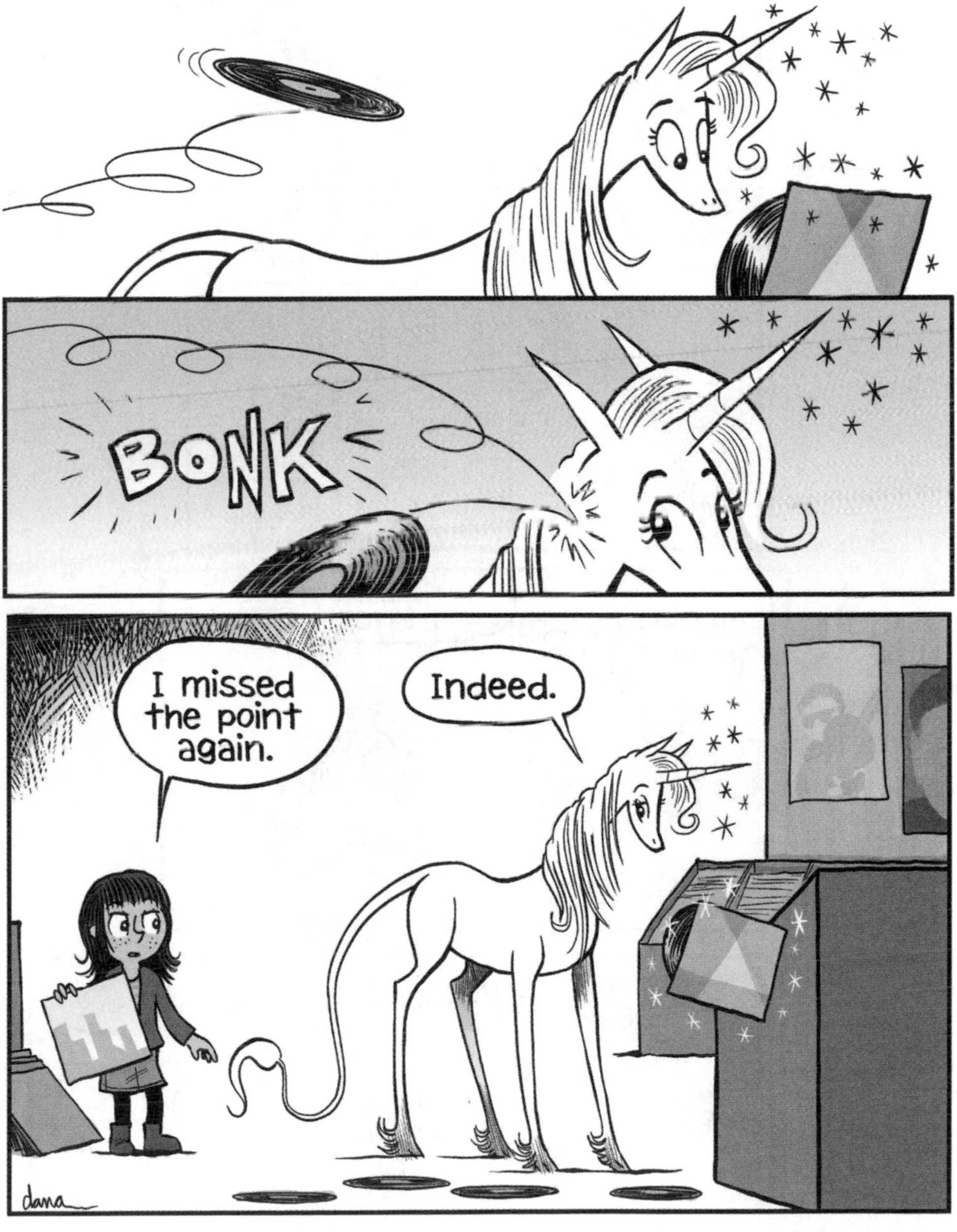
BONK
I missed the point again.
Indeed.
dana

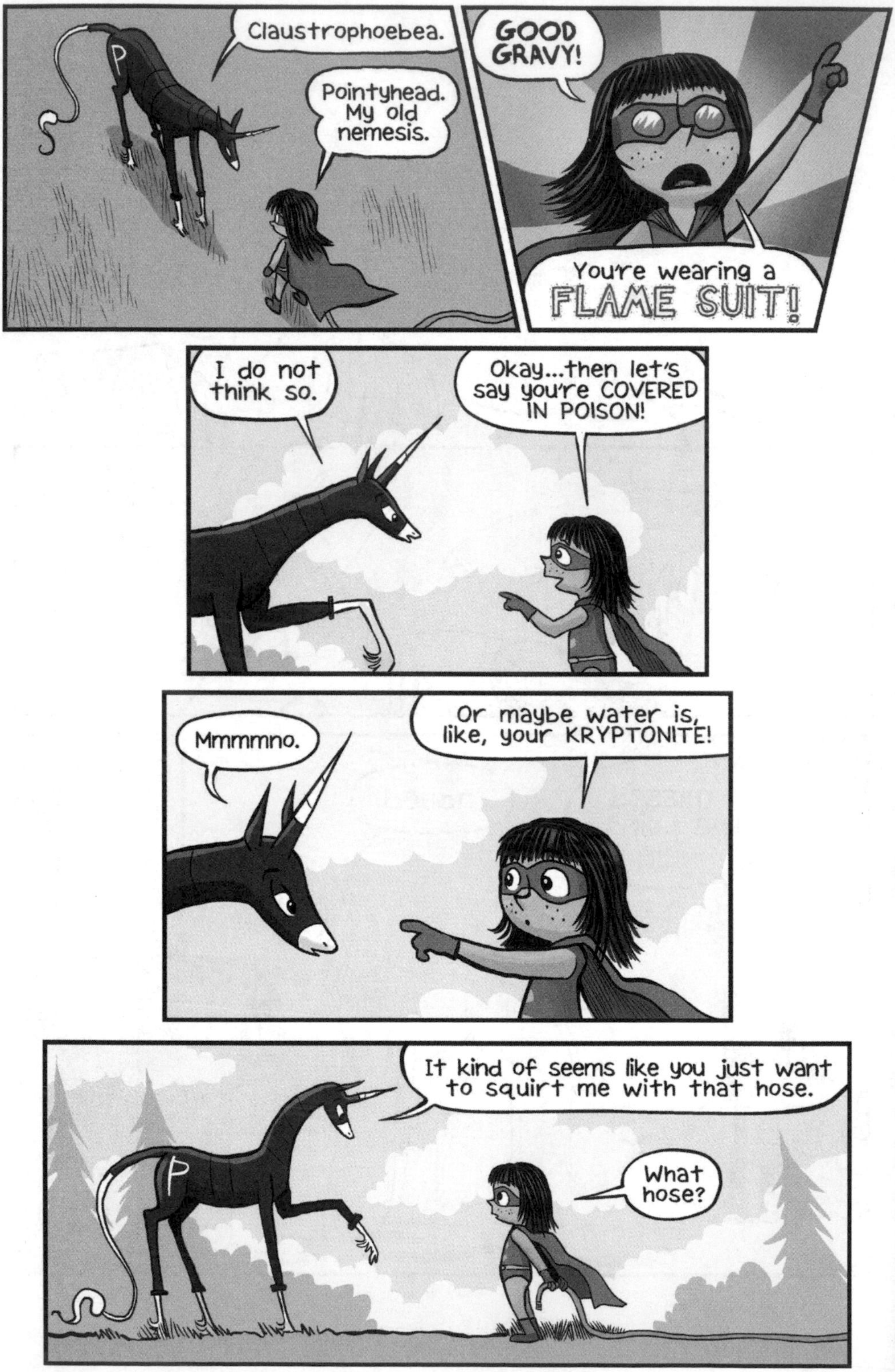
Claustrophoebea.
Pointyhead. My old nemesis.
GOOD GRAVY!
You're wearing a FLAME SUIT!
I do not think so.
Okay...then let's say you're COVERED IN POISON!
Mmmmno.
Or maybe water is, like, your KRYPTONITE!
It kind of seems like you just want to squirt me with that hose.
What hose?

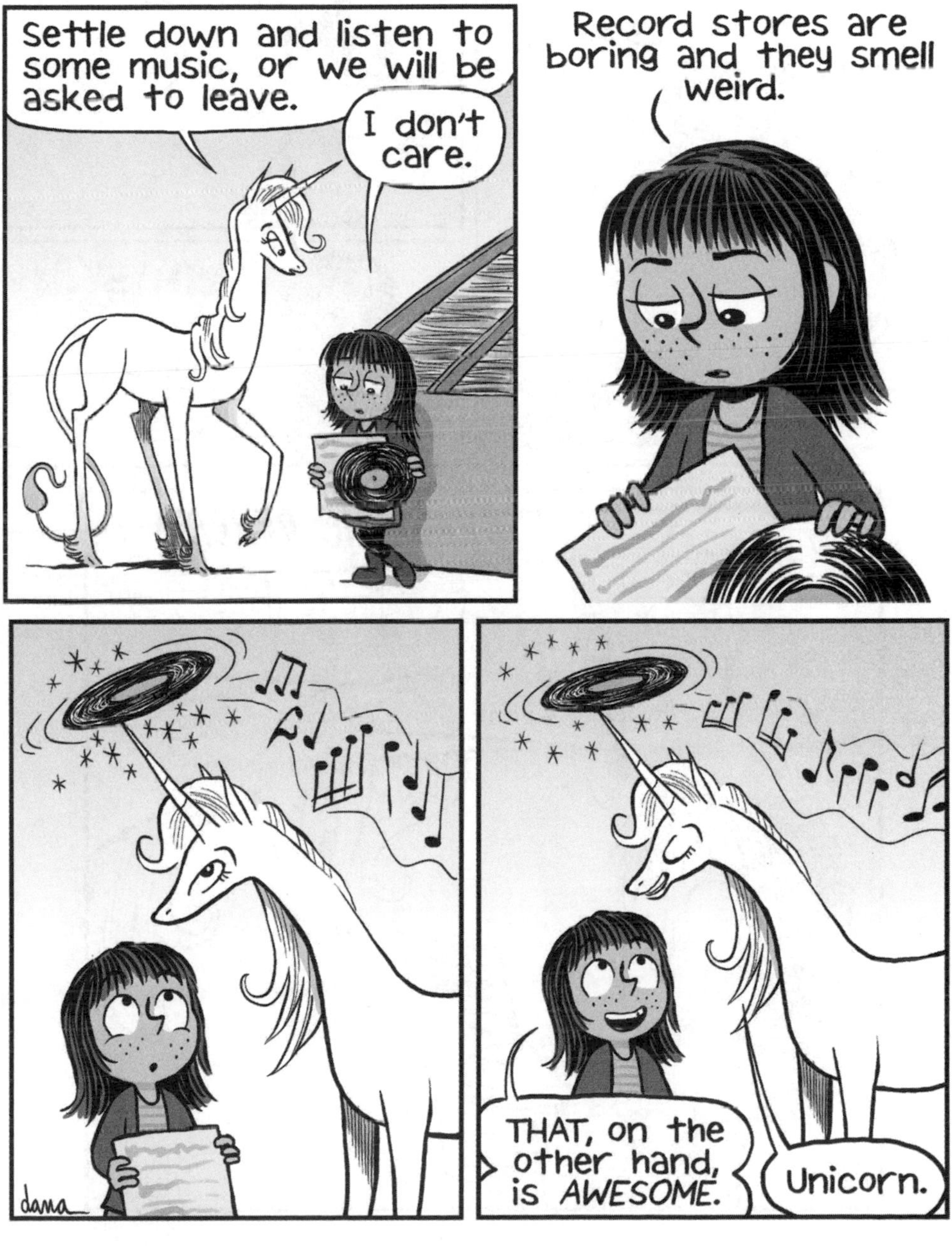
Settle down and listen to some music, or we will be asked to leave.
I don't care.
Record stores are boring and they smell weird.
dana
THAT, on the other hand, is AWESOME.
Unicorn.

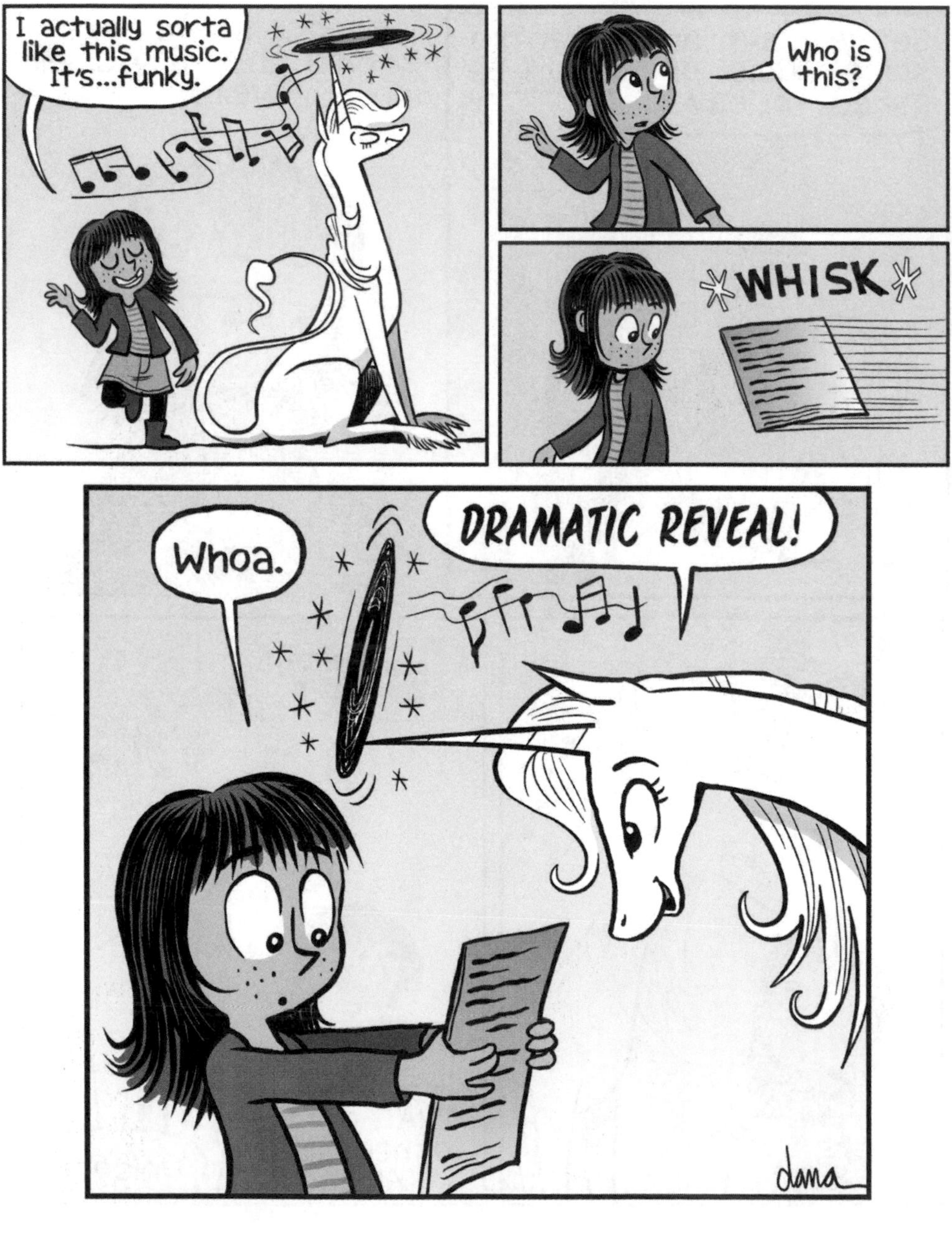
I actually sorta like this music. It's...funky.
Who is this?
WHISK
Whoa.
DRAMATIC REVEAL!
dana

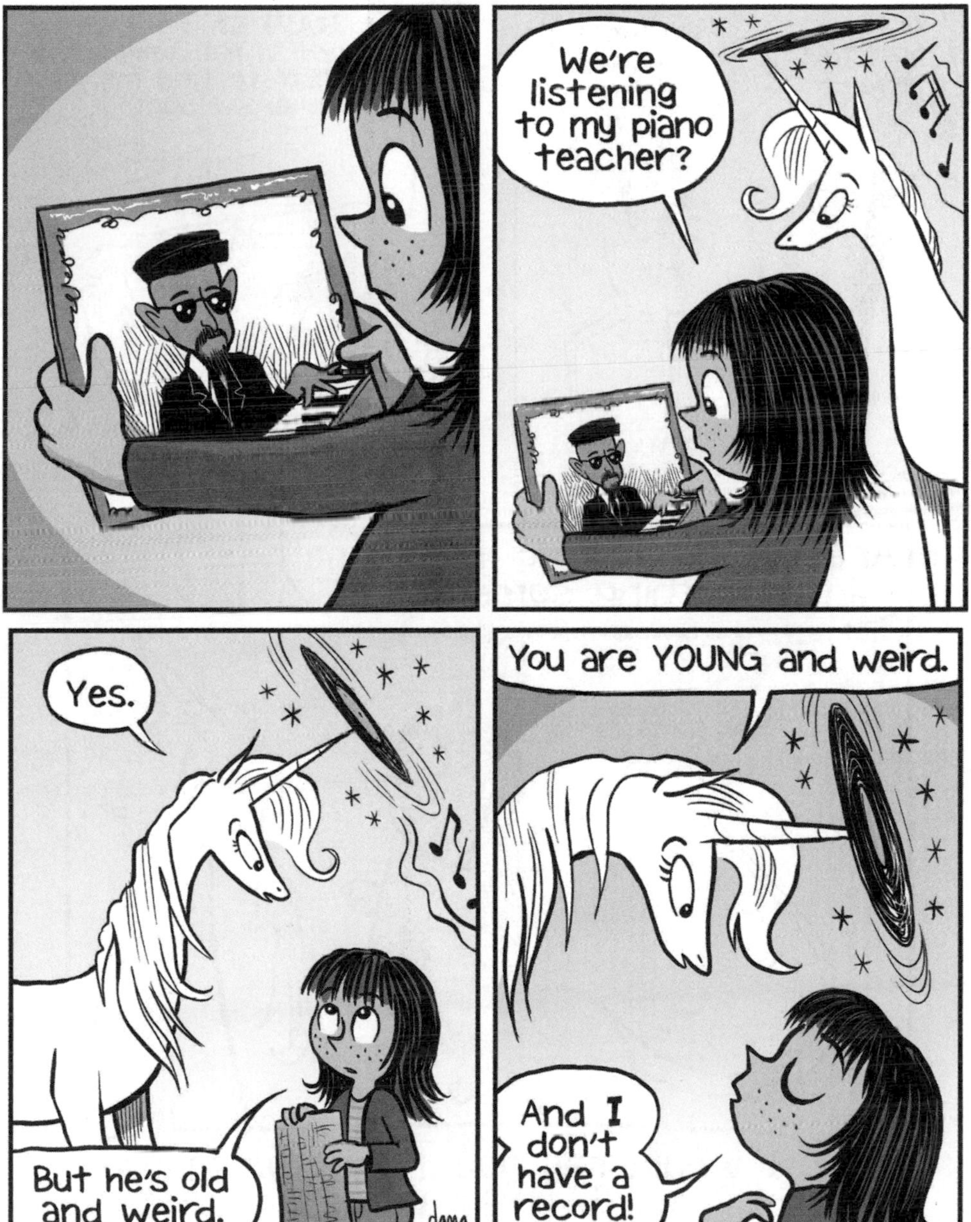
We're listening to my piano teacher?
Yes.
But he's old and weird.
dana
You are YOUNG and weird.
And I don't have a record!

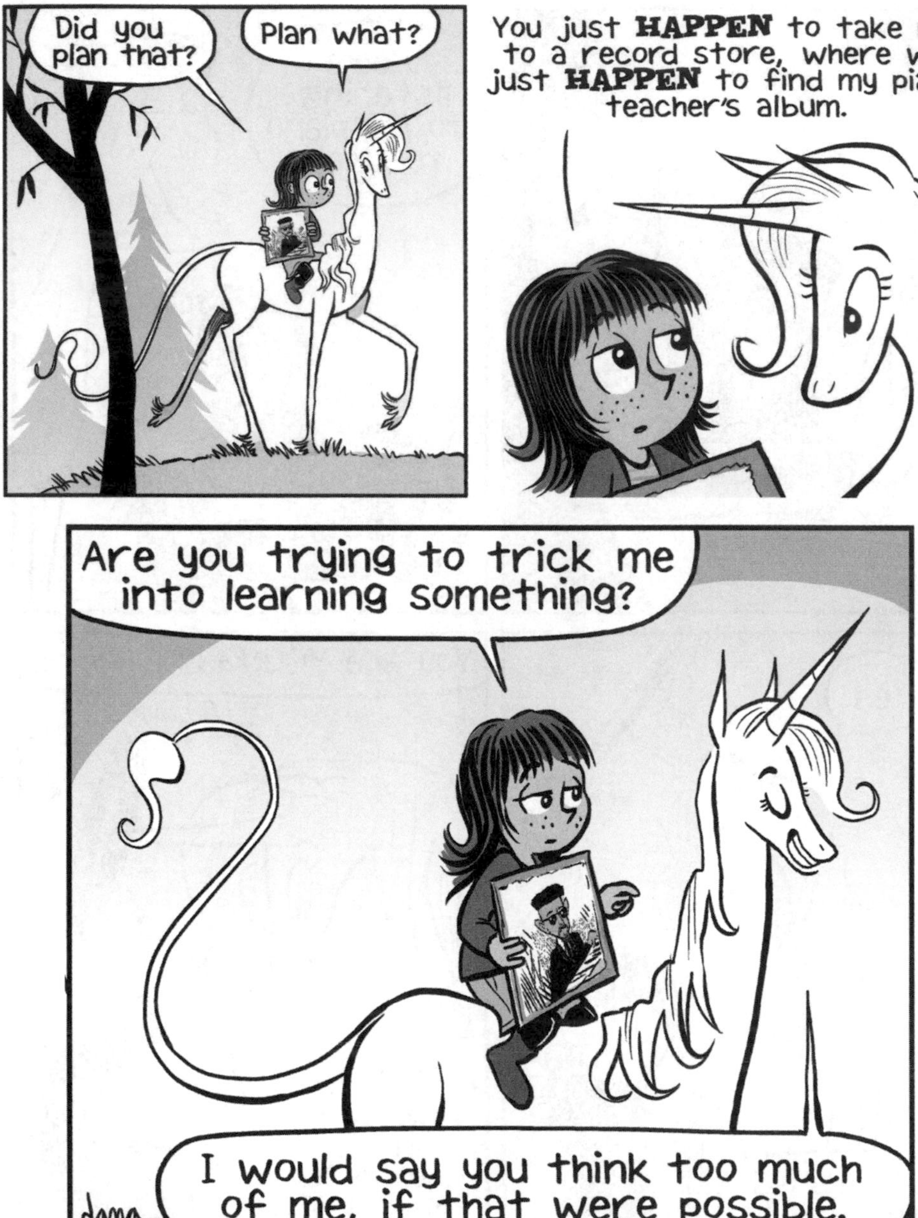
Did you plan that?
Plan what?
You just **HAPPEN** to take me to a record store, where we just **HAPPEN** to find my piano teacher's album.
Are you trying to trick me into learning something?
I would say you think too much of me, if that were possible.
dana

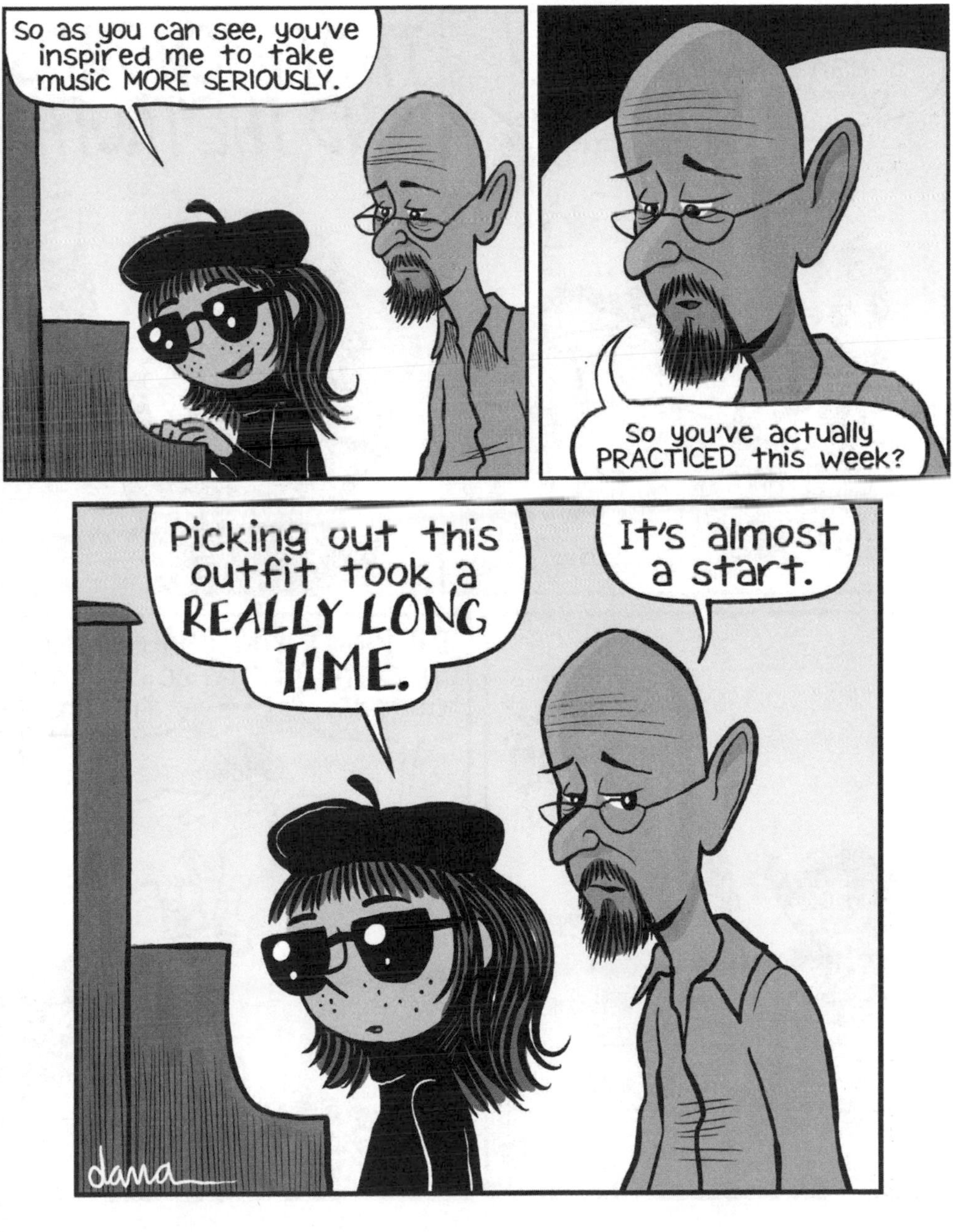
So as you can see, you've inspired me to take music MORE SERIOUSLY.
So you've actually PRACTICED this week?
Picking out this outfit took a REALLY LONG TIME.
It's almost a start.
dana

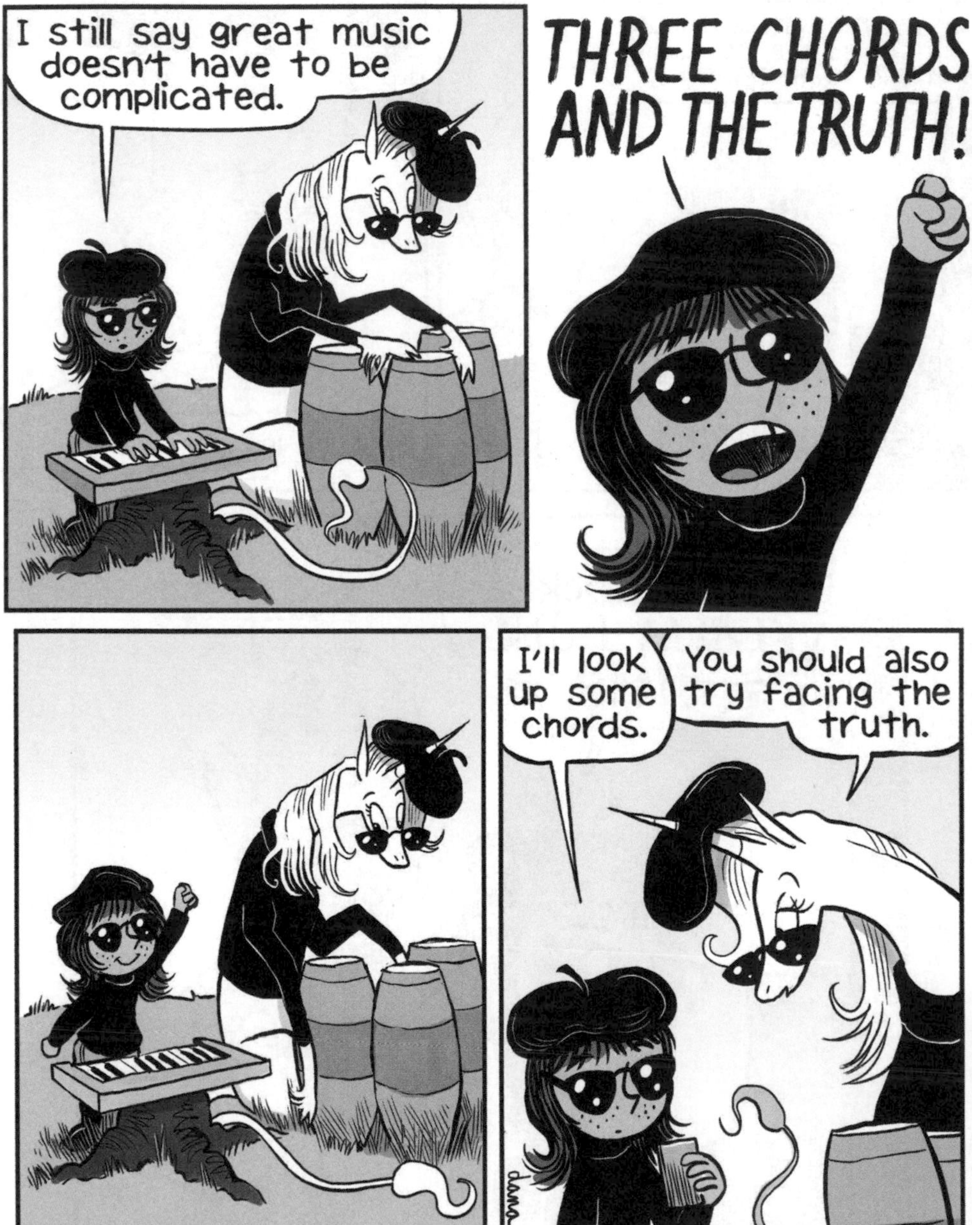

I still say great music doesn't have to be complicated.
THREE CHORDS AND THE TRUTH!
I'll look up some chords.
You should also try facing the truth.
dana

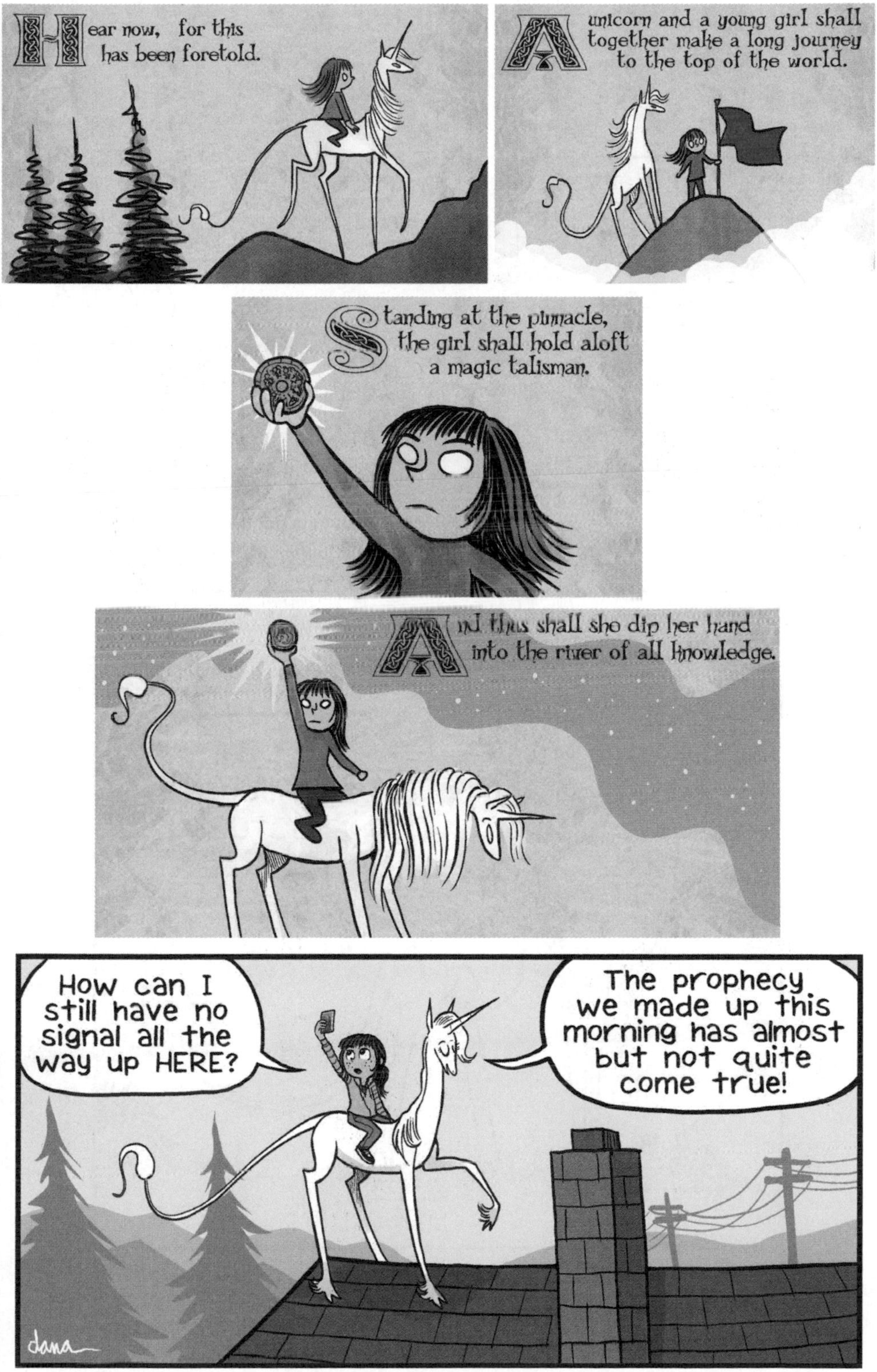
Hear now, for this has been foretold.
A unicorn and a young girl shall together make a long journey to the top of the world.
Standing at the pinnacle, the girl shall hold aloft a magic talisman.
And thus shall she dip her hand into the river of all knowledge.
How can I still have no signal all the way up HERE?
The prophecy we made up this morning has almost but not quite come true!
dana

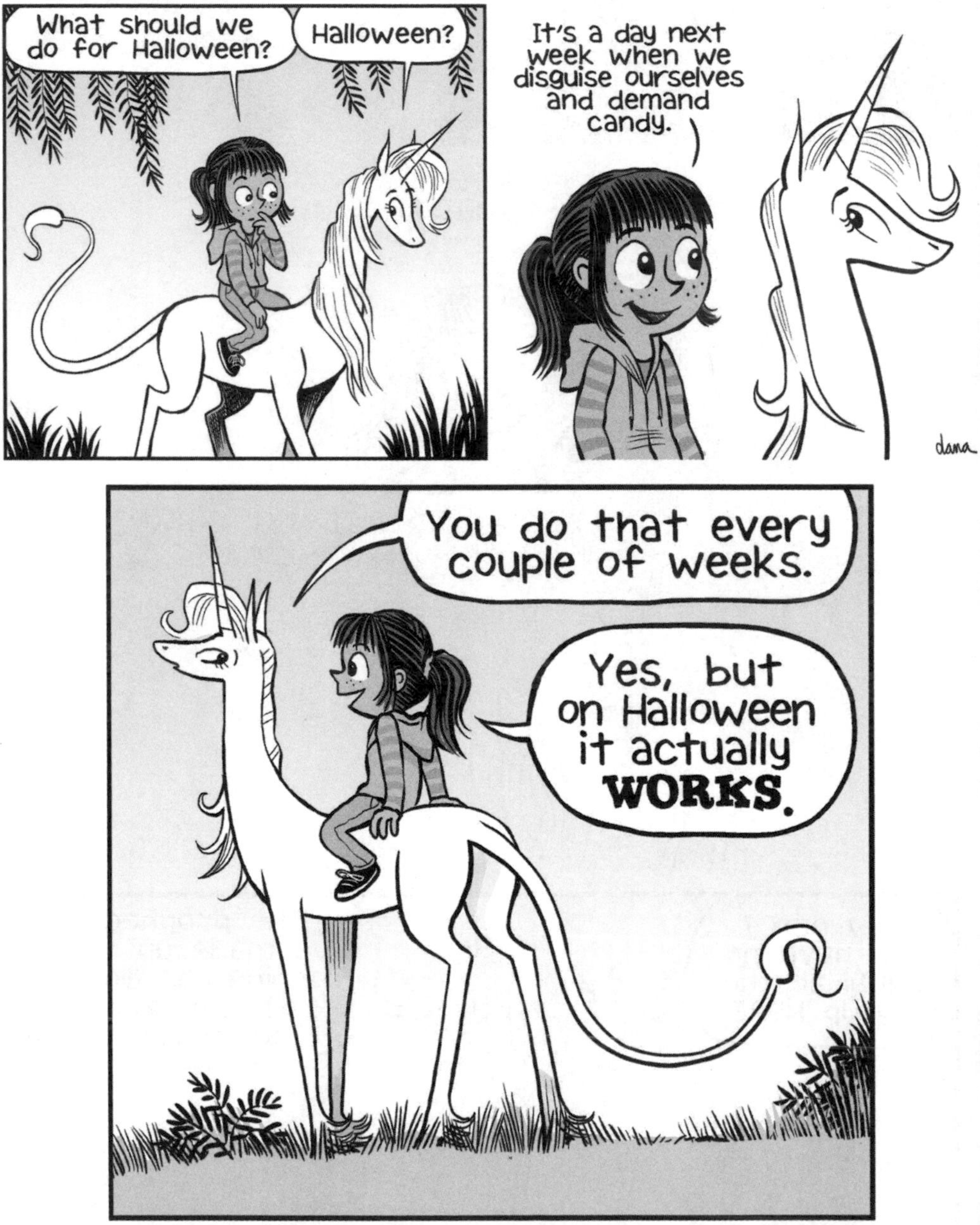
What should we do for Halloween?
Halloween?
It's a day next week when we disguise ourselves and demand candy.
dana
You do that every couple of weeks.
Yes, but on Halloween it actually **WORKS**.

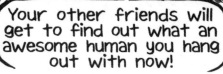

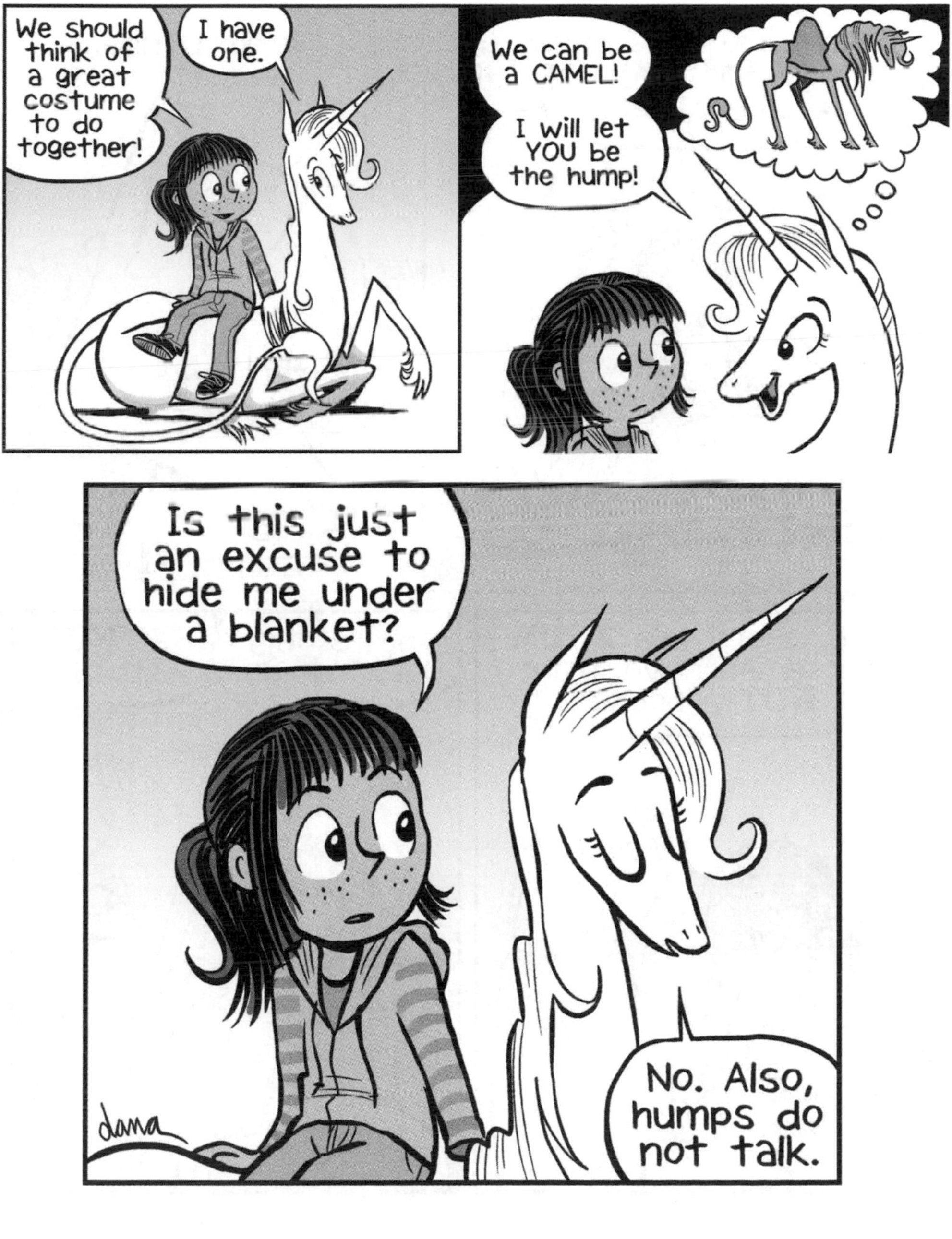
We should think of a great costume to do together!
I have one.
We can be a CAMEL!
I will let YOU be the hump!
Is this just an excuse to hide me under a blanket?
No. Also, humps do not talk.
dana

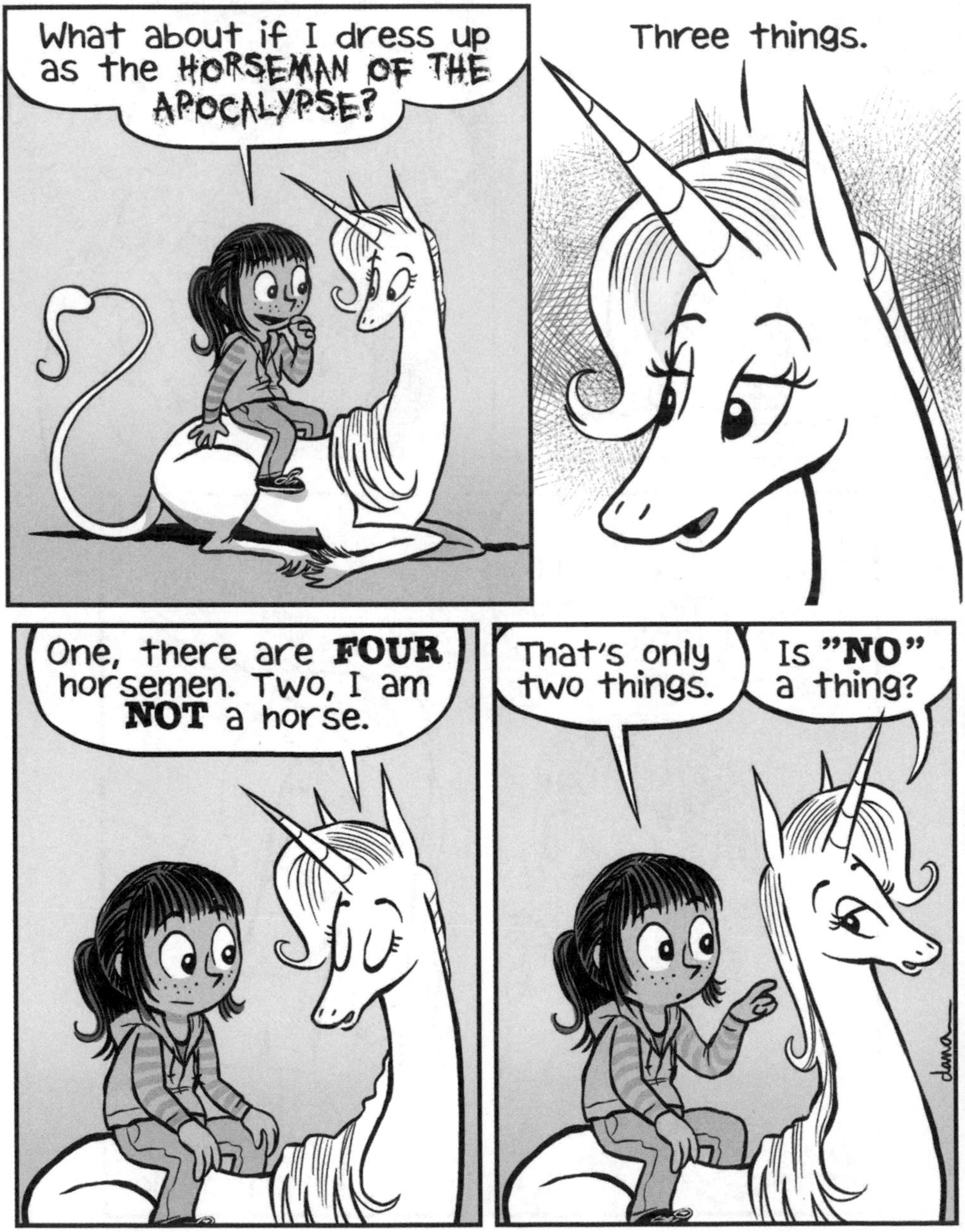
What about if I dress up as the HORSEMAN OF THE APOCALYPSE?
Three things.
One, there are **FOUR** horsemen. Two, I am **NOT** a horse.
That's only two things.
Is **"NO"** a thing?
dana

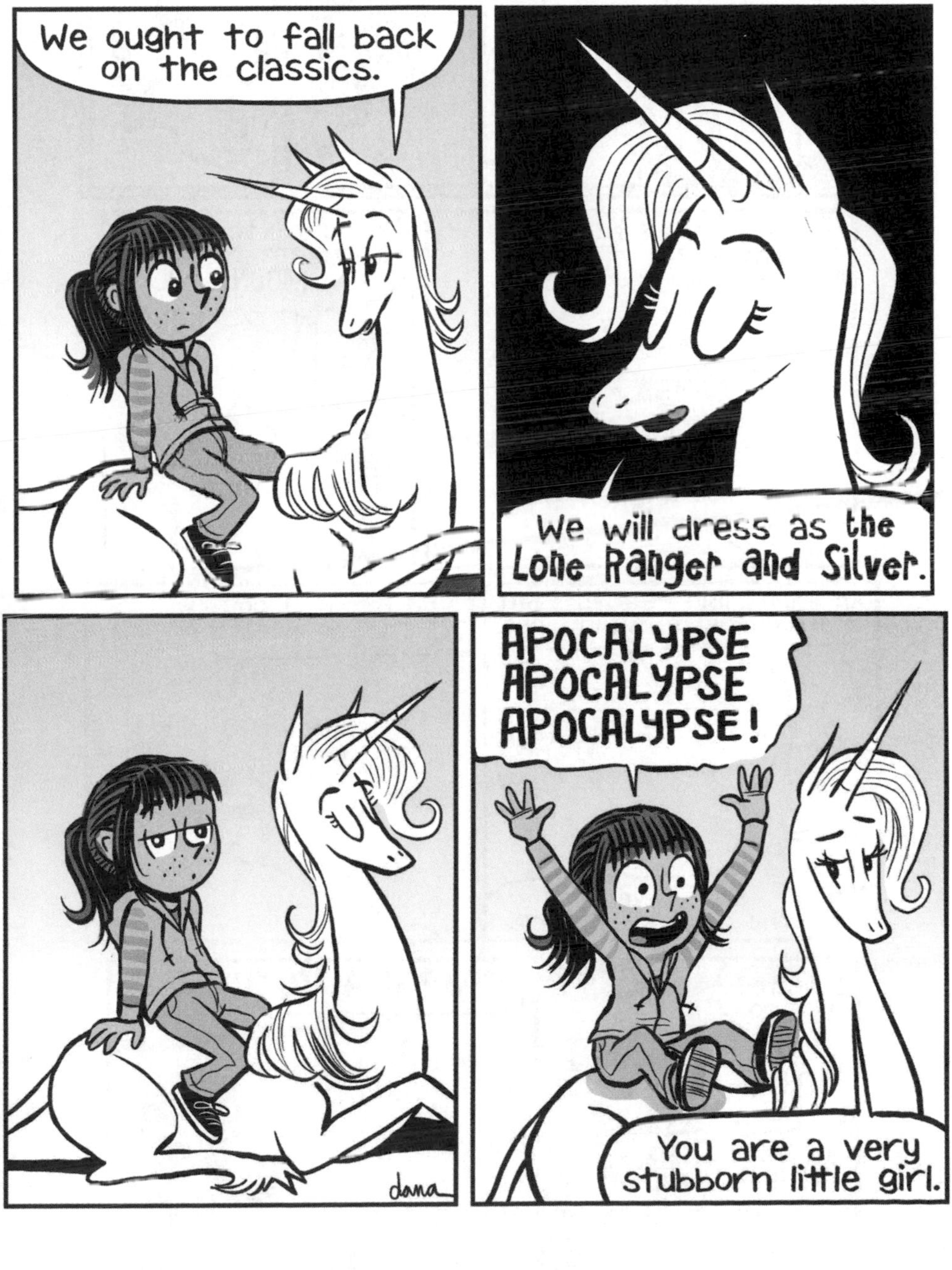
We ought to fall back on the classics.
We will dress as the Lone Ranger and Silver.
APOCALYPSE APOCALYPSE APOCALYPSE!
You are a very stubborn little girl.
dana

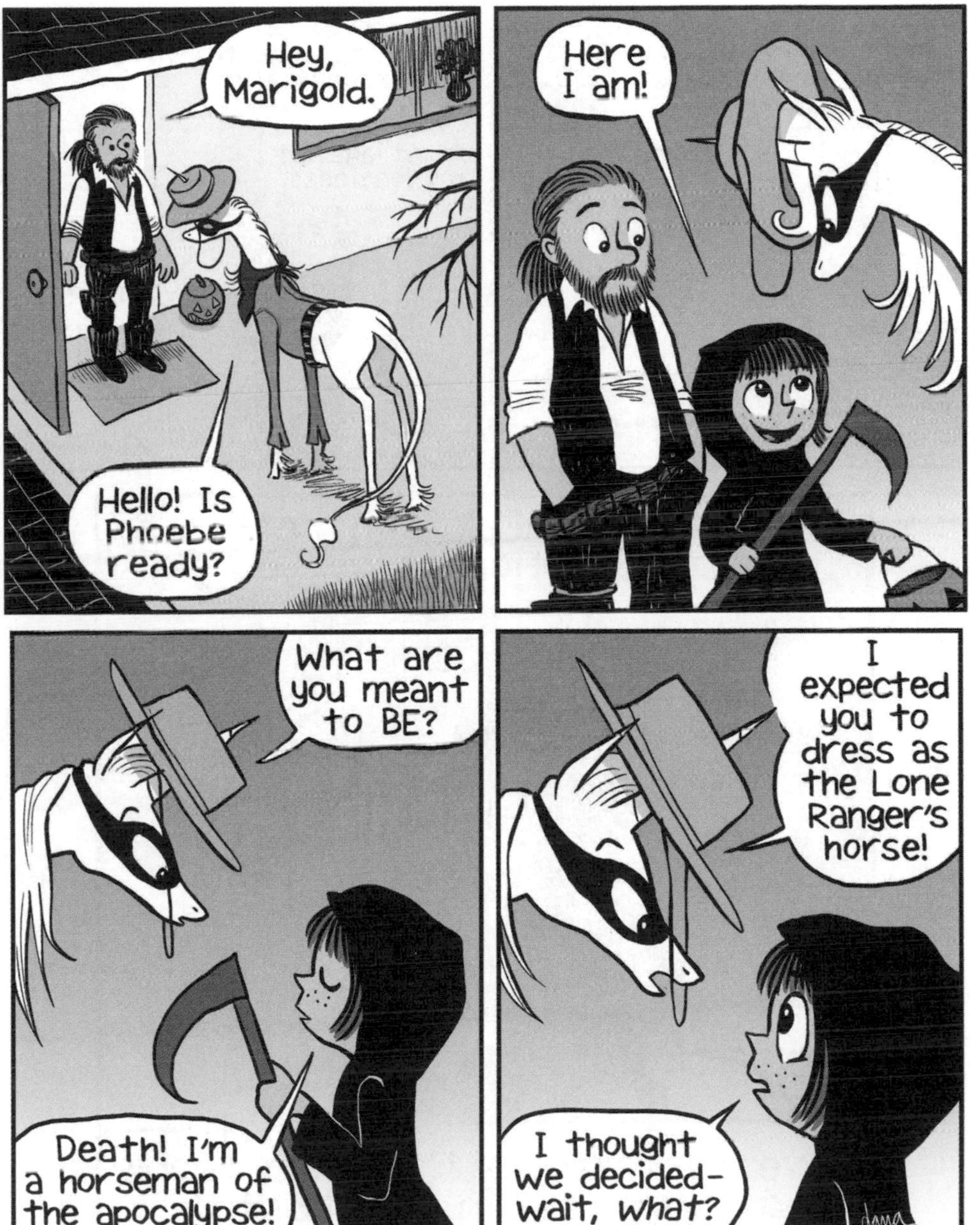
Hey, Marigold.
Hello! Is Phoebe ready?
Here I am!
What are you meant to BE?
Death! I'm a horseman of the apocalypse!
I expected you to dress as the Lone Ranger's horse!
I thought we decided- wait, what?
dana

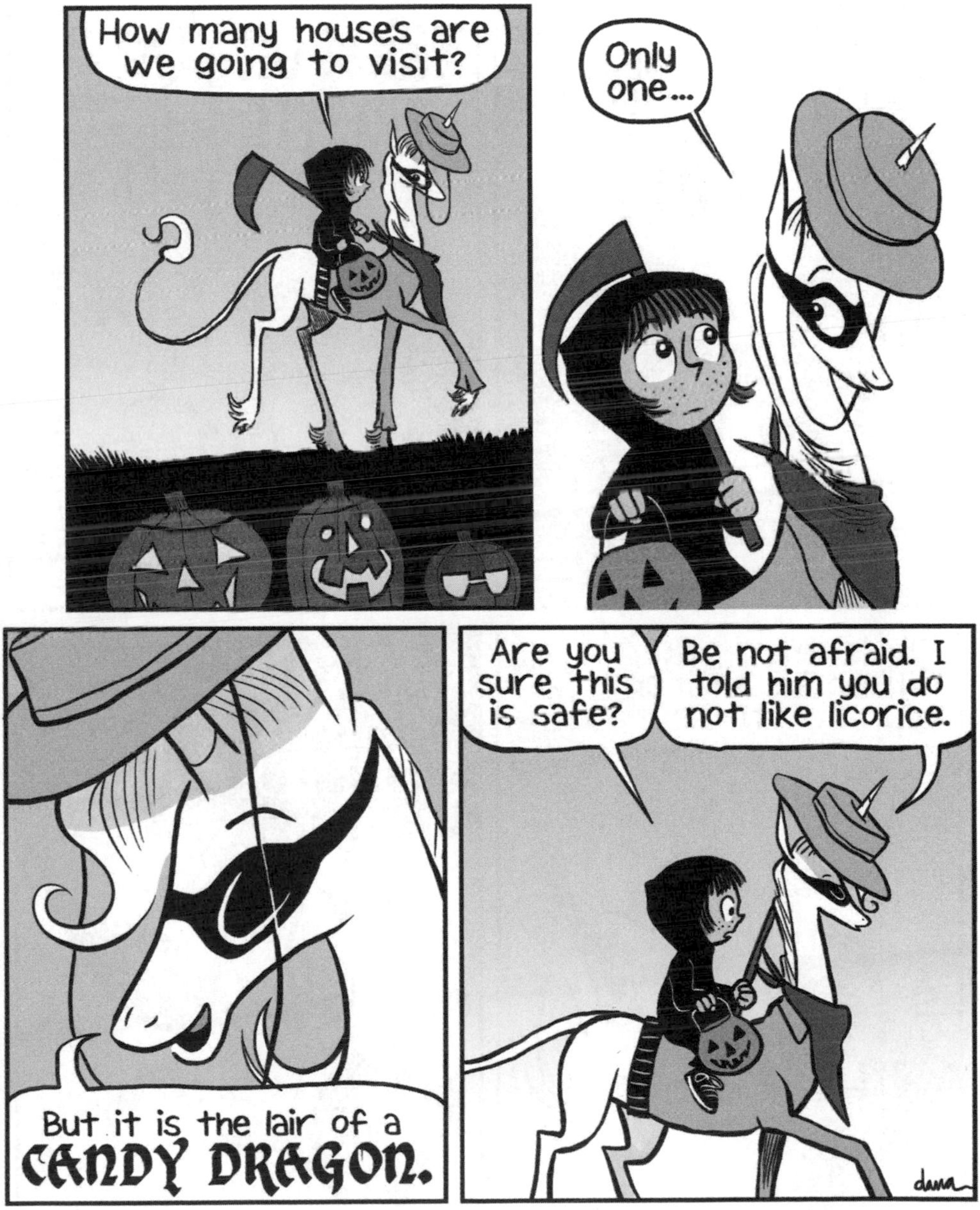
How many houses are we going to visit?
Only one...
But it is the lair of a CANDY DRAGON.
Are you sure this is safe?
Be not afraid. I told him you do not like licorice.
dana

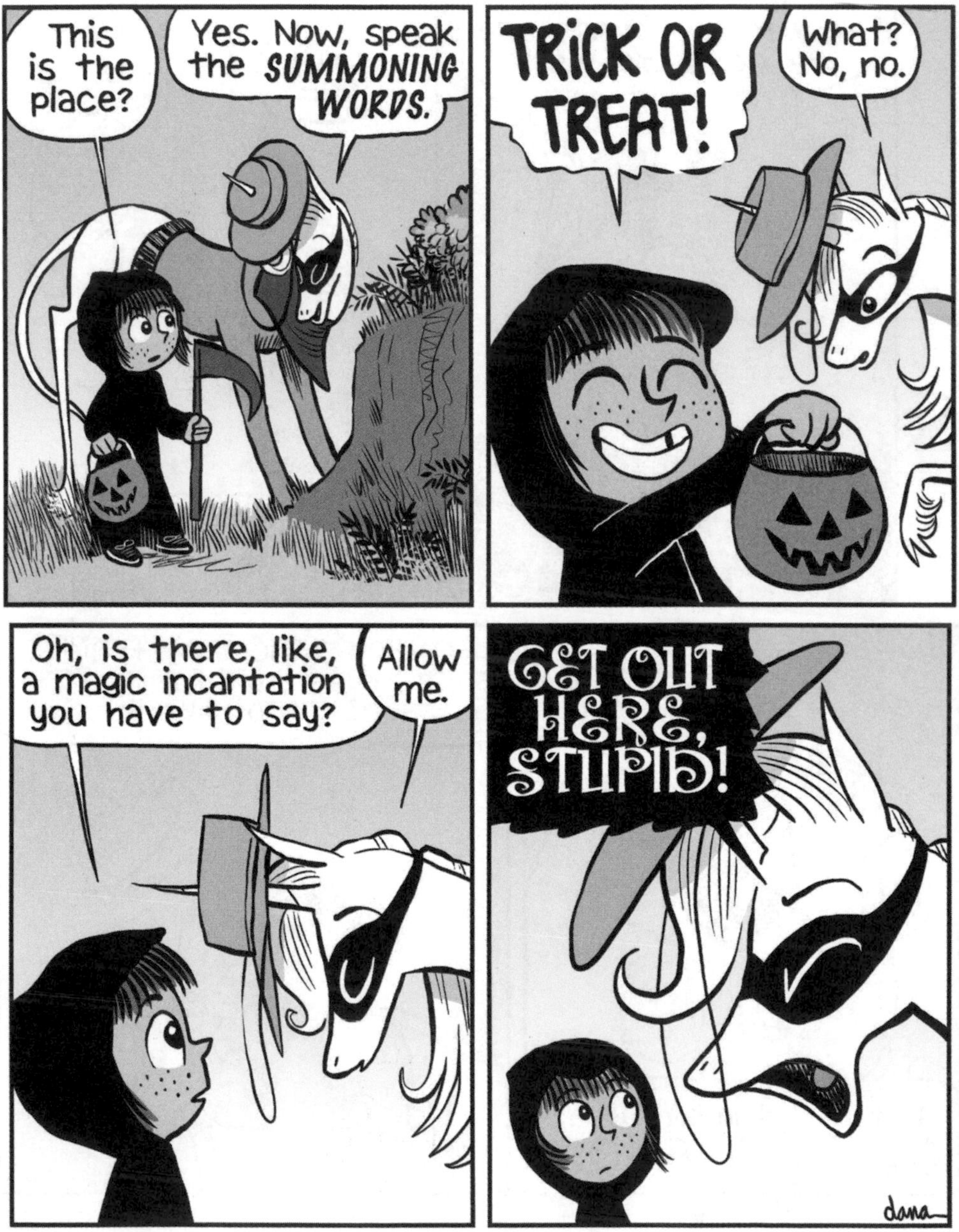

This is the place?
Yes. Now, speak the SUMMONING WORDS.
TRICK OR TREAT!
What? No, no.
Oh, is there, like, a magic incantation you have to say?
Allow me.
GET OUT HERE, STUPID!
dana

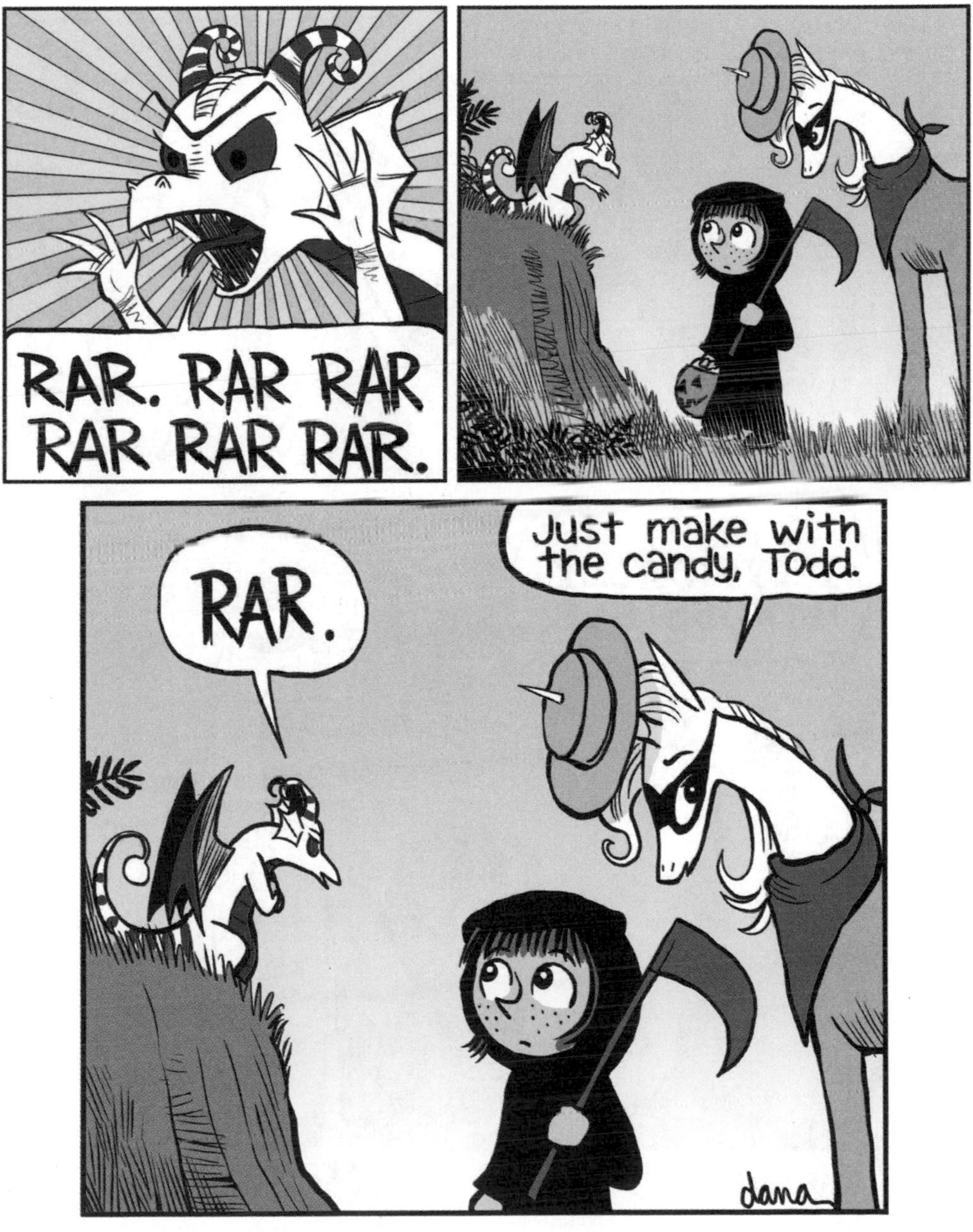
RAR. RAR RAR RAR RAR RAR.
RAR.
Just make with the candy, Todd.
dana

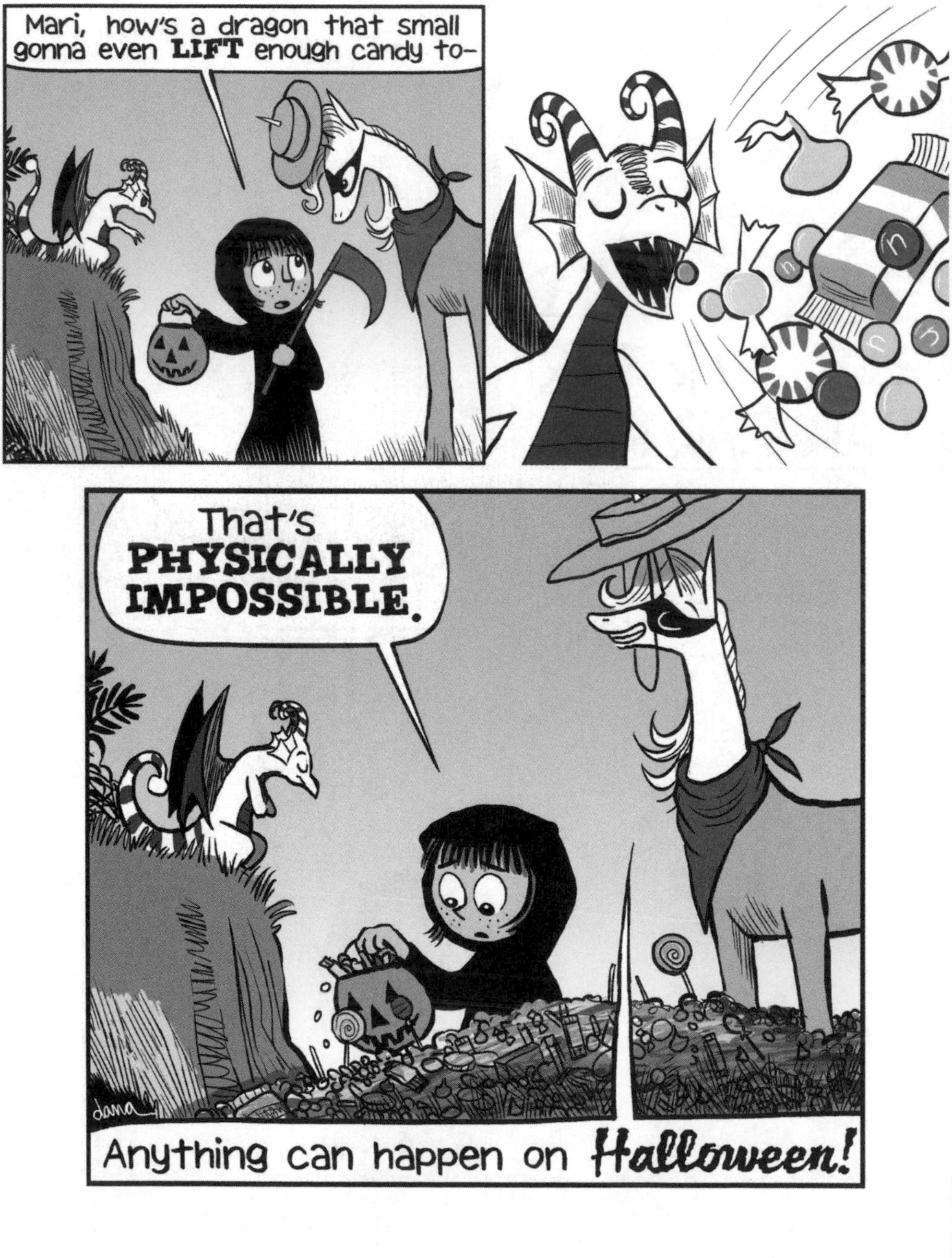
Mari, how's a dragon that small gonna even **LIFT** enough candy to-
That's **PHYSICALLY IMPOSSIBLE**.
dana
Anything can happen on *Halloween!*

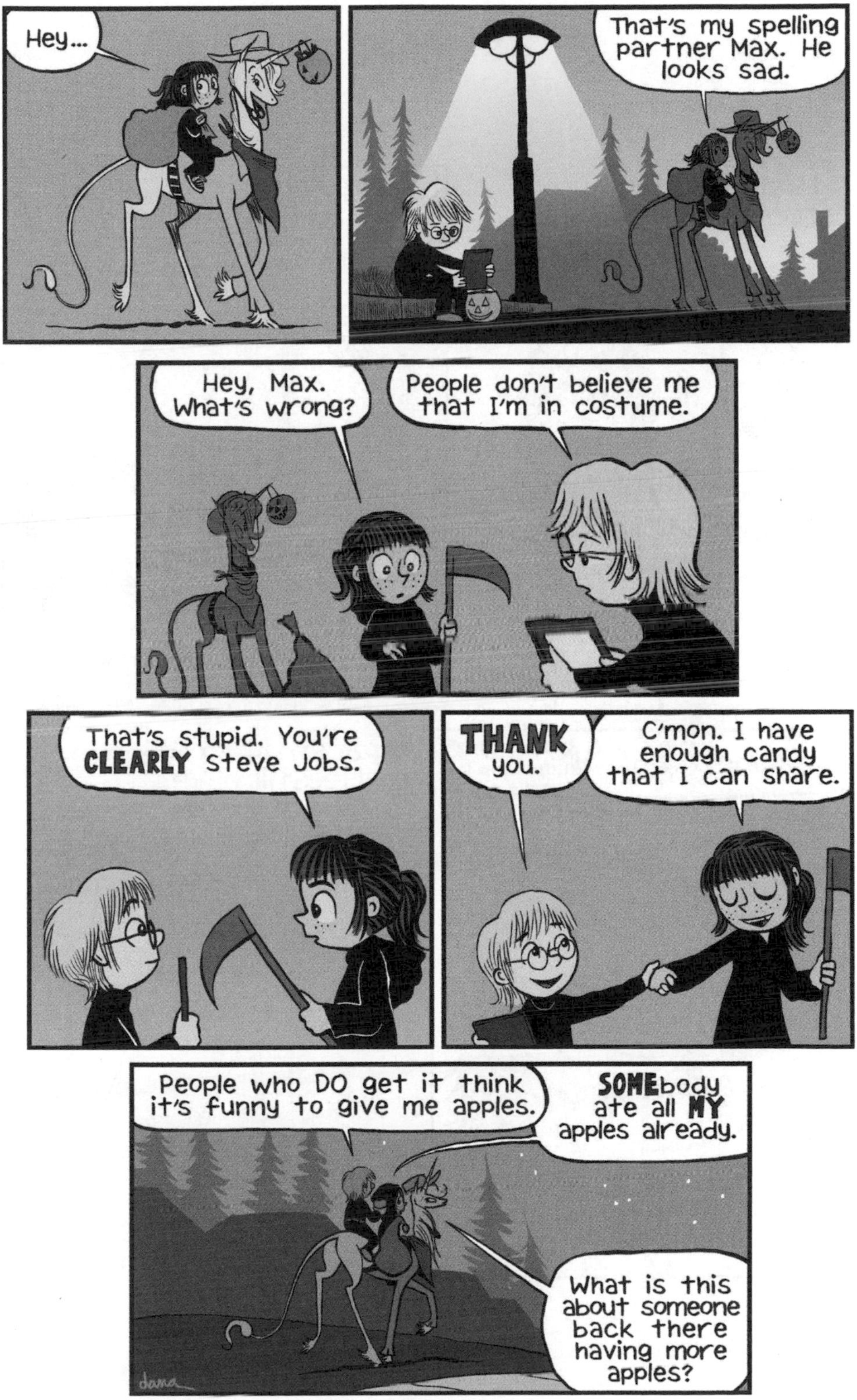
Hey...
That's my spelling partner Max. He looks sad.
Hey, Max. What's wrong?
People don't believe me that I'm in costume.
That's stupid. You're CLEARLY Steve Jobs.
THANK you.
C'mon. I have enough candy that I can share.
People who DO get it think it's funny to give me apples.
SOMEbody ate all MY apples already.
What is this about someone back there having more apples?
dana

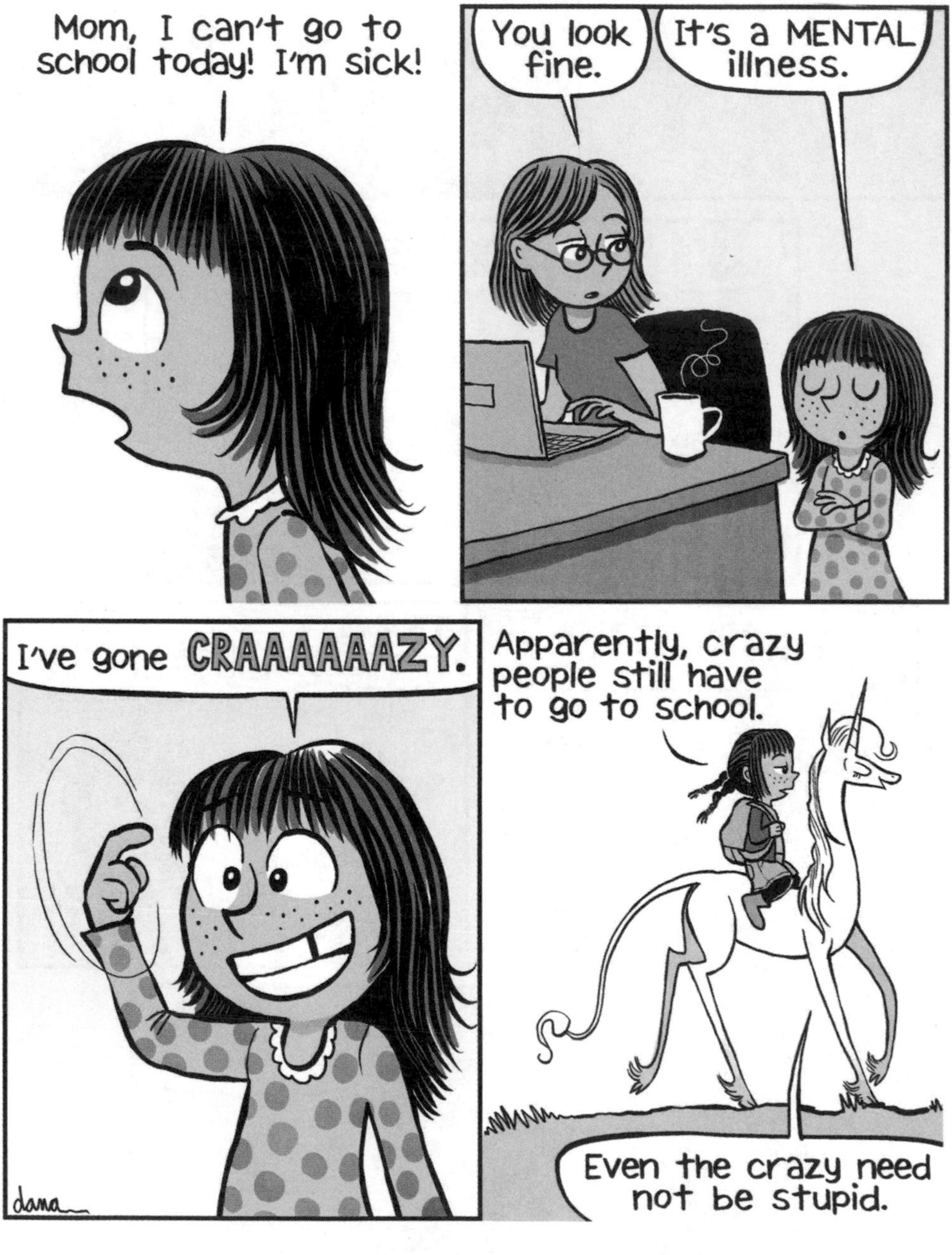
Mom, I can't go to school today! I'm sick!
You look fine.
It's a MENTAL illness.
I've gone CRAAAAAAAZY.
Apparently, crazy people still have to go to school.
Even the crazy need not be stupid.
dana

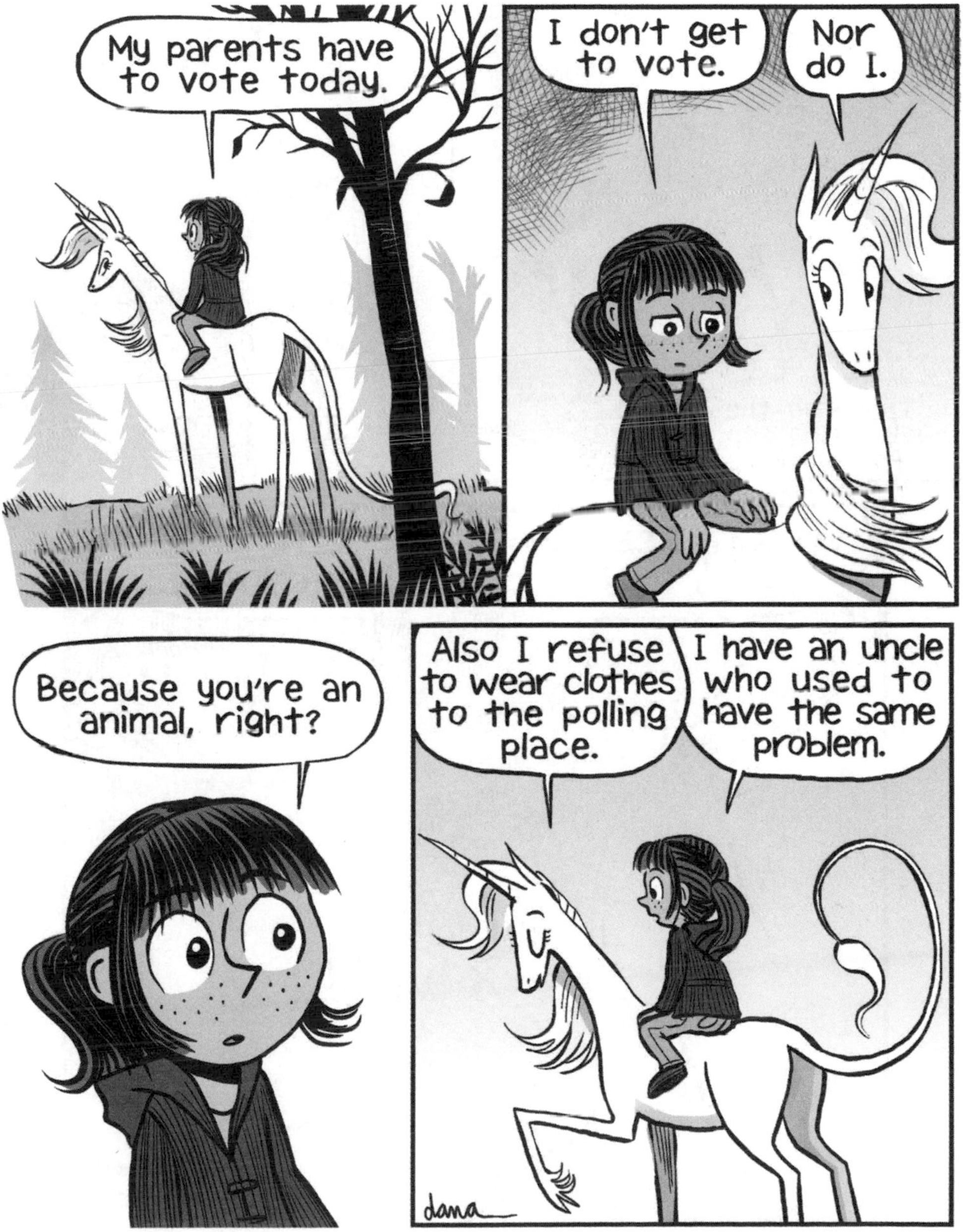
My parents have to vote today.
I don't get to vote.
Nor do I.
Because you're an animal, right?
Also I refuse to wear clothes to the polling place.
I have an uncle who used to have the same problem.
dana

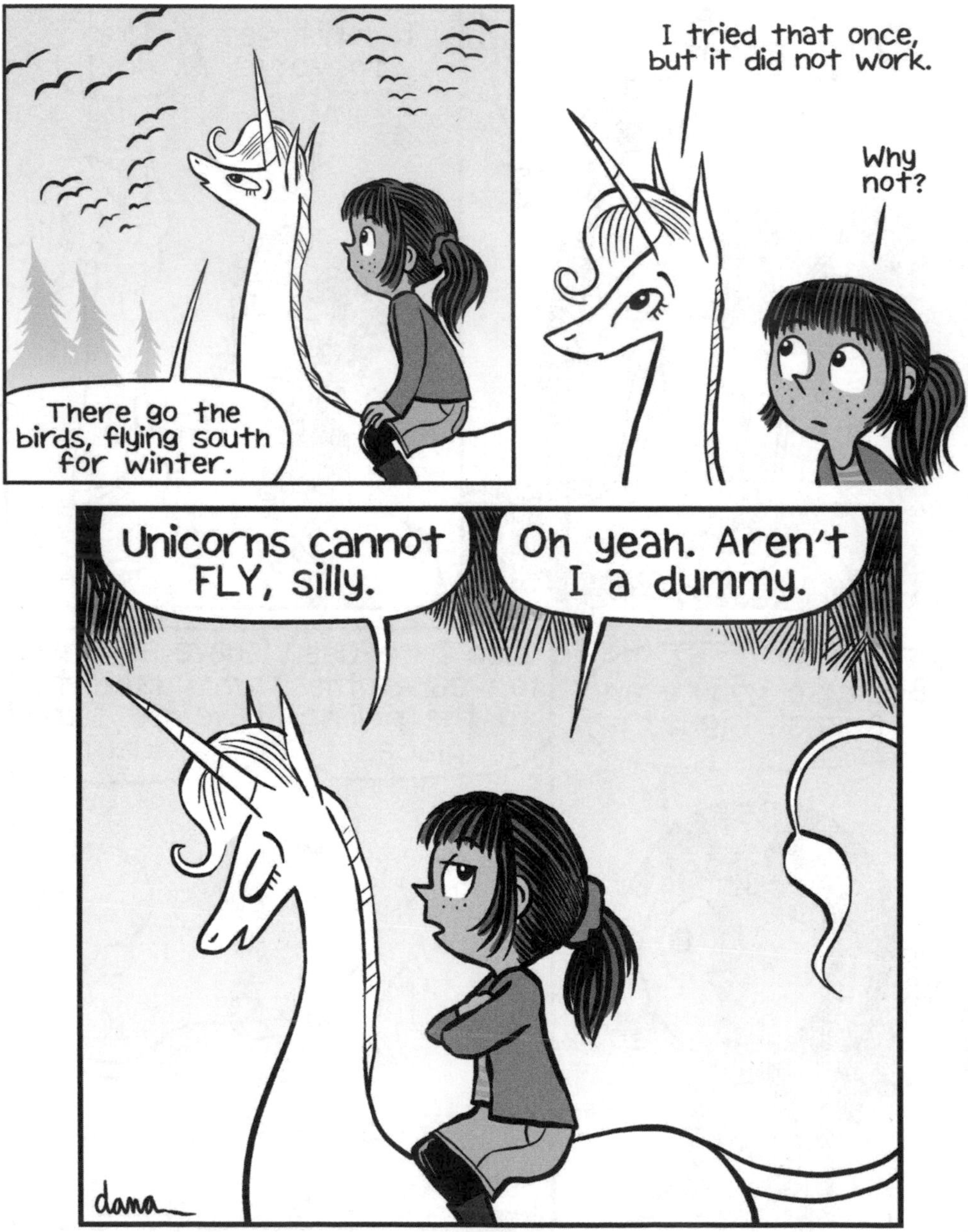
There go the birds, flying south for winter.
I tried that once, but it did not work.
Why not?
Unicorns cannot FLY, silly.
Oh yeah. Aren't I a dummy.
dana

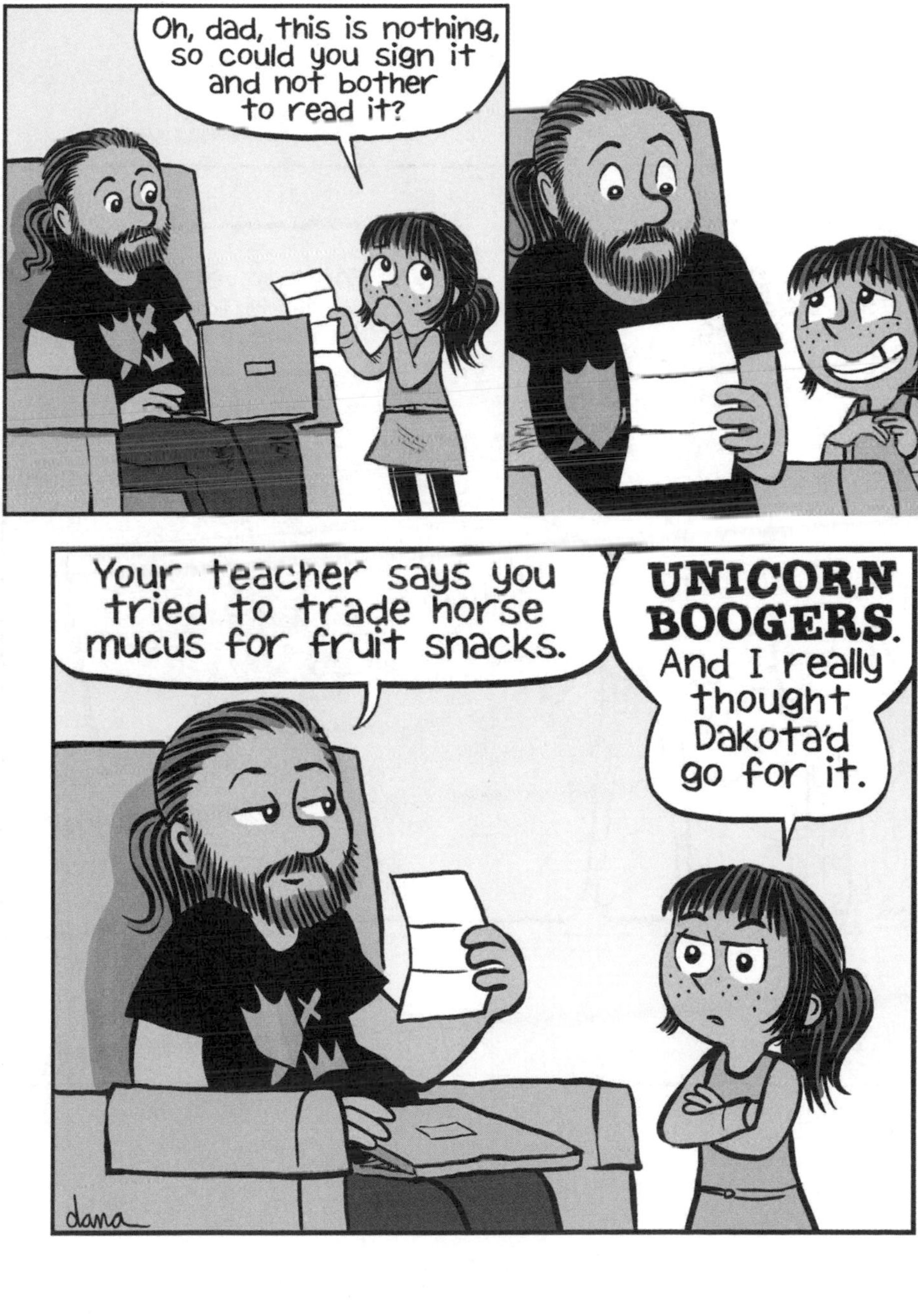
Oh, dad, this is nothing, so could you sign it and not bother to read it?
Your teacher says you tried to trade horse mucus for fruit snacks.
UNICORN BOOGERS. And I really thought Dakota'd go for it.
dana

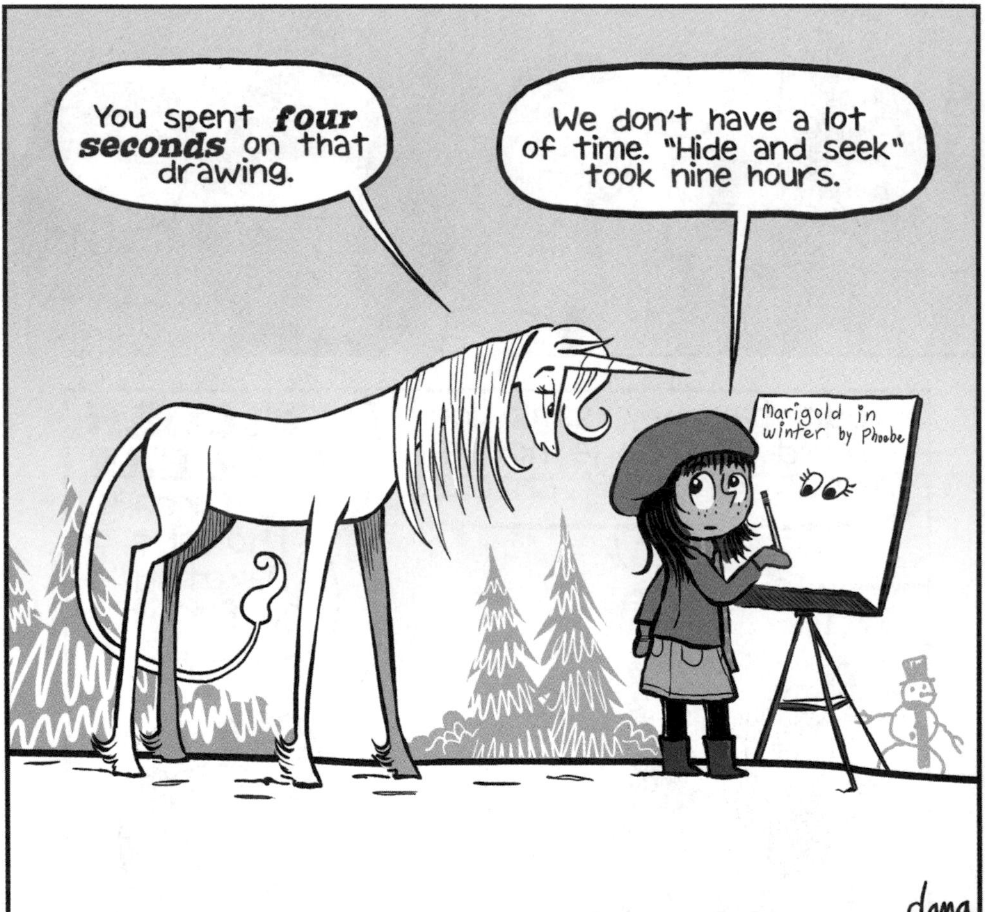
You spent **four seconds** on that drawing.
We don't have a lot of time. "Hide and seek" took nine hours.
Marigold in winter by Phoebe
dana

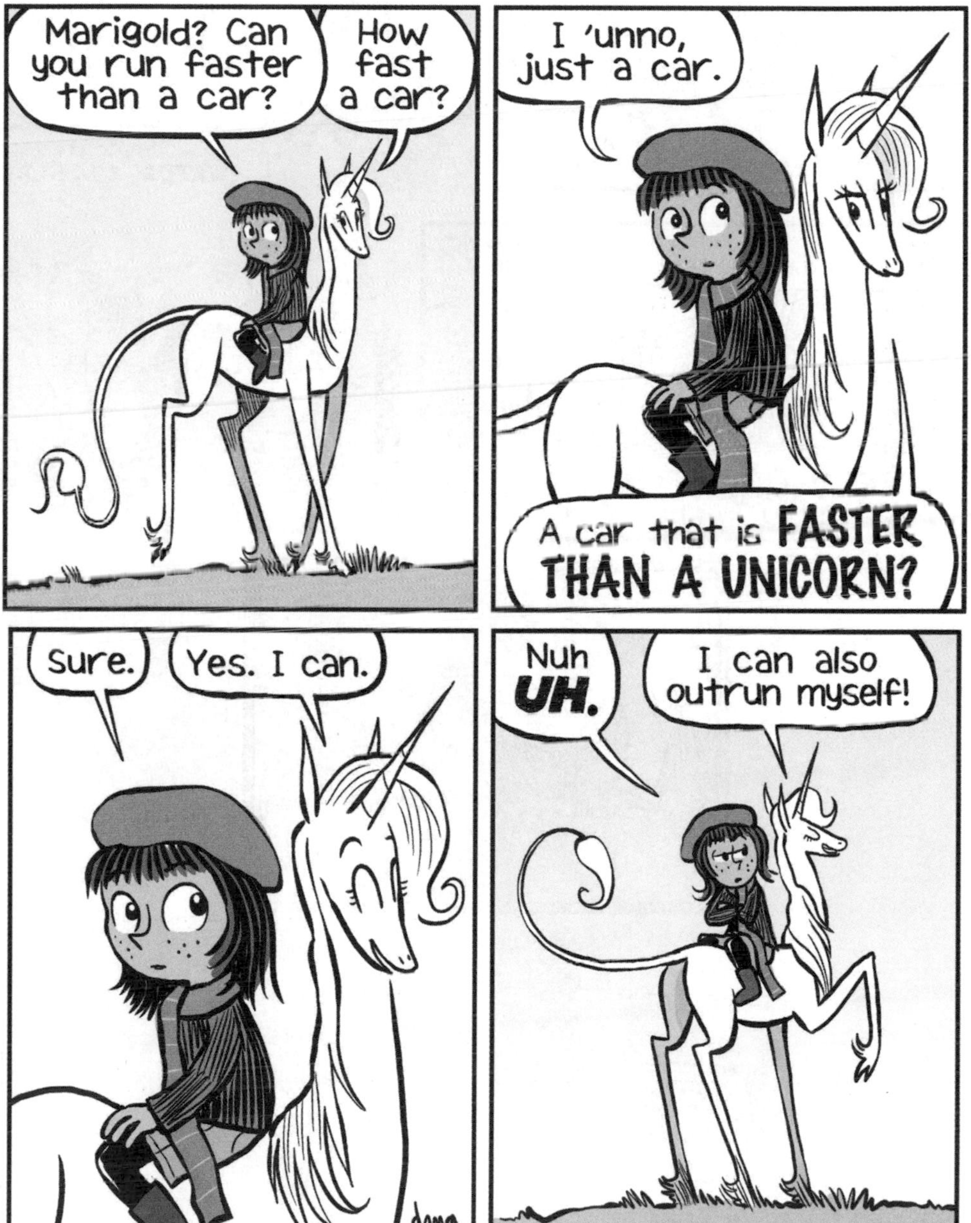
Marigold? Can you run faster than a car?
How fast a car?
I 'unno, just a car.
A car that is FASTER THAN A UNICORN?
Sure.
Yes. I can.
Nuh UH.
I can also outrun myself!
dana

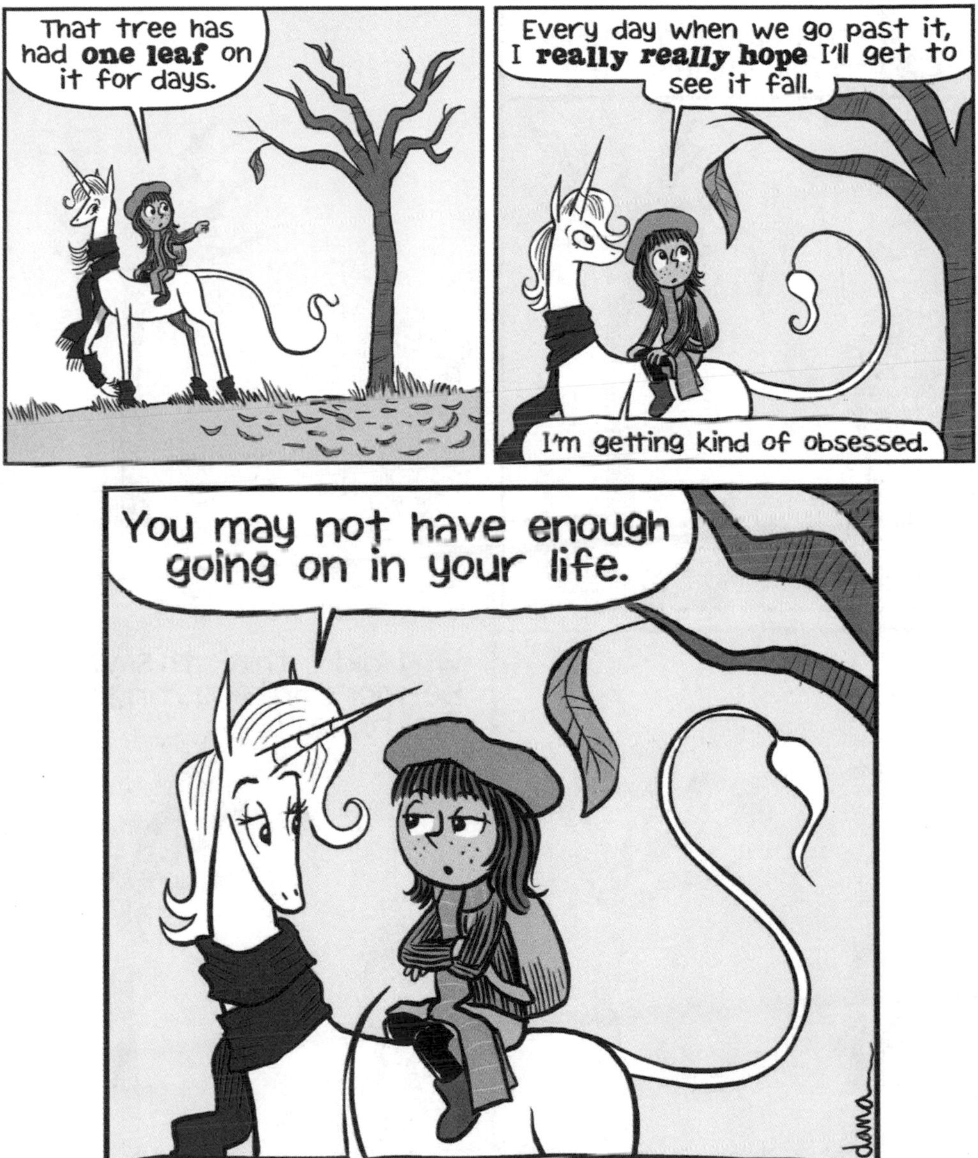
That tree has had **one leaf** on it for days.
Every day when we go past it, I **really really hope** I'll get to see it fall.
I'm getting kind of obsessed.
You may not have enough going on in your life.
Dude, I ride a **unicorn** to school.
dana

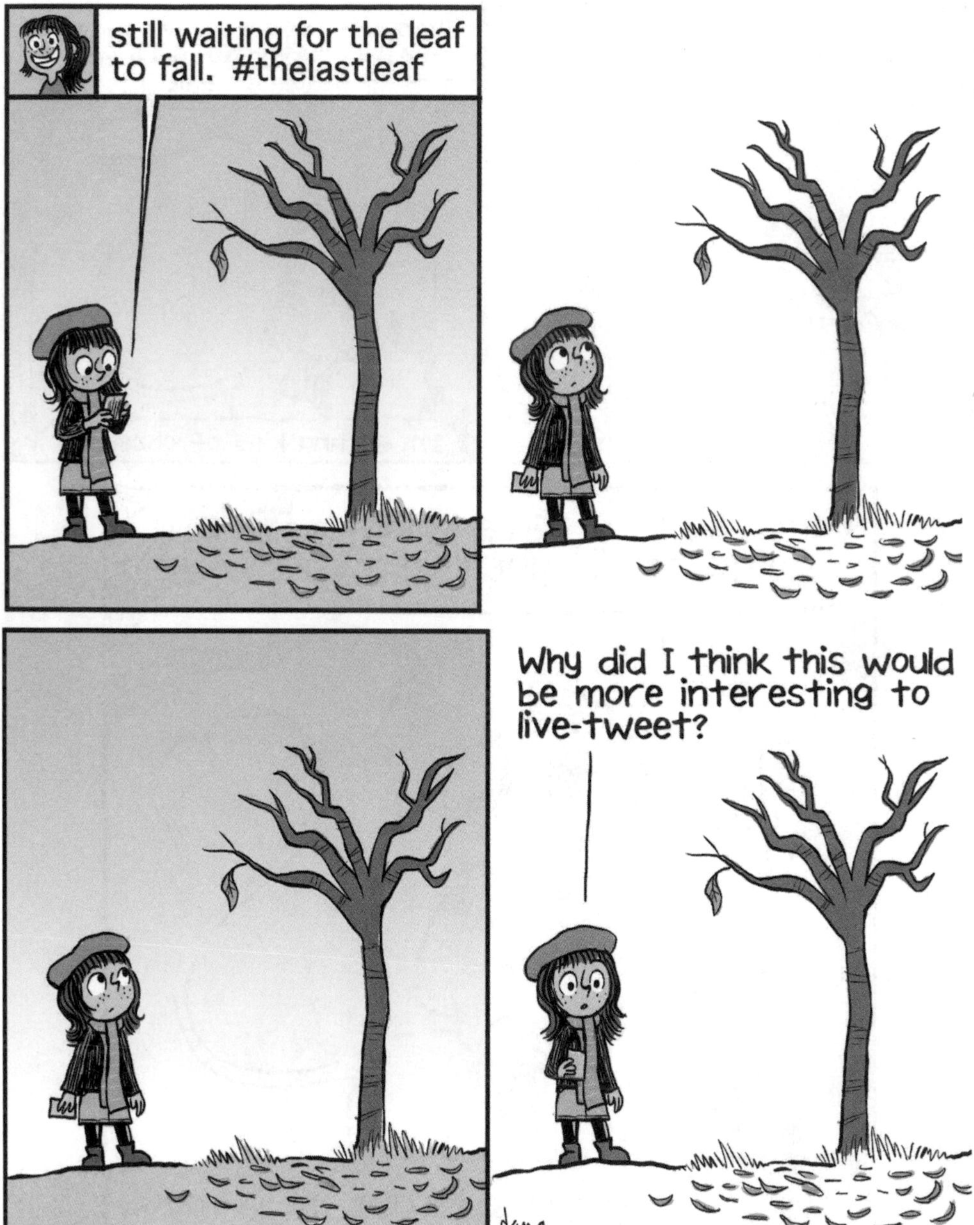
still waiting for the leaf to fall. #thelastleaf
Why did I think this would be more interesting to live-tweet?
dana

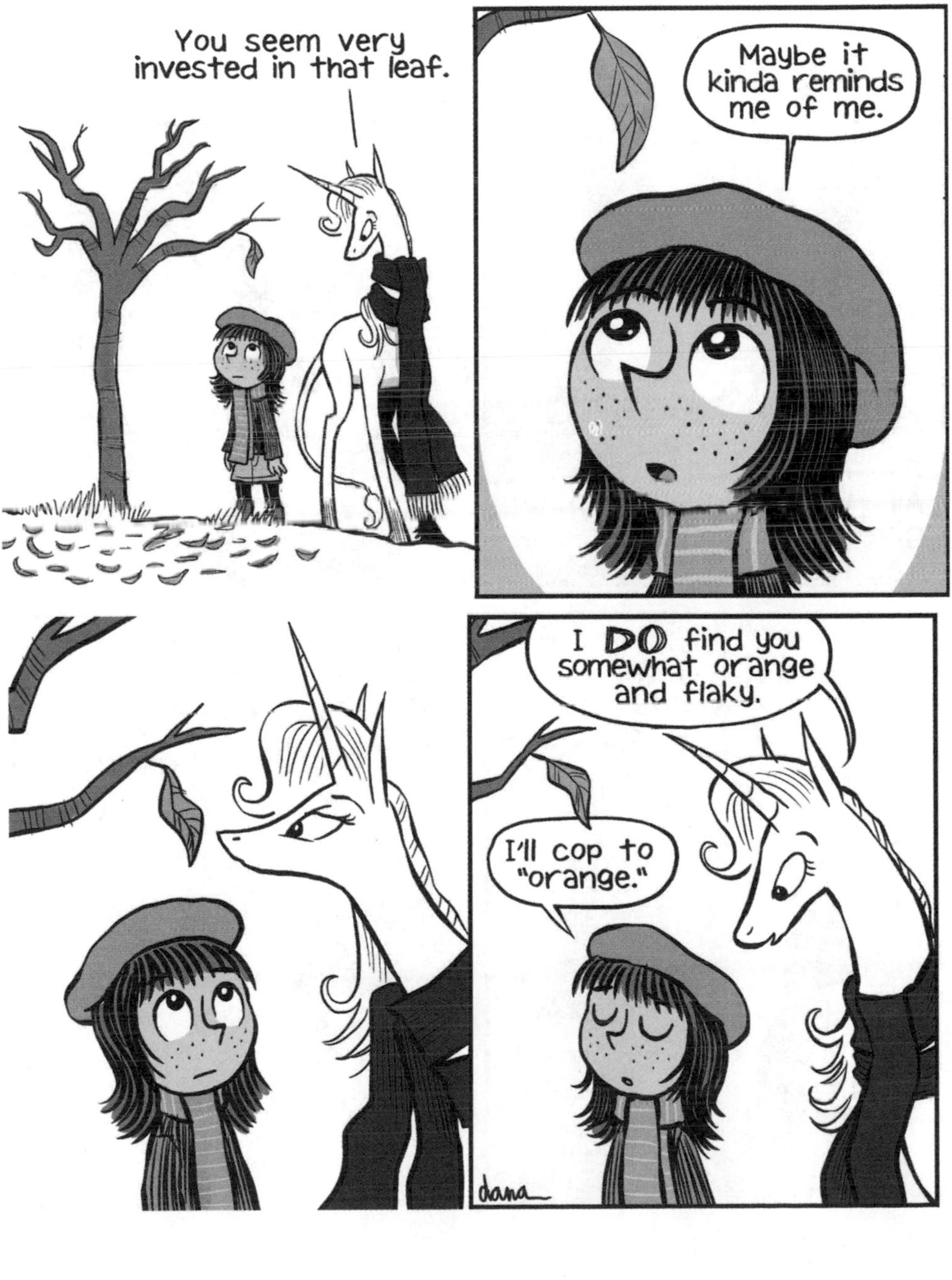
You seem very invested in that leaf.
Maybe it kinda reminds me of me.
I DO find you somewhat orange and flaky.
I'll cop to "orange."
dana

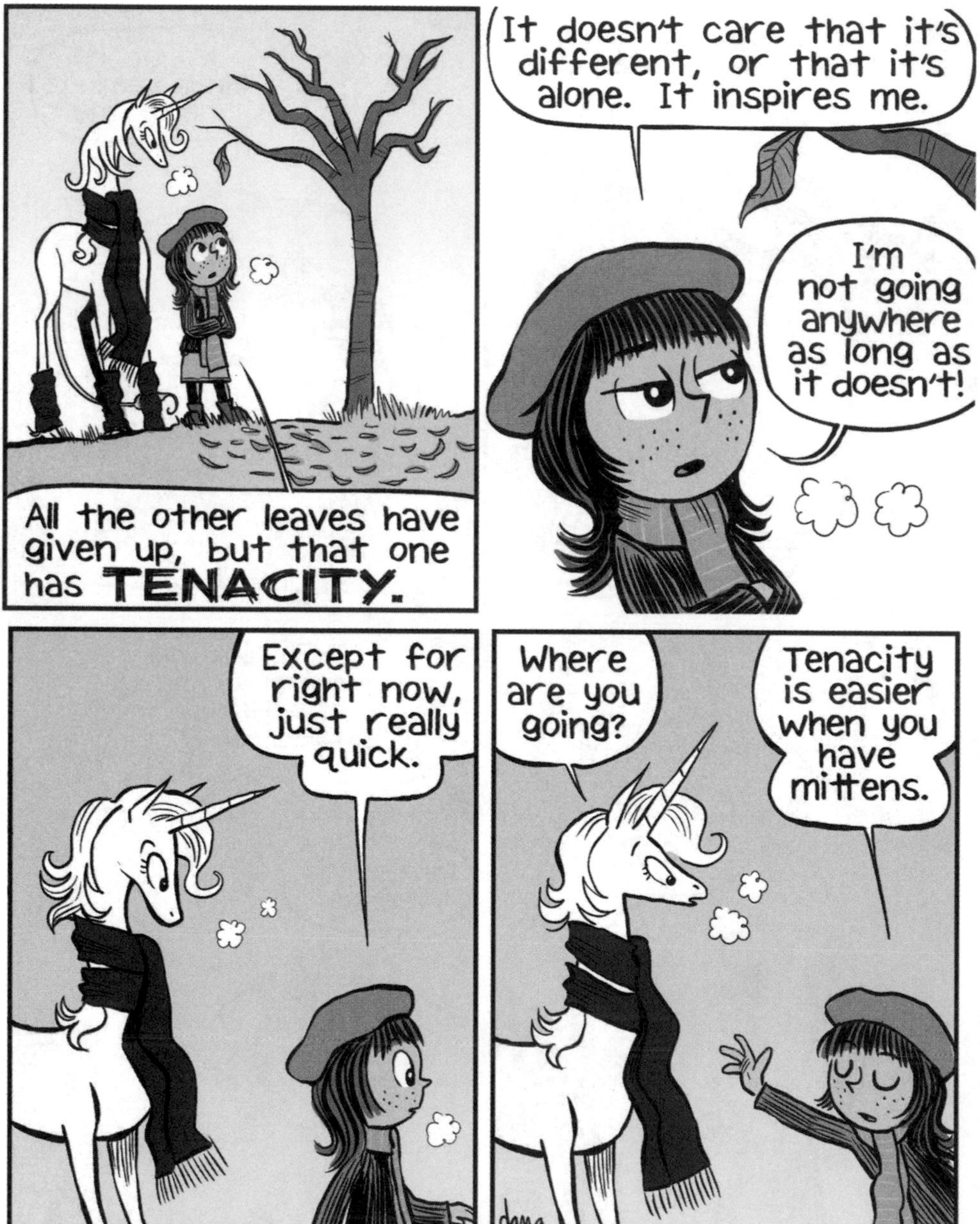
All the other leaves have given up, but that one has TENACITY.
It doesn't care that it's different, or that it's alone. It inspires me.
I'm not going anywhere as long as it doesn't!
Except for right now, just really quick.
Where are you going?
Tenacity is easier when you have mittens.
dana

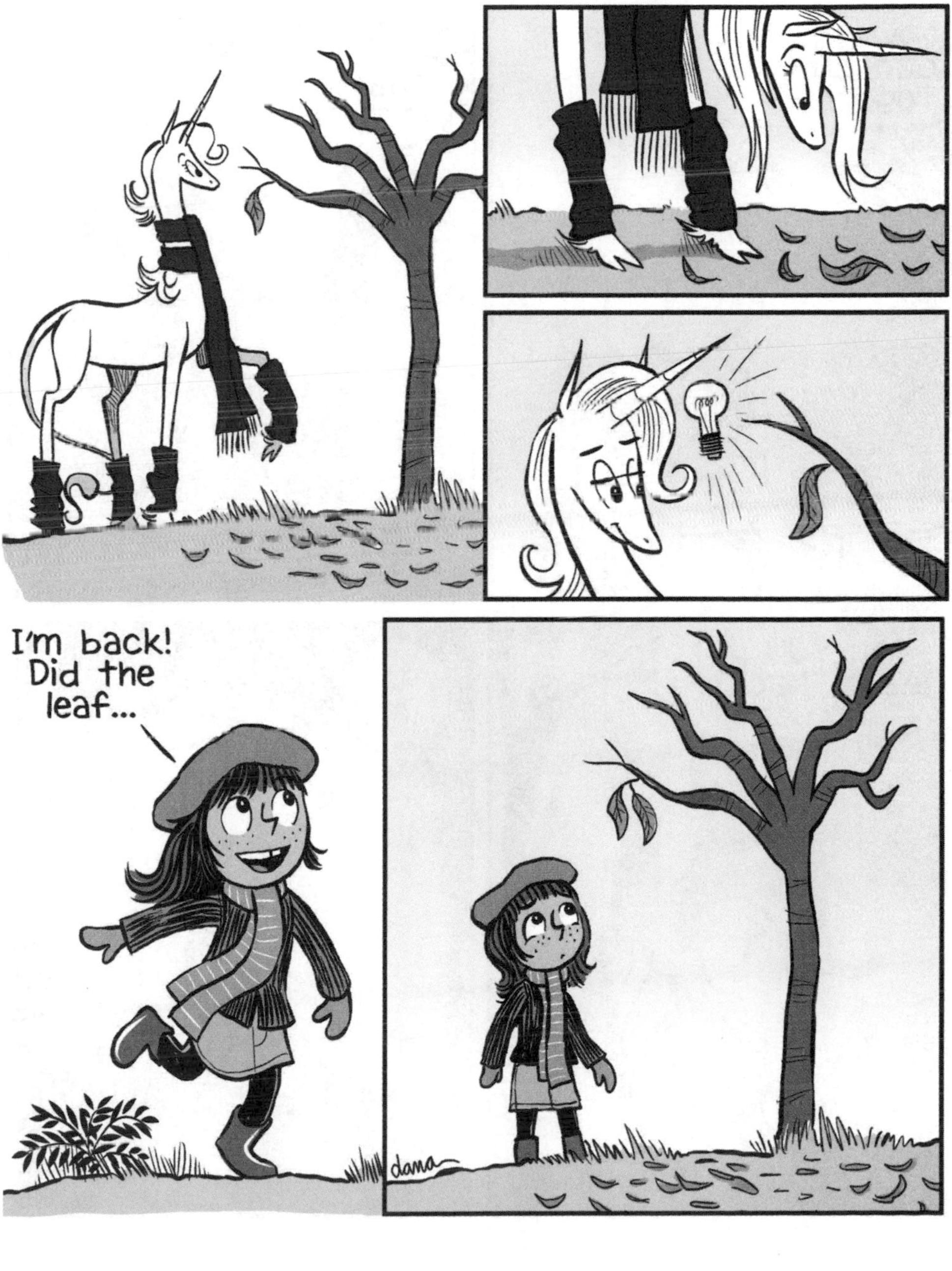
I'm back! Did the leaf...
dana

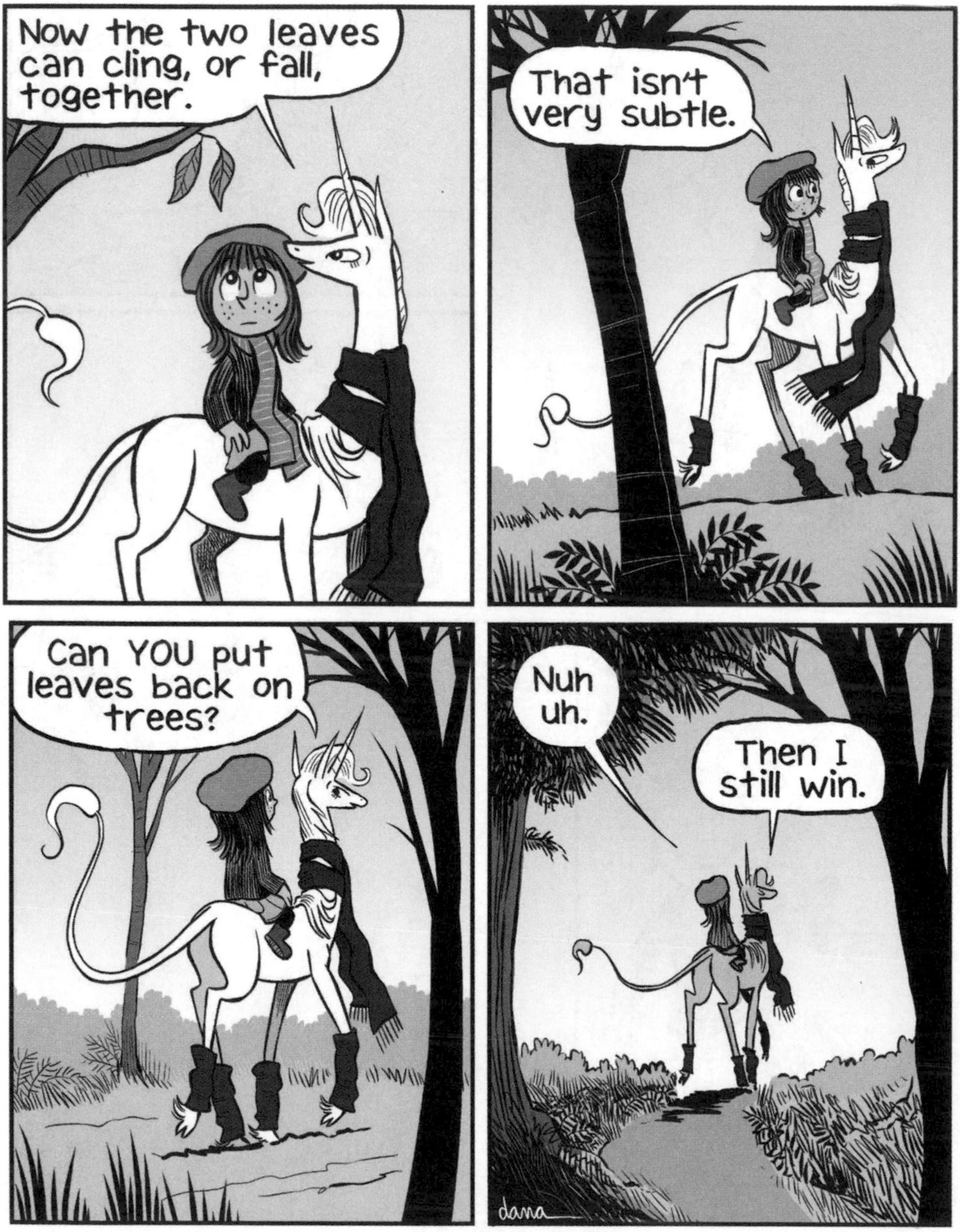

Now the two leaves can cling, or fall, together.
That isn't very subtle.
Can YOU put leaves back on trees?
Nuh uh.
Then I still win.
dana

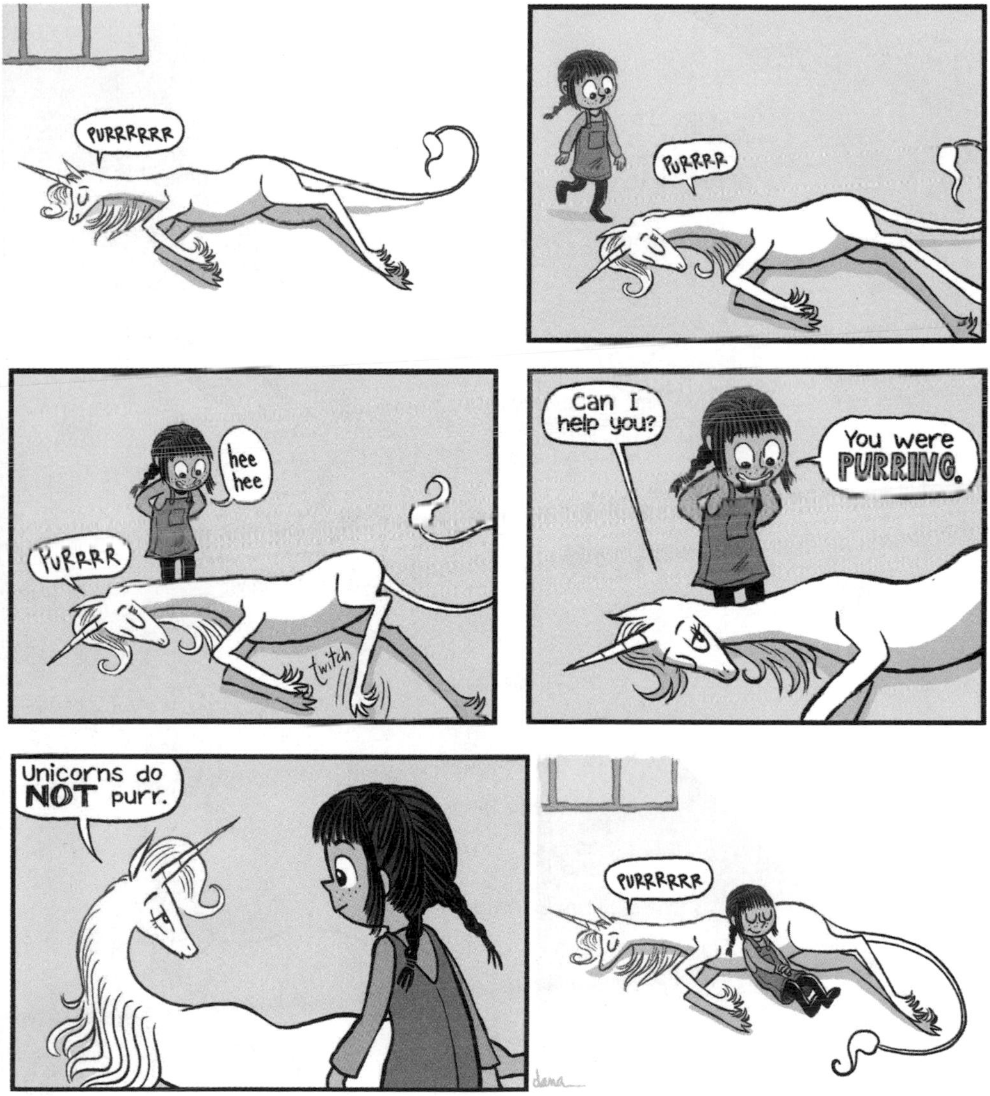
PURRRRRR
PURRRR
hee hee
PURRRR
twitch
Can I help you?
You were PURRING.
Unicorns do NOT purr.
PURRRRRR
dana

MORE TO EXPLORE!
A special section featuring fun facts and activities!!

How to Draw Marigold

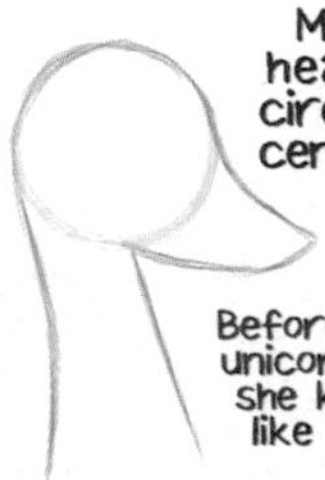

Marigold's head has a circle at the center of it.

Before I draw her unicorny features, she kind of looks like a dinosaur.

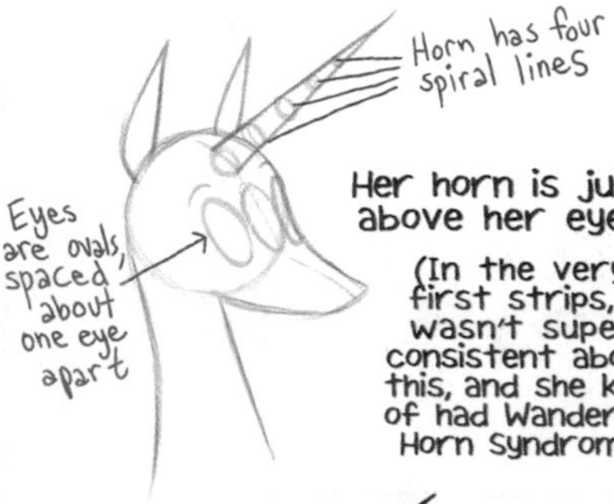
Horn has four spiral lines
Eyes are ovals, spaced about one eye apart

Her horn is just above her eyes.

(In the very first strips, I wasn't super consistent about this, and she kind of had Wandering Horn Syndrome.)

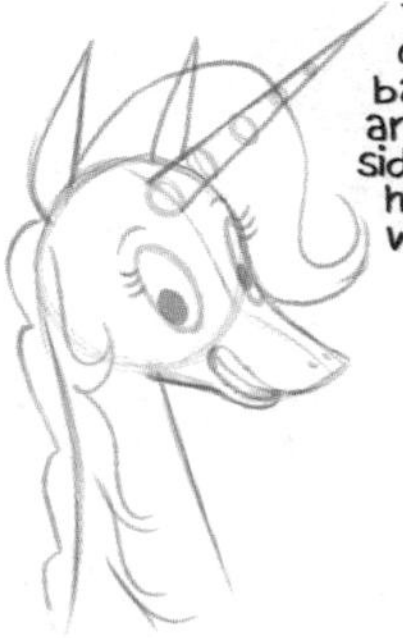

The front part of her mane is basically a swoop, and is on the far side of her head and horn no matter which way she's facing.

(It's magic.)

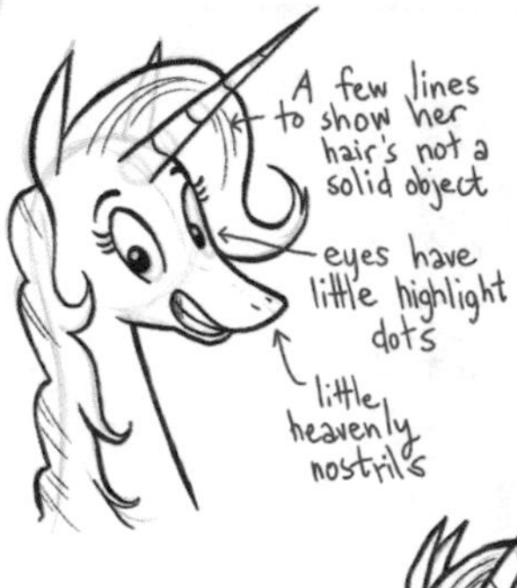
A few lines to show her hair's not a solid object
eyes have little highlight dots
little heavenly nostrils

Marigold is kind of swan-shaped, with a long slender neck.

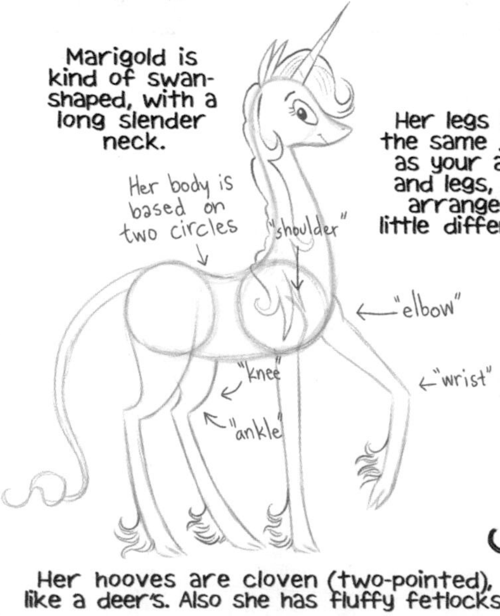
Her body is based on two circles
"shoulder"
"elbow"
"wrist"
"knee"
"ankle"

Her legs have the same joints as your arms and legs, just arranged a little differently.

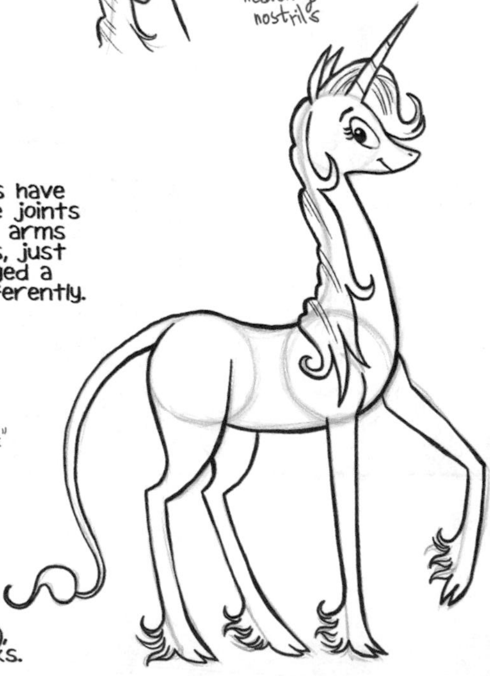

Her hooves are cloven (two-pointed), like a deer's. Also she has fluffy fetlocks.

How to Draw
Phoebe

Phoebe's head is very round.

 She has oval eyes and a little point for a nose.

 Her hair has a lot of lines in it.

She usually, but not always, wears a ponytail.

Eyes have little highlight dots

Freckles!

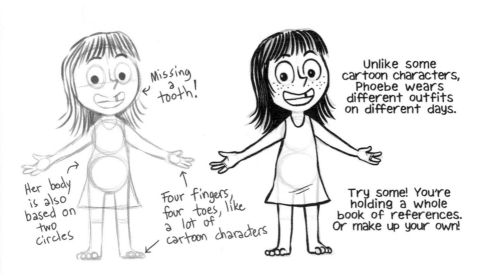

Missing a tooth!

Her body is also based on two circles

Four fingers, four toes, like a lot of cartoon characters

Unlike some cartoon characters, Phoebe wears different outfits on different days.

Try some! You're holding a whole book of references. Or make up your own!

Make a Marigold Heavenly Nostrils Stick Puppet

MATERIALS: white cardboard or white paper plate; scissors; pencil; large craft stick; markers; glue; tape; yarn

INSTRUCTIONS:

 Photocopy or trace the picture of Marigold, below.

 Color the picture with markers.

 Cut out the picture and glue it on the cardboard or paper plate.

 Cut the cardboard or paper plate around the picture.

 Tape the picture to the craft stick.

 Glue yarn for mane.

Make an Animated Flip Book

Cartoonists create stories in cartoon panels. Often cartoonists are also animators. An animator must capture a broad range of movements in order for a cartoon to look continuous. Animation is possible because of a phenomenon called "persistence of vision," when a sequence of images moves past the eye fast enough, the brain fills in the missing parts so the subject appears to be moving.

MATERIALS: paper, index cards, or sticky notes; stapler and staples, paper clips, or brads; pencil or marker

INSTRUCTIONS:

 Cut at least 20 strips of paper to be the exact same size, or use alternative materials, such as index cards or sticky notes.

 Fasten the pages together with a staple, brad, or paperclip.

 Pick a subject—anything from a bouncing ball to a running Marigold or a shooting star.

 Draw three key images first: the first on page one, the last on page twenty, and the middle on page ten, then fill in the pages between the key images.

Make Unicorn Slumber Party Snack Mix

Marigold's favorite food might be luscious, tender grass, but snack mix is required at a slumber party! This is a yummy, easy-to-make treat.

INGREDIENTS: 1 bag Bugles (they look just like unicorn horns!), 1 bag cheddar fish crackers, 1 bag round pretzels, 1 cup nuts (either cashews or peanuts), 1 package ranch salad dressing mix, ½ cup vegetable oil

INSTRUCTIONS:

 1 Mix the vegetable oil with the dressing mix in a small bowl.

 2 Put the Bugles, crackers, pretzels, and nuts in a large bowl.

 3 Add the dressing mixture to the large bowl and mix.

 4 Store in airtight container or storage bags.

Fun Things to Know About Unicorns

Even though the unicorn is a fictitious animal, it is one of the official animals of Scotland and was used on the royal coat of arms of Scotland in medieval times. (The red lion shown in the shield on the crest is the other official animal.)

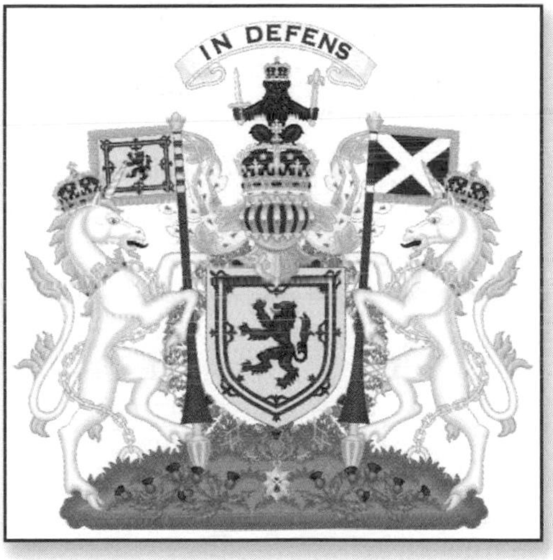
IN DEFENS

Lake Superior State University (through its Department of Natural Unicorns of the Unicorn Hunters) issues Questing Unicorn Licenses. Check it out at: www.lssu.edu/banished/uh_license.php.

Unicorns have appeared in folklore and art since ancient times in such different places as China, Greece, and France. One of the most famous depictions of unicorns is the *The Hunt of the Unicorn*, a series of seven tapestries that is in The Cloisters, which is part of The Metropolitan Museum of Art in New York. You can see them and learn more about them at: www.metmuseum.org/collections/search-the-collections/467642.

Create Your Own Cartoon Strip

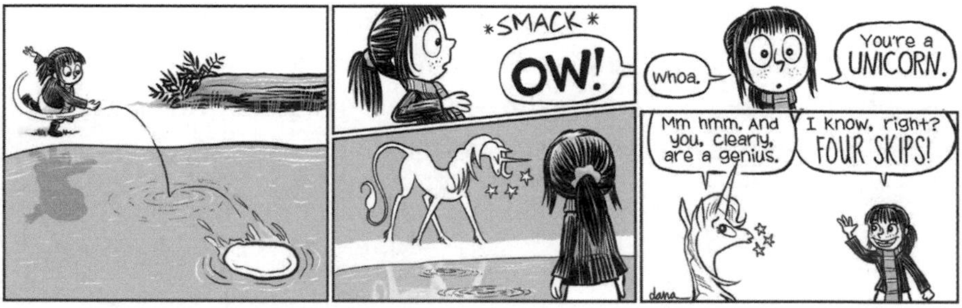
SMACK
OW!
Whoa.
You're a UNICORN.
Mm hmm. And you, clearly, are a genius.
I know, right? FOUR SKIPS!
dana

The comic strip *Phoebe and Her Unicorn* began when Phoebe met Marigold and they became friends. Think about how you met one of your favorite friends and draw a comic strip about it.

MATERIALS: blank piece of paper, pencil, markers, or colored pencils

INSTRUCTIONS:

1. Make three blank cartoon panels.
2. Look at the example above to see how Dana Simpson set the stage for the meeting and ended with the punch line.
3. Once you have decided on the story you want to tell, draw it in three panels. Remember, it should have a beginning, a middle, and an end.
4. In the first panel, give your comic strip a name.

> *"We'll be friends forever, won't we, Pooh?" asked Piglet. "Even longer," Pooh answered.*
> —Winnie the Pooh

Andrews McMeel Publishing
a division of Andrews McMeel Universal
1130 Walnut Street, Kansas City, Missouri 64106

www.andrewsmcmeel.com

16 17 18 19 20 RR2 10 9 8 7 6 5 4 3 2 1

ISBN: 978-1-4494-8348-7

Library of Congress Control Number: 2013957200

Made by:
RR Donnelley & Sons
Address and location of manufacturer:
1009 Sloan Street
Crawfordsville, IN 47933-2743
1st Printing—8/5/16

ATTENTION: SCHOOLS AND BUSINESSES
Andrews McMeel books are available at quantity discounts with bulk purchase for educational, business, or sales promotional use. For information, please e-mail the Andrews McMeel Publishing Special Sales Department: specialsales@amuniversal.com.

Check out these and other books at ampkids.com

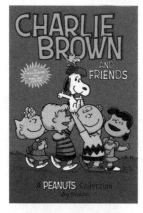

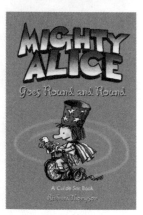

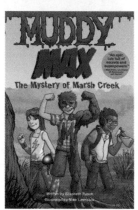

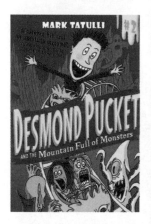

Also available:
Teaching and activity guides for each title.
AMP! Comics for Kids books make reading FUN!